"Only the Dead Endure"

The Great War Memoir of Felix D Strachan

Cover Illustration:

Detail from "Ghosts of Vimy Ridge" by William Longstaff (1879-1953)

To my late friend Marco (1970-2022), who was, by all accounts, a *Mensch*

Part One:

"They Shall Not Grow Old as We Grow Old"

Canada, January, 1936

There is a photograph on the mantle. It stands in a delicately edged pewter frame among a serried rank of mis-matched frames of no like shape or size from any other. I was just able to pick that one photograph out from the odd grouping while remaining in my chair, which I kept almost the room's length away as the fire heated the room sufficiently to not need to be near it. Not that the lounge was of any sort of grand room to begin with. It was a suitable size in which the family could gather, the children usually sitting upon the intricately patterned Persian-style carpet as proximate to the radio as possible without risking deafness, my wife and I in matching armchairs, plush upholstered high-backed pieces of rather modern design. There was also a settee directly opposite the fire which was saved a lot of wear due to my kids' peculiar habits. Furniture and fireplace put together seemed to make the room seem closer than it really was, but overall, the size of it was just enough to hold all five of us; six if we counted Malachai, our cat, without being directly on top of one another. A small room in which our family time was spent suited more than comfort. It cost less to light and heat. These days, it was especially wise to be frugal. We weren't wealthy but we didn't want for anything, and keeping things that way meant avoiding unnecessary waste. Besides, far too many people were having to go without from experiencing reversals of fortune that too much in the way of extravagance would be very bad form. It didn't bother me to use a little less coal and not have so many electric lights on at any one time as I had done just fine without them in my youth.

That whole row of framed pictures, running the length of the mantle's ledge, were as such things are; memories of a single moment. A few were mine; some were Adelaide's and the rest were ours together. It was a different sort of collection than had even been imagined a generation ago. My mother, for instance, only possessed a single photograph, a studio portrait of my father taken shortly before he left with his regiment for South Africa. Nothing exists of her wedding day, or myself and my siblings as children. Our past life in Banchory, where we'd lived before coming to Canada may as well have existed only in imagination. These days, with everyone wandering about with a Box Brownie, there was scarce an event, formal or casual, which wasn't captured on film. Our wedding, each of our three children as bairns, the family at Christmases and church fetes, these were so many that they crowded for space along the mantle and told a story, one instant at a time, of what seemed a perfectly ordinary, mostly cheerful life; an unassuming existence. That was largely the case in reality, or so I would like to think. I'd have to look farther into the past to see that ordinary cheerfulness wasn't always so for me. Along the ledge, that past was on display. There stood the first portrait I'd had taken of myself, entirely like my father—in uniform prior to embarking for war, and alongside that was the one which had just drawn my attention.

This, which my eye had fallen upon, looking up from some guff in the evening paper depicted me, so frightfully young; not but a few years older than Hamish, our eldest. Despite the setting, with me abed in an army hospital, I'm grinning, right enough. In my left hand, there is a cigarette which had prompted a cross letter in return from Ma when she had first been sent the image. I had been in hospital over Christmas for a trifle of a wound and on New Year's Day, 1917, my cousin Bill—there he was, the both of us posed, touching our tin cups in a toast—had tracked me down to 'First Foot' me on Hogmanay. At the time that photo had been taken, I had not seen him since he and his brother Alec had gone to join up in 1914, at the war's start. In those August days, I recall no feeling of any emotion in their departure other than jealousy. Here was the greatest event in human history and while my cousins, neighbours and friends had gone off to death or glory on far off battlefields, I would remain in the tedium of working. Working, at that, all the more for Bill and Eck having left. With the whole thing projected to being decided by year's end, by measure of my youth I would miss out entirely. I had only just turned sixteen a fortnight before the declaration. To try to take part would have involved a great deal of subterfuge on my end, and my mother was far too vigilant to allow me any chance of that.

"Now, laddie," she had said the same evening my cousins departed, "don't go getting any notions of stealing off in the night to chum along. I will find where you have gone and drag you back hame by your lugs." My mother never having made an idle threat in her life, I was sufficiently warned to stay put. Escorting me home by pinched ears might have been an embellishment, but none too far from what she'd be capable of.

That summer's evening, the last time I saw the two as they went off to war would be the last time I ever saw Alec, who vanished to nothing in the spring of the following year. When the picture of me in hospital had been taken, it would be the only time Bill and I saw each other while overseas. Half a year gone from the event captured in still life, Bill would be cruelly wounded by counter-battery fire directed against his gun. It was a severe enough set of injuries to have him sent back to Canada in a series of leaps from one hospital to the next, the discharging unit having only done for Bill enough to ensure he'd survive the trip to the receiving end. He's made of strong stuff, our Bill and though it took time, he returned to work at the vineyard, the family business of a modest acreage in the back country of Falls Parish, Ontario. Inchmarlo Estates had been founded by Bill's father at the close of the last century. Uncle Isaac had taken the name from the village just beyond Aberdeen in which he and his younger brother, my father, had first seen the light of day.

Bill's injuries meant he couldn't walk all that far without pains, any physical effort tiring him quickly. That was fine, his role was mainly directorial. The running about and managing the different works of the estate was taken up by me and my brothers-in-law the O'Leary twins, who had proven to be quite competent in that regard. It was an arrangement which was very cooperative and had developed into a routine we'd settled into some years ago when Uncle Isaac had gradually ceded his business in anticipation of a retirement he never got. We buried him, what, eight years ago now? Certainly, it was before the crash which had threatened to shatter the legacy not quite moved into its second generation. The Depression had such a bad effect and ruined so many in agriculture that it was very fortunate the vineyard remained productive, if not perhaps as vibrant as it had been. Its survival had all been upon Bill who had carried forward his father's program of diversification which had begun in small measures during the war and a prohibition act which forbade the domestic sale of wine. Such things had seen the end of a number of vineyards. Inchmarlo was being kept going by policies and plans I had no hand in, giving leave to worry as to what would happen once I was in charge. This was something that bore some thought as I trusted Bill knew what he was doing much more than I trusted my ability to comprehend the complexities of this business. I might have a better grasp on those things, had I dedicated more time to being on site in recent years. Precedence had always been given to balance the care of our children with Adelaide's teaching and my other job. I was still in the army.

Such as it was, in the time being. At the end of it all, the majority of us faded away to lives the war had interrupted. Some, a fractional minority in which I am counted had been invited to stay with the colours in the Non-Permanent Active Militia; the part-time force intended to be the frame upon any expansion world events might require. In the case of my unit, as with many others, our authorised strength had been much reduced. The King's Own Canadian Scots Regiment had gone, in a blink, from a fully established battalion of four companies to that of a single rifle company and support staff. A smaller force gave less room for upward mobility, and as I approached my twenty-first year of service, I'd moved exactly one pay grade higher than the rank I'd achieved at war. It could be worse, as a great many units had been folded altogether. On the face of it, not being permitted to swell our ranks was an indication that we didn't have any need to. This was a set of circumstances I found infinitely more appealing than its opposite for what requiring a full-strength force would indicate. Practically, however, I would have to admit it was a very real prospect, what with that squat Austrian peacock running the show over yonder. I really don't want to speculate about any such future, but it's hard not to with everything in the news these days. That, and ignorance, especially wilful, is no refuge from wide reality.

This evening, it wasn't the notion of dim and possibly martial events yet to come which had bounced my eyes from newspaper to a particular photograph. Rather, it was a piece on the monument being built in France. The dedication was to be this summer, and I had begun to think about bringing up the subject with Bill one last time. What the war had cost my cousin was, perhaps, reason for him not want to return to the same fields which had altered his life so much. Not that it hadn't altered mine, and it's fair to suppose my inkling to tread old ground had to be linked to events I could not undo. I did have to consider what he had said the last time I opened the subject of the dedication. Six weeks ago, perhaps, I'd called into his office, on the ground floor of Inchmarlo House. The year's hardest work was over with, and Bill had been busy closing out the books on the season passed. I'd lobbed the question at him, trying for an air of casual indifference by doing so while studying the landscape of bare vines and plucked orchards which spread beyond the bright windows opposite his immense oak desk. It was usually a captivating view, particularly in height of summer with deeply leaved vines and splendidly heavy trees, or in winter when the fields were dressed in a blanket of snow upon which even a faint sun brightly set frozen crystals sparkling. Transitioning from one idyll to the other left little but a grubby and bare display, soil worked to mud by late, chilly rains. The vista from these windows, nearly as tall as the room in which they were set, went sloping gently away from the prominence upon which the house had been built to the horizon. At more active times of the year, Bill could survey his holding—a good share of it anyway—without more effort than crossing the plain wooden floor from his desk to the chair he kept to the one side of the triple set of grand panes. That chair, his desk and its chair, with the two for visitors placed in front of his work surface were not company to any other furnishings. Bill had no taste for decoration, leaving the walls, nude plaster except for the windows and one length which was uncovered brick, exactly as they were. He hung no artwork or photographs; he hadn't even felt the need to splash a colour coating on the plaster which leant to the room all the charm of a bandage. The spare setting of his office and the dismal view beyond the glazing was quite reminiscent of the war. Except that in my two years in France, one of the world's famed nations for wine, I never saw a single vineyard.

"Do you have to go?" was his immediate response to my question.

"You mean with the army? No. Some other plugs will be going over official-like. We didn't draw a straw on this one." Sure, if the Regiment had been invited, I'd have got over for free. Then again, that 'free trip' would have come with a lot of bollocks for spit and polish; the King would be present. Given the option, I'd much rather go out of pocket in mufti and avoid a lot of needless fuss and bother.

"You'll go without me?" It's hard to hear him sometimes, his voice often caught between his hoarse wheeziness and my less than stellar listening skills. Plus, I was still at the window, my back towards him, and knowing Bill as I do, he hadn't looked up from his work, addressing me indirectly from the surface of his blotter. I turned about.

"That a question, Bill?"

"Aye," a nod. I shrugged.

"Suppose I would."

"Then go, Felix. It's a long time to be gone, in summer no less." I had no sensible rebuttal prepared, forward thinking not being a strength, and there wasn't much chance to give thought to any response for what he said next changed the tone entirely.

"I'm dying, Felix."

"Nonsense. No harm, Bill, you aren't the picture of health but that doesn't mean it's fatal. You worry too much, that's what this is."

"I'll nonsense your nonsense. I've got a scrapyard of iron they couldn't fetch out of me all along my right side and shite for lungs. It is killing me."

"Bit dramatic, what, Bill? That's years you've got. You going to tell me you've set a date or something?"

"Don't," he had to pause, the poison he'd breathed never having entirely left him, "don't be daft. I'm not long for it, that's just how it is. What I've got left to do is as much to hand over Inchmarlo when the time comes as viable a business as it was left to me." I said nothing further, he bears little contradiction. He made a show of getting on the telephone just then and I had followed his eye to the frosted glass door which let from his office to the hall. His predicted demise hadn't yet arrived. A month and a half later, and he was still upright. I might not be able to change his mind, about going to France, or dying for that matter, but I'd have another crack at trying. In the case of France, at least.

"Will you not see the children to bed?" Her voice from just putting her head round the lounge's passage from the corridor brought me back to where I was. She stopped, came in.

"And how long have you been off and away?" Bless her, Adelaide had a knack for catching me mid-mental wander. Must be some trade secret school teachers shared.

"Not long," I lied. I had no idea; never did. All my life I've been subject to such absences. It may have been that I'd been blank since I'd settled back into my chair after turning the radio off and sending the weans up to bed. It was not unusual to find me lost in thought at this time of evening. After dinner, the kids and I would tidy the kitchen and move to the lounge. This gave Adelaide the peace to prepare for her next day's lessons. The trade-off was that it was I who was subjected to the blether of the children's favourite programme. "Antoine and Belfry" it was called, and it involved two grown men putting on silly voices and pretending to be half-wits who, despite lacking sense always managed to extricate themselves from whatever ridiculous pitfall they came across in the span of thirty minutes. Perhaps I didn't care for it much as I got enough similar nonsense with the army. Once set for their continuing adventures to be lived the following night, I would cast Antoine and Belfry to Oblivion by means of the off switch, which my three rascals knew was their signal to do their revisions and prepare for bed. I would then wind the mantle clock and sink back into my chair, my mind not anchored to anything but the tiny cadence of the clock's gears and the smouldering pops of the waning coal fire.

My hands might be holding the newspaper, fingers folding the pages, eyes moving over the print, but I wasn't really reading it, in any sense of absorbing the information. Some things did stand out, like this article on the monument. Besides that, though, most items didn't particularly interest me. I've got no stake in politics, no real sense of commerce and care little for sports. Generally, me going through the paper was an exercise in appearances and whatever might be passing across my mind could be any number of distracted thoughts; most of which bear no relation to the subjects within the pages. There were times that I had begun to read a story, all the words absorbed by sight, yet I could get to the final sentence and realise I had journeyed off in another direction mentally and had not a clue as to what I'd supposedly just read. There is a great deal I continue to think about; a mess of tangled memories made difficult to resolve because of the duress and relative brevity of time in which they were accumulated. At least, if I'm deliberately mulling these bits of my past in a solitary moment, I'm in some form of control. When they caught me unaware, creeping upon me in a moment of waking distraction or when I'm defenselessly asleep, I am at the mercy of my past.

Her brow furrowed; she never believed any claim I made to the lengths my mind wandered. She bent down, kissed my cheek.

"Where were you this time?" I pointed to the picture which had caught my eye. She saw the one I meant.

"France, then." I don't know why she said that, it's always France. Unless it's Belgium. It's always the war, and that's what Aidie really meant by saying 'France.' "That's the first picture I ever saw of you." I had forgotten that in the moment. We had not known each other prior to the war. Our connection had begun through a correspondence of my condolences to her family's loss, which had branched into her introduction

17

to my relatives, principally my mother. Ma had wasted no time in brokering our match.

"Aye, I suppose it was. I'm going to talk to Bill again." There, having said it out loud to her, I committed myself to it.

"Oh, don't, Darling. He doesn't want to go. Why is it so important he make the trip with you?" Another mystery to how my wife operates is in her ability not just to put good questions to me for answering, but doing so in such a fashion as requiring me to discover an answer deeper than the question asked. Meaning, I couldn't tell her why the whole idea was so important until I was certain what about it was so important to me alone. I didn't think I could tell her; my reasons would include things about which I had not ever disclosed. As she was the person I trusted more than any other, I would have to have a damned good reason for any kind of taciturnity. I stood, kissed her in return, set my paper on my chair and went up to say goodnight to our children.

Much later, I lay awake in the enveloping darkness of a mid-winter's night, Adelaide gently snoring beside me. I would never live through the wrath she'd descend on me if I ever had the lack of sense to mention her night breathing. It wasn't of any roof-raising quality, rather petite and adorable in a way. My own raspings were far more disruptive as evidenced by the frequency of which her elbows jostled my ribs over a night's sleep. It not only saved my hide and her embarrassment by keeping mum on Aidie's snore. Had I the thoughtlessness to bring up the subject, her self-consciousness might inspire her to eliminate the habit, if she could. If that were to happen, I would then stand to lose one of the things which reassured me I was safely at home and not in the perpetual nightmare of the years I had spent abroad. 'Nightmare' may not be a strong enough word and doesn't apply to memories rather than dreams. I use the term, ill-fitting it might be, as there is no entirely comprehensive way to explain how what I have lived through has had such a lasting impact. Relating the events as observed isn't difficult, as I can describe what my senses recorded. Divulging how it has affected me inwardly is altogether different. War occurs on a level at which there is absolutely no room for sentimentality. A lapse of mood was nothing more than a distraction when distractions could be fatal. In the extremes of environment and circumstances where the norms of moral behaviour have been suspended, something as delicate as emotion must be denied. Of course, such forbearance is neither rational nor possible. Deprived emotions have nowhere to go and thus a period of more than two years of getting from one moment to the next in one piece had fashioned this self-imposed stoicism into a tightly wound spring in my guts I could do nothing about but keep winding tighter. This had remained with me for no other reason that there was a great deal of it all I had yet to be able to make any sense of.

The nature of a damaging self-denial was some of what passed through my mind as I sat up in bed, working over the question Adelaide had posed. My reasons were something I had come to some time ago, which were not dissimilar to what inspired me to rethink addressing Bill on the subject, which was, as the paper's story had reminded me, to do with the purpose behind the monument's construction. The immensity of industrial destruction visited upon France and Belgium had created a curious phenomenon. There were untold scores of men whose whereabouts could not be determined or whose remains left little but an infinite anonymity. So prevalent were these great unknowables that the fashion had arisen to memorialise the missing by raising monuments which could be inscribed with the names of those graveless men. The paper's byline on the story had related that our monument would be no different. There would be no shortage of chiseled names of men I had known, but for Bill's sake, that long list would include his younger brother. I knew, in a slightly different way, that empty and inconclusive feeling of an unknown and unreachable grave. My father's plot was that of the latter, he having died of typhoid while on campaign in South Africa. He may as well be buried on the moon for all the remoteness of his resting place. It's not, I admit, quite the same, as in a yard somewhere near Paardeburg there definitely was my father's body beneath a stone bearing the name of Sergeant Hamish Strachan, Gordon Highlanders. As I had never seen it for myself, his mortality hovered in a strange limbo of the mind unprepared to confirm fact absolutely without proof of personal experience. It may not be an apt comparison between my father and Bill's brother any more than a vague similarity. Even so, I really had little notion how my cousin might feel about a symbolic memorial of a loss now twenty years in the past. In all that time, I could not recall Bill even mentioning Eck from any point of memory. He had, by that, only been continuing the silent grief begun by Uncle Isaac and Aunt Ruth. The nature of their mourning manifested itself only as an intangible tension, that some element of life as it had been was awry and to acknowledge it in any way would confirm its reality. As I wasn't aware of how other households moved through tragedy, I couldn't comment on any such behaviour as being normal. The only thing I might say which contributed to it was the elongated process of Alec's status from life to death.

Both brothers had been part of the First Contingent, Canada's initial response to the Call of Empire. Whether Bill and Eck had contrived to serve together in the same unit or not had been immaterial. My elder cousin, with a sharp mind for mathematics would have those skills welcomed in the artillery where precision with figures was crucial. Alec, a little less prepared in that fashion was destined for the infantry where the need was for numbers of men, not particularly men of numbers. I believe he had intended his occupation to be within a rifle company anyhow. The First Contingent had arrived in England with far more men than would fit into a properly established division, which had meant paring composite units down to size. I can only guess at any level of enthusiasm my cousins would have had to be among those selected to be part of the vanguard. It made no difference, anyway, as feelings are given little consideration by those charged with making such decisions. Alec would remain on his battalion's rolls when the 1st Canadian Division crossed over to France. A lack of available field guns would keep Bill's battery in England. If they had a chance to visit each other before the Division sailed, and I don't know whether they did, it would have been the last time.

Not long after its arrival to the Front, in the spring of 1915, the 1st Division was given a rough handling when the Germans attempted to reduce the salient of defensive lines protecting the Belgian town of Ypres. As battles go, this one had an ignoble beginning in which the Canadians had been completely outclassed by the enemy who had mounted a swift and thorough attack behind a concentrated dispersal of chlorine. Casualties had been severe. Many of the forward most Canadian positions, composed of poorly constructed and segmented trenches were infiltrated and isolated by the assaulting wave. Cut off from supporting units, these positions were defeated in detail by subsequent attacks. Most of the casualties from a grim total were in fact a large count of men taken prisoner as a result. The first news which arrived at Inchmarlo was that within the tumult of battle, Eck was 'missing.' It's an uncertain status, to say the least, but not one without a small measure of hope. For some months following, other families began to receive supplemental notices that their relatives had been counted among the prisoners taken on the field. I'm not one for calculating probabilities, but odds didn't favour a similar outcome in Eck's case. His battalion had been at the very crux of the German attack.

Time continued onwards, and no informative notice from the Red Cross came to our door. The following year, I too had left, and while awaiting my unit's deployment from training fields in England to the battlefields of France, Ma had written me a note to say that Isaac and Ruth had received a telegram notifying them that for 'official purposes,' Private Strachan, A E was presumed to have been Killed in Action on or about 25 April 1915. No trace of him had ever turned up and if his remains had ever been interred, they would be marked by a plinth bearing the legend 'Known Unto God.' Even all this time later, there wasn't anyone among the survivors who had been able to relate anything certain about Alec's final moments. The various possibilities of what happened are numerous and entirely tragic and were just another thing to add to the unknown of where he finally lay. His name, one among thousands, engraved on our national monument was the best that could ever be hoped for to finalise his memory. It might be a lot of bother to drag Bill all the way across an ocean just for that purpose, especially if I didn't know if it would in any way be to his benefit to put Alec's death firmly in the past where it belonged. I only had knowledge enough as to how I feel about such things and although Bill and I are different people. I would find it difficult to believe he felt no pull towards closing out a chapter long in the past. It would be reason enough for me to go. I complicated matters by not being able to say which bits of my past in particular could be put to rest by being back in the places where they had happened. Coming home from the war was supposed to have been the start of the rest of my life, not at all unlike having a sentence of death commuted. It had been my intention to move beyond it all without any kind of backward glance. It would not unfold to my desire. Whatever I had tried to deny thought or feeling in the instant would remain exactly as it was when experienced. So much of memory is tied to emotion, which itself is inextricable from morality. For me to face how the war had impacted my sensibility would require having to face the influence my own deeds had upon it. I wasn't much concerned about anything I had done in the course of my duty. Odd as it may seem to be dismissive of certain actions I took which I would not have otherwise because of that base nature of war. Those memories were vivid and terrible, but anything of regret was rare. That particular quality was more to be found in the things I hadn't done. By my failure to act, by mistake or indecision I can count myself responsible for lives lost which perhaps shouldn't have been. Not the least of those was my wife's father, Kelley O'Leary.

France, October, 1916

A small glade by the roadside, despite the austerity of most trees having shed autumn leaves seemed at first a calm oasis for us to begin our break from the days we had just spent on our battalion's first trip up to the line for an offensive action. This place may have been such, an oasis, if not for the fact that the noise of war is not as easily distanced as are its sights. We had not been part of any huge campaign, but as long as they were over there and we were over here, unrelenting effort had to be placed to retain that vague status quo until such a time as we would be able to deliver a killing blow and send the Hun packing. Meaning that even without the fury of a dedicated bombardment, the air was still punched by the reports of our field guns and howitzers, answered in like terms by theirs. The area directly in rear of the trench system, a netherworld reaching back from the front lines for miles further arear was atmospherically dominated by the artillery. Drifting smoke carried with it the odour of carbon, grease and cordite, overruling any natural scents. Hanging heavy, this cool industrial pall seemed entirely mechanical as it was accompanied by the constant flash and bang of outgoing fire. My throat was dead raw from this acrid air, not nearly enough water and days of having to shout just to be heard. There never was such a racket, and it never ended, only going in one direction of intensity or another. It was like living in a thundercloud. The roadside we had come down was lined alternately by stacks of shells, boxes of charges and fuses and mounds of expended brass casings, indicating that the guns had been at this for a while and were well set to continue for a while yet. Apparently six weeks, the length of time we had been in France, was not enough to get used to the incessant rumble of artillery.

Our journey so far had been transformative in that we had left a great deal of what was usual and familiar behind and had begun to act the part of soldiers. Indoctrination to the point of departing for the Western Front had shifted how we carried ourselves and added both functional and expressive terms to our vocabulary. A year's worth of drills and route marches had hardened us physically and demanded us to test beyond what we had thought our limitations were. All along, knowing what purpose this work was serving was the rather naïve idea of what lay ahead. That being a mistaken apprehension where once embarked to be ferried across the Channel to France we would be completely prepared for our part in all this. Our ignorance had been well exposed these past six weeks, which had cumulated with brief orienting tours of front-line occupation and defensive routine. Nothing of our imagination could have predicted such noise and chaos. Everything we had done the preceding year had not been without the practical lessons of soldiery but it all had done nothing to prepare for the sensory impact of the real thing. I had thought I knew what it was to be afraid, but that concept melted away to a shadow my first time up the line. Realising that my mortality was substantive rather than abstract forever changed my understanding. It was up to me to learn how to keep functioning with the knowledge that my life could be forfeit at any moment. At that point, it might have been natural for us all to think, after spending ten days rotating through the incremental lines of defense, from reserve, support and firing lines, the latter being the very face of it—beyond was nothing but contested ground and the enemy, that we had seen the war. While it was ugly and uncomfortable, it wasn't really all that bad. Even though that first assignment had deliberately been in a 'quiet sector,' we might have been excused our belief that we had become soldiers more than in appearance. That idea was not much more correct than having believed it at any time before, we had only taken another step towards it. Our only accomplishment was a further, moderate reduction of the fallacy of our belief. We had one thing yet to do for us to truly become the soldiers we were mistaking ourselves for; go into a fight with the enemy.

Coming into this rough wood were those of us who'd had that particular lesson and were able to come away from it. Aside from the magnitude of everything enclosed in combat, which no amount of training could have sufficed to mitigate was an incredulousness that we could have deigned to think ourselves ready for what reality was. Where we had been brought, this little copse, was behind our brigade's gun line, so the noise of infrequent firing was diminished but still stupefyingly loud. A cambered stone road was at all times, day and night as heavily travelled as a city street with lorries and limbers providing a continuing line of supply. These were passed in the opposite direction by wagons and ambulances moving much more slowly to not further aggravate the wounded being carried towards advanced dressing stations. We had stopped here for a rest. For how long, no one had been told. Presumably, after that we would continue moving further rearward for a proper period of relief from the line.

It was early morning, right then, that strangely solemn time between the loneliness of night and the liveliness of day. Knowing exactly what hour it was had become an impossibility as through the previous evening menacing and darkly heavy clouds had gathered, obscuring the sky above. The air, steeped in the thick reek of the big guns hung damply chilling made worse by a weariness of body lowering my ability to withstand a dreach environment. Passage of time seemed to matter very little. I'd lost count somewhere a while back, and quite honestly, I was occupied by other things. Practically, there was no difference to me if I were to be killed on a Monday I thought was a Tuesday.

The battalion, one reduced company at a time had been led into this wood, and I was able to quickly claim a hearty tree to prop myself against in 'B' Company's area. This, as it was not our final destination and that we had come directly from the lines meant we were without amenities such as blankets and other comforts which could be found with battalion transport, if only battalion transport could be found. I contented to keep my bare hands under my armpits and shiver in the chill damp of dawn. If I drew up my legs to sit Indian style, I had just enough hem to cover my knees. I would later be savvy enough to carry mitts, a knit cap and a scarf; I had no such things in that moment. Even with those items, what I could not do very well, if at all, was insulate the six inches of exposed skin left open from the tops of my puttees and bottom of my kilt.

Borne upon the cold air, the pattern of clouds delivered their burden on us in volume and variety from the faint damp of dewed fog, the plainly wet of a deluge; light whispers of fairy flakes or whipping needles of ice. Day was no different than night. One sky was only slightly brighter slate than the other, an overhead field to all horizons of solid gloom. I would eventually learn that in this part of the world, continued and complete damp was normal between the end of summer to the break of spring. There is something ever so squeamishly and awkwardly uncomfortable about a continued state of wet. My clothes were damp through, clinging to my skin kept puckered as from too long a bath. The ground beneath me was either solid and cold as a stone slab or clammy and viscous saturated earth. I had not made any thought about what weather I might have to contend with when I joined up for the war. My mate Andy Ferguson seemed little bothered by weather and had curled up his giant's frame, laid on his side and was already sawing away in a heavy sleep. I shuffled a little closer to him, big lad that he was, he kicked out a lot of heat. I blinked.

A moment—how long, of course, I could never tell—later I was being shook awake.

"Hullo, Matt, I said, recognising Norton.

"Corporal Norton," he corrected. Not a day into his stripes and he was having this formality?

"Really?" I'd been, we'd all been calling each other by familiar terms; first names, nicknames, since we'd started. He chucked his head back, a movement indicating the train of men he had with him.

"Yes, Lance Corporal." Oh, right. It was hard to keep track of all these new appointments as they were so recent that none of us had yet a spare moment to attach indicative chevrons to our sleeves. As it seemed we were exchanging pleasantries on a formal level, I stood to my feet.

"New men for the section," he informed me. "Chaps, this is Lance Corporal Strachan, One Section second-in-command. Do not go beyond his eyesight, we'll be moving out soon and I don't want anyone wandering off. Lance Corporal, these are," he paused to discreetly consult a slip of paper concealed in his palm, "Privates Denison, Finch and O'Leary."

"Hullo," I said, and received each with a handshake. Denison and Finch don't bring forward too much in memory, neither would last to the New Year. However, even if O'Leary had gone the next day, I could not have forgotten him. He was old, far older than any man in the platoon. Clear and icy eyes were framed by deep lines, his face and chin round and dense, his body short and broad; a compact but powerful frame. I shook his hand, a paw which swallowed mine and though I sensed a great deal of strength, his grip was soft and his grasp gentle. He had no need to apply any force to prove he could crush my bones to dust. O'Leary grinned, a narrow expression which didn't part his lips to show what was an eclectic collection of teeth, but merely shifted his jowled cheeks slightly upward. He had less than six months to live. Of course, there was no way to have known it then, as with the fate of the other new chaps, or even Matt Norton, for that matter. If I didn't notice too much about any of them in that moment, it would have been due to my mind being pulled into distraction by the fatigue of endless days and a collection of vivid new memories of what those days had contained.

"I think," Corporal Douglas had said, "that was the easy bit." Easy? I hadn't given any thought that Douglas was prone to understatement and my own estimations of the preceding quarter-hour had no inclusion of ease. He'd said it as he, I and Andy Ferguson stood reviewing the mess of metal and men which had only recently been delivering heavy fire on our approach to this redoubt of a tumbled stone and plaster wall. Much of this slick mess was the result of several Mills bombs we had tossed as soon as Lieutenant Thorncliffe had brought our party by means of a dash along shallow ground beyond the sightline of the machine guns, close enough to do so without much risk of catching a bomb splinter ourselves. A fair deal of the force of the grenades had been absorbed by the thick walls which in turn required us to finish off the crew left alive or unharmed by our iron calling cards. Corporal Douglas had been first through, sticking his point in quick jabs into the mass of grey figures spread about the two guns. Andy followed, bringing the butt of his rifle in a wide muscular swing across the temple of one who had been regaining his feet. The crunch of impact was loudly like a gourd splattering from a drop of height. It caved the man's face, shattered his features and was delivered in such a hard sweep as to take the man upward, landing roughly across the stone spill of the wall, and remained, legs and arms wrongly placed by momentum. If the strike hadn't been enough, Andy in his follow through punctured the man's breast with his bayonet. I was right behind him and while Douglas was stitching his quarry and Andy clubbing his, I spotted what must have been a loader, some yards off. On his way to deliver more ammunition to the guns as we arrived, he'd dropped the cans he carried and turned to quit the field in a sprint. I leapt over the mess being dealt with by the other two, took a knee, raised point of aim to consider the muzzle's balance with bayonet fixed, and pulled. Nothing happened. I'd not cleared the action from the last shot I had taken—an oversight of excitement. Rapidly righting this by flicking the bolt back and forth, I fired. I don't know why I was surprised at the result, but I was. My bullet smacked through his back and he dropped with a complete lack of elegance mid-stride; the last thirty inches of his life.

There's an awful lot of stuff inside a human body, not one bit of it pretty, especially if exposed by crimped shards of iron. Moments ago, these stilled forms, or parts thereof, had been living, thinking men. Their present condition, as horrid as it was could be rationalised as well-deserved considering the damage they had delivered in the moments before we had ability to vengeance. We had been taken completely unaware by those machine guns which had lain in wait for our extended order formation to approach the broken wall which surrounded the abandoned French farm we had been ordered to secure. It lay at a length of more than a hundred yards from the concealed positions we had moved to from our front-line trench. Under cover of a bombardment and the darkness of midnight we took up this advanced point for our jump-off at the appropriate time. We waited through dawn and sunrise; the length of time spent was to ensure that we could rely upon moving forward in precise coordination with the general advance. Daylight showed that the land between us and our goal was flat and wide. Barren soil, dry and loose was flecked with withered stalks having been left unproductive since the war began. The field was broken by one feature, a raised track of packed earth which was a dyke road marking a point just about half-way from our starting point to objective. Apprehension was supplanted by relief when at last we heard the order to move out. We were eager to get moving after having been cramped up at the jump-off for so long through a chilly night. That, and at last we were advancing towards the enemy. Our footsteps over the disused land kicked up pockets of dust in an uneasy rhythm of two platoons' worth of boots crunching the arid clots. The artillery had lifted, and going forward its absence made the relative silence seem uneasy for want of noise. Just the planting of boots, huffs of breath and the tin taps of our rifles' stacking swivels bouncing against the stock.

Ten yards forward became twenty, the distance falling away, our eyes fixed straight ahead at the stucco wall wrapping the farm which stood it out as a solitary, cleanly white feature atop a gritty grey-brown field. Fritz must have been somewhat puzzled that we had provided such a wide and inviting target. Arms at the high port, advancing at the quick-step we were dressed, that is, properly spaced, as if on review. We hadn't known of any better way of delivering men under adequate control to a distance from which to launch an assault. That control, such as could be given by two officers and their NCOs who, lacking as much experience in their roles as the rest of us had in ours, had broken down entirely as we came upon that raised track. I clearly remember being told when we were all getting our instructions how easy it was all going to be. This may have been what Corporal Douglas had been referring. The enemy, so went the pep talk we had been given with our rum, had been under pressure over months of continual attacks which although having yet cracked the Front wide open had decimated German manpower. Our strategic gains meant that the Hun were now fighting from less well-prepared defensive works far arear to the firmly constructed lines now in our hands after the summer's battles. All we would need to do was to turn them out of hasty entrenchments and scattered strongpoints. Our battalion had been given the task of reducing an angled bend the German trenches were obliged to make to follow the contour of a curving stream which ran along their frontage like a moat. The river, actually a runoff canal built long before the war to drain low-lying farm land was neither wide nor deep but its length was overlooked by the enemy positions making a direct fording assault a difficult concept; notwithstanding we had never learned how to do such a thing. However, the river did interrupt a contiguous line of defense, the trenches terminating at a short length after it switched rearward along its return. The river at that point disappeared via a culvert running under a wide road. Smashing into the German line there would negate having to cross the river and taking that rump end might carry the whole position on the flank. We would have to get there first. 'C' and 'D' Companies were to demonstrate against the main German line, supressing the enemy enough to permit 'B' Company to make its approach. Our objective, the French property we had named "Spoon Farm" made up for the German's loose end by having command of the ground over which our advance was to be made. This we did, two platoons abreast, in a depth of two platoons. The leading wave, of which my platoon was part, was going to capture this strongpoint, permitting the second wave to pass through and assault the German main line. Listening to all of this in the sleepy hours before heading to our starting line, about moves parallel and flanking over rivers and roads I had never seen and incorporating terms such as 'oblique' or 'enfilade' did not strike me as anything easy, rather than appearing quite complex involving details beyond my comprehension. That really didn't matter very much as all I was required to know was what Six Platoon would be expected to accomplish. This had been delivered to us with utmost simplicity as "Six Platoon, in coordination with Five Platoon WILL take and hold the redoubt known as 'Spoon Farm'." Heavy

35

emphasis had been placed on the word 'will' as it was meant to impress upon us that doing as we had been asked was definitive.

We had also been told that the Hun was only moments away from being licked—understrength, poorly fed and equipped, morally broken and, of course, in possession of inferior positions. Absolutely none of that was true. If that which was imparted upon us was what our intelligence johnnies really believed, they were in want of new jobs. More likely, we had been sold a softer bill of goods with a paved road to Hell of being able to undermine any trepidation we might have in going into action for the first time. I rather think we didn't know enough for trepidation to be an issue.

My mind wasn't on much of that at the time, and so far as I felt anything I could only describe an excitement of a slightly fluttery nature, and for the first while of our advance, enjoyment. The air was pleasant; crisp but not cool, a lovely clear sky, sparkling blue under a brilliant sun. These fields, flat and spare were bordered with sparse stands of trees, fully in autumn ochre. Just above the height of the farm's white wall, the red clay tiles of the chateau's roof stood in contrast, the building of such plain colour as to blend in with the enclosure. Beyond the roof line were several tall trees, dressed in golden leaves. It must have been a matter of some pride for the Frenchman who had owned this property, as although it was simple in style and muted in no extensive decoration it stood as an example of a practical simplicity. It was the first really pretty scene I'd clapped eyes on since coming to this country, where every place I had been so far was either altered or destroyed by two years of war. It was such a shame, I thought, that even this thing of small beauty had not remained whole; its looks diminished by a craggy tear of tumbled masonry making a wide gap in the otherwise egg-smooth wall which embraced the farmyard. Coming to that raised road, which required a hop over a swampy ditch and a few steps up the incline, I was bothered by some flies snapping quickly about my ears. I made to wave my hand about my head to scatter them before I came to realise that they weren't flies. We hadn't even heard the sound of the German guns firing before men started to fall. Sergeant Merrick had been torn apart by several bullets in all the time it took to draw breath and Cutler, right next to me, had caught one in the shoulder in the next moment. In the panicked frenzy of that first ten seconds under fire, I launched myself forward into the soggy ditch on the other side of the dyke and tried to collapse myself into the smallest figure I could, entirely forgetting everything about my supposed purpose. I stopped being a soldier the very moment I became a target. My eyes squeezed shut to stop taking in the sights only made the sounds worse; a constant whining buzz of bullets overhead, sent our way by long ripping stutters of the guns, every so often the skree of a ricochet or a heavy thud as rounds struck one surface or another accompanied by a chorus of low groans and high screams.

I never wanted to do that again. All of my enthusiasm, my willingness, my impatient desire to see the thing for myself which had been couched at home for a year due to my youth and another year yet in drills and training first at Niagara Camp and continued in England had evaporated in that instant. I had been positively put off the idea, but at this point, I was far beyond the liberty to decline further participation. Worse, there was little indication that the last few moments were out of the ordinary and was instead rather more likely to become a regular feature of what may well be my short life. If Corporal Douglas was correct, things could stand to become nastier yet.

"Easy, Corp?" I must have given him an astounded look. This was no time for jokes.

"I mean it, Catscratch," he continued, applying my nickname—a 'portmanteau' I've heard it be called; taking that my surname is often mispronounced with full value given to the 'ch' near the end instead of allowing one's voice to glide over it as a mere suggestion. This led to, at first, my mates having a go at my insistence my name be said properly by corrupting it further to "Scracthin'." I disliked this, and began to encourage those same mates to just address me by my first name. It helped little that 'Felix' is a name often given to cats. It may well have been Andy who had put the whole together for the first time, and now even Mr. Thorncliffe called me "Catscratch." I dunno, there are worse things to be called.

"Once their bosses find out we've got Spoon Farm from them, they're going to want it back and they'll waste no time in the effort." Inside the walls, aside from the damage we had lately caused, it could be believed

38

that the war was someplace else. Even the sound of fighting nearby seemed at a greater distance than it was. The three buildings, chateau, stable and shed were in good repair, only a few smashed panes in the windows and some roof tiles out of place, all sitting tidily together on a pebbled courtyard. An avenue of trees stood astride the path which led to the road under which that tiny river flowed. The large and brilliant boughs I had seen on the approach were the thick and older growth of the orchard by the wall across the courtyard from where we stood. These, like the buildings, had seen some damage. Exposed wood from fractured branches threw stark contrast to the rough, dark tone of bark, but not so much in the way of harm done that it couldn't be supposed that hard weather, rather than hard iron had been the cause. If I didn't pay any mind to what was at my feet, or the immobile figure oddly toppled and staining the yard from the thorough rent my shot had made; this piece of France was a perfect little homely island upon a turbulent sea. It was a powerful and confusingly peaceful image, while so much chaos was near to hand. Although it was built differently than farmsteads back home, and that whatever this farm had produced were crops I had never worked to grow, what this place was, its purpose, was unmistakeable and for someone who had grown up tending land and as such made me rather homesick.

I looked away from Douglas and studied the charnel display once again. If the Corporal was right, and I didn't have much doubt that he was, only a measure of time separated me from the man I was to these crude parodies of men, in sloppy bits and pieces. If the Hun wanted this place back, they could have it. Most unfortunately, that was not my decision to make. We here at Spoon Farm were supposed to be preparing to defend it. "Take and hold," had been the verbiage used. The other two platoons of our company, supposedly following along our advance would need a secure spot from which to pierce the rump end of the German trenches beyond road and river. I had not been informed as to how long we would have to hold this position, nor the methods by which we intended to do so. Times such as these would show those possessed of good intuition were invaluable. We had lost our platoon's only combat veteran, Sergeant Merrick who had gone to South Africa at the turn of the Century, in the first seconds of being under fire. All of us were reliant on those in positions above the ordinary private to know what was best to do next, forgetting perhaps that our trust was being placed in our superiors who were also emerging through this from a like level of absence of experience. Corporal Douglas had years of service in the pre-war Militia and from that alone he now was the most veteran among us, if only for the fact that he might know 'a thing or two.' Mister Thorncliffe had only just informed him he was the ranking NCO of those of us who had made the crossing. The Lieutenant had not even the mote of military experience of Douglas, his elevated position a result of higher education rather than prior service. However, he had demonstrated in our attack with the way he had led us obliquely towards the redoubt an inclination towards sound tactical decisions. Now that we had Spoon Farm, he credited himself again by consulting with Corporal Douglas on what to do next.

"The only way in besides this breach is the gate beyond the avenue letting on to the road. We need to block that in such a way as to deny Fritz from using it, but not so completely that it becomes difficult for Captain McCormack to pass through when he arrives with the rest of the company."

"When, indeed," Thorncliffe had said and although we heard it, the comment was probably not meant for us to. "Have you got anything in mind?"

"Yes, sir. Have some men scrape out rifle pits, over by the orchard at an angle to the gate, using the trees as cover. If we can make use of these machine guns, position them in the second floor windows of the farm house, overlooking the gate."

"Sounds good," the Lieutenant replied. "See to the machine guns with Strachan and Ferguson, Corporal. I'll organise a party to get those pits dug. I've a runner out to find Captain McCormack, watch for his return through this breach." He turned to leave for the orchard.

"Sir," Douglas said, before Thorncliffe had gone five feet, "lose your tunic and find a rifle. You're the only officer we've got and your fancy dress will invite unfriendly attention." I would have thought it impertinent for a corporal to speak thus to an officer. Only later would I learn that it was normal and, in some cases, critical that an officer be open to receiving advice from subordinates.

I didn't want to think about what our chances might be if the Hun were to pitch back into us in large numbers, especially as we had no heavy weapons other than the outside chance the German guns had not taken too much abuse to be ineffective.

"So," Andy said to me, "how d'you want to do this?"

"I think we should unload it first, before we move it."

"Go ahead, then," he invited.

"How? I don't know anything about these things."

"Well, I thought theirs were much the same as ours, so." I shot him a look.

"What difference does that make? Do you think I went to some machine gun lecture I never mentioned before now that took place within the five minutes we've been out of sight from each other this past year?"

He held his palms up, a calming gesture. "Alright, Felix. Let's not get you all wound up." Tapping the barrel jacket with the toe of his boot inquisitively he then said, "I don't suppose we could move it as it is. How hard can it be?"

"About five hundred rounds a minute in the wrong direction would be my guess."

We were not permitted, by the unfolding situation at large, to find out. Not a few moments after Mister Thorncliffe had left us to assess the functionality of the guns, the runner he'd dispatched returned, stepping lightly through the bodies we'd been gathering the stomach to move aside.

"Hi, fellahs," he said; an exuberant youth of ineradicable smile called Dewey, "Seen the Sir? Got a message for him." Douglas pointed to the orchard where

42

digging had commenced, Thorncliffe incognito among the men. Dewey trotted off without pause.

"Hang on," Douglas called after him, "what's the message?"

"Orders, Corporal," he answered, still moving towards Thorncliffe, but backward as he had turned to not put his back to us while talking, "from the Captain. We're moving back." That was unexpected. Hadn't anyone told our company commander how much it had cost us to get here? We had done as we had been told, this object was in hand. All that needed to happen was for Captain McCormack to bring the other half of 'B' Company forward and carry the attack through. Seemed to me only fair since we'd accomplished our task that everyone else attempt theirs. The desire I had just moments ago of leaving Spoon Farm to the Germans vanished with a rise in pride of ownership in the instant I heard that leaving was exactly what was going to happen. Being afraid of facing an enemy counterattack transmuted into anger at leaving without a fight. The seemingly insensible order to withdraw from a hard-won objective was infuriating; but those of us at Spoon Farm had no appreciation of how badly the entire attack had gone. Dewey had only given us the gist of the Captain's orders, not the reason for them. All along the axis of our advance, the situation was particularly bad. We at Spoon Farm had reduced only one strong point which did little to aid 'C' and 'D' Companies' demonstration against the mainline of resistance. Their assault had been blunted by overwhelming machine gun and artillery fire and those two companies had been unable to adequately suppress the enemy for the other part of 'B' Company's attack—Captain McCormack's flanking move via Spoon Farm—to proceed. Most other units involved in the day's fighting had been likewise stalled, making the whole effort a wash except for a few cases of isolated gains. Nearly everyone else had been obliged to retire to their jump-off positions.

"Meaning," Thorncliffe had told us where we'd gathered in the courtyard to hear the news properly, "we are further forward than anyone else and have no friends on either flank. We go back the way we came. Corporal Douglas, Ferguson, Strachan, take position by the shed and keep watch on the gate. I'll be at the breach. Lance Corporal Norton, lead the file through the breach and fall back towards our jump-off, double quick. Sloane, you will be last in file, be sure to tell me as you go, and for Heaven's sake both of you make sure you have everybody with you. Corporal Douglas, I will signal you by whistle to withdraw your covering party once everyone else is clear. Now, move!" Norton and Sloane went off to round up the rest of our number while Douglas brought Andy and me over to the shed to keep eyes on the laneway. The evacuation took a few minutes, but was made with all urgency. When the Lieutenant blew his signal and we moved back to the broken wall, it occurred to me that we were now the only Canadians in these parts. Thorncliffe told Douglas to lead, that he would bring up the rear. The first group led by Norton had made tracks and were well across the dyke road when we started our retirement.

It had not been a moment too soon. We were a handful of yards away from the narrow depressions we had sprung from earlier that afternoon when the German counterattack began. These positions were only meant to obscure us from the enemy as close as we could manage before having to advance over open ground. Improvised from roughly joining shell craters to create a long ditch, this line was never intended to be either shelter or fighting positions. I felt an awareness of the ground's inadequacies as a great shelling commenced. Gritty bursts of shrapnel flung out over the field we had abandoned. For most of us, for me, this was the first serious bombardment experienced at the receiving end. Further on, I would be able to reflect on this and find it laughable that I was so petrified. Fritz had only wanted to regain what he'd briefly lost and walked his shells far enough to ensure the capture. This display was minimal in effort, intensity and range, but each sparked flash and smutty cloud reached into my core and made me certain my moments were few; this groove of earth in which I cowered too shallow to protect against splinter and blast, but perhaps deep enough for my grave.

We remained stood-to, ready to repulse, until well after last light, but nothing happened except a change in weather, the clear skies of the day ceding to a full cover of wet clouds. Under a cold rain, we moved back in stages from jump-off to the main trench line where we remained for a few hours more until we were relieved and hustled to the rear. The entire confusing, frightening events of a single day had failed to completely settle in my mind, and I was bothered that it was sticking with me such that it was enough to distract me when I was meeting the new men Norton had brought up. It was then I would learn that some things would evade any attempt at finding sense. The worst of it was knowing that there would be uncountable times ahead of more such days this wretched place would present to me and I couldn't fathom how I could stand it more than once. Whether or not I could didn't matter at all. I had no choice one way or other.

Canada, January, 1936

"Hey," she whispered; a soft warmth of breath in my ear. Her arms crossed over my chest, she cradled me, sweetly gentle. "Hey, you're at home, you're with me, you're safe." I must have woken her, as I do from time to time as what I see when I close my eyes can cause me to stir in my sleep.

"I'm sorry," I said; a weak voice.

"For what?"

"That this keeps happening."

"Don't be, Kitten. You've had to go through so much." She stroked my hair, and I fell deeper into her embrace. I never know what to tell her with these episodes. Not about the details of my memories or how they can wash over me like a summer storm of quick and complete fury breaking as rapid as it formed. No, I never knew what to tell her about how good she was to me, how having her near kept me from being lost forever in the wreckage of my past. So, I told her what I always did, simple and very true.

"I love you." Her arms squeezed me tighter. "Was I shouting?" That happened too, sometimes, and it could be enough to wake the children. Hamish was old enough now to have some understanding, but Irene and Philip were quite young and a terrible midnight wail would frighten them.

"No. You were fussing about, but. I was worried you were going to launch yourself out of bed."

"I was dreaming," I said, in the candidness I felt secure in sharing with her, "of the time I first met your dad."

"Oh." We didn't discuss the war in any great detail, and her father's part in it hardly at all.

"Will you visit him when you go?"

"I expect so. He's buried none too far from where the monument is." Another squeeze.

"Good. He'd like that."

I didn't go back to sleep. I never could after one of those nights. It was still very early, that fearful indeterminate time of dark and quiet between night and dawn. I went down to the kitchen, put the pot on the stove for coffee and communed with Malachi. The mog was my excuse for airing my thoughts out loud without seeming to be talking to myself. He was a good listener; a stolid confidant who rarely interrupted.

"Meow," he said.

"Really? That's your answer for everything." My criticism didn't bother him, he only repeated himself. "Ah, ye big lump. Fine thing to be a cat. What have you got to worry about?"

"Meow."

"So you said." Oh, it's downright silly, chatting to him in this way, but being a little silly helps me, always has, in coping with the difficult. I sat at the table, keeping an eye on the stove for the water to begin popping in a lively fashion over the fresh grounds. He followed me, from stove to table. I stretched my legs out over the cold tile floor. Malachi slalomed through them and came to rest at my feet. A very small cast of purple sky was beyond the window above the sink, the briefest herald of the approaching day. Another difficult night was now almost entirely behind me. I knew it wouldn't be the last. There were such a number of things which could have me slip actively into my war years, and on any given night I could be visited by one, or by several, piling on in a crushing weight seamlessly blurred into each other in a continuity which left me with the same feelings the events had inspired in reality; fear and guilt. Guilt in particular is what had roused me so early in the morning and that alone was the reason beyond decent propriety as to why I had not ever been candid with Adelaide about her father's death. Decent propriety in this case being the platitudes of a quick and painless end; that the deceased had not suffered and was among friends in their last moments. Often, very little of that was entirely true, but little was served to the grief of relatives in not sparing the fine details. The way in which some men struggled to their deaths would, if shared, only detract from the memory of who they had been in life. With Kelley O'Leary, it so happened that all of those overused assurances were true. My problem with how he had died, and what I hadn't revealed to his daughter, my wife, that it was all my fault.

"It was all my fault," I told Malachi. He just stared up at me, winked one eye, then the other and licked his nose. The problem surrounding this was not only having withheld my culpability from Adelaide, but having done so for so many years and with its consistent gnawing away at me and her seeking to comfort me, I was in actuality receiving succor for my role in the orphanage of her and her brothers. I didn't kill him; though for my part in the circumstances I might as well have. Not only did I not do enough to prevent his death and that of Andy Ferguson at the same time but by a rather bizarre episode I had provided the man who did kill them with the weapon by which he did so. It was, in my view, more than negligence, although it was a great deal of that. I was by some extension an accomplice to their deaths. As usual, I resolved to myself and my cat that I'd never get beyond that event until I told Adelaide the truth; provided I do so at the right time. Such a time, though, always seemed to be in an unreachable future.

My mornings usually consisted of getting Aidie and the youngsters over to the school by car. Hamish had just started secondary school and preferred to walk with his pals than have his dad drop him off. After the school run, I might return home, run the errands or fulfill any task Bill may have set for me. I had none of that pressing on me, but decided to head over to Inchmarlo anyway. I was going to strike while the iron of my idea was hot. The drive to the Estate would take me through the town. Much of what had been built in Falls Parish beyond the intersection of the primary roads of Main Street and North Lake Avenue was original to the town's foundation. Pulling away from the robustly red-bricked primary school, which to me seemed a tiny building for tiny people, the spire of the grey stone church; a sharply tapering peak, could be seen clearly through empty branches of street-side trees. Houses along this stretch, 'South Main' as it's known for the collection of blocks below North Lake Avenue, are turn of the century beam and clapboard brightly painted with brick chimneys and tar shingled dormers giving features to otherwise flat facades. Others were older still, highly pitched roofs above lengths of block walls anchored either end by widths of lumpy stone and mortar which proceeded upward to flat-stacked chimneys. No two were quite alike and were grand character to a stretch of road which grew more uniform and squatly square through the commercial district past the Avenue which was called, incongruently 'Upper Main.' A great deal of Upper Main was new; that is, from after the war. The two-block stretch of Main Street divided by the Avenue, bordered by Station Road in the south and George Street to the north had been tarmacadamed in the twenties. Other core roads beyond those boundaries remained largely of paving stones, a few were set in brick. Any place beyond the painted lanes of proper road which delineated the optimistically named 'business district' which had a rudimentary hard surface ran only for a mile or two before giving way to dirt tracks of old and rutted wagon paths. The spurt of improvement projects which had begun enthusiastically immediately after the war had by now stalled in light of the present financial crisis. Ours remained a largely farming community and being well situated between Hamilton on the one side and Toronto on the other was cause for the hope that Falls Parish would grow into a hub feeding, in some ways literally, both cities. When the bubble had burst in 'twenty-nine, very little of what had been planned had been built, and the town remained confined to being an isolated dot on the map, largely self-sufficient but often not more than in a subsistent way.

At its most dense, Main Street was little more than town hall and church, fire station and bank with a dash of small stores and services spread on either side of the road in long, uninterrupted rows of brick and mortar. Taking Main all the way to George Street to reach the Second Concession beyond the town and along that line to Inchmarlo was a slightly longer route for me to take, but this morning I made the choice to avoid a more direct drive going along North Lake Avenue to spare myself any memories that may be provoked by what occupied space along its verges. Closest to the town was the slowly growing campus of North Lake University. It had been founded but a few years before the war and drew students from the wider rural areas of Falls Parish Township; the municipality rather than the town centre of the same name. There was no connection between the university and myself—I'd never get in the front door with my incomplete scholastics. It was, as it happened, the alma mater of many officers under whom I had served; some of them named on a plaque mounted within the main administrative building. There was scarce any need for me to call by, so any memory of men I'd known wasn't part of my desire to bypass the institution. What it would bring to mind was that I had yet to provide Paddy with a response to his proposition. That would be Major Patrick Desmond Thorncliffe, MC and Bar, who had been my commanding officer from my very first day in the army and remained so to the present, he being the officer commanding the only extant company the King's Own had been permitted to keep on establishment. When 'dressed up' we were required to live within the strata of officer and NCO. At all other times, which was most of the time, at Paddy's insistence, we treated each other as equals. After the war, he'd returned to NLU to further his education, in quick succession defending his Master's and PhD in Classics. Following his bestowment, he was immediately taken into the faculty. At about the same time I had begun to lobby Bill to come abroad with me, Paddy had laid out for me an opportunity which could lead to more consistent employment. I'd demurred as for what he had in mind, I was of no real use; or so I felt, anyhow. As Adelaide would be more likely to take Paddy's side, I'd not mentioned anything about it to her lest I be outnumbered. Just beyond a wide playing field circled by a clay track which marked the edge of campus was an imposing—perhaps purposefully so—great stone building which only last year had been re-dedicated as Sinclair Barracks. I think it had been built to resemble a fortress, with an enclosed court accessed by an iron gate set in a deep bricked archway. Its style of narrow, barred windows and corners of circular turrets cast upwards from huge sandstone block foundations made it seem to belong to an age beyond that of the town in which it stood. It was from that building my Regiment parades, and was my place of business about one day every fortnight. The new name—it had been North Lake Barracks previously—was a tribute to Colonel Barclay Archibald Sinclair DSO. He had founded the King's Own

Canadian Scots Regiment, meeting the extra cost of Highland uniform from his own purse and had been at its head from that beginning to the absolute finish of the war. If he were about to ask my opinion, I'm sure he would loathe that he died in bed, but a peaceful end of a long life was more suiting as brave, generous and kind figure he was. The man was unflinchable, even as the worst was happening around him, he always showed the most absolute coolness. Our 'Old Man' as he had been, he was never unreachable and through deed he consistently demonstrated he cared a great deal about the men he'd commanded both during the war and afterward. With her father dead and her eldest brother, Kelley the Younger having fallen off the face of the Earth, Adelaide had no one of majority to stand for her on our wedding day. Colonel Sinclair was only too happy to substitute as father of the bride. I was able to repay the favor, if less happily, when Missus Sinclair asked me to help bear his casket.

Much further along the Avenue, at the edge of town was a place I never went to or past if I could reasonably avoid it. Tremaine and Sons was the automotive garage I brought my Packard to when it needed to be taught a lesson, but it had once been a livery stable run by the titular patriarch, my good friend Tim Tremaine. Colin and Gregory, the sons, had succeeded to joint ownership when Tim had passed, the year before the Colonel. I don't visit them often outside of mechanical need ass in their presence I felt his absence the most.

Just then, on the jolting unpaved track outside of town, I worked the clutch and brought the car out of gear, allowing it to come to a rolling stop. Somehow, I had managed to make all the required turns to put me in direction of the estate, but I must have been too deep in thought as I remembered little of the drive. My mind on all the places I was avoiding kept me rather lost upstairs as even though I was on Second Concession as I should have been, I had driven right past Inchmarlo's front gate and had proceeded a mile or more beyond the property. It worried me, as it always does, these little mental holidays of mine. They were bad enough, a little embarrassing, when they came upon me sitting in my lounge. When they occurred while I was in command of a car on the road or men in the field, why, the results could be catastrophic. Times like these, my first name seemed to suit. I was lucky—felicitous, I think the root is—that I hadn't been the cause of an accident in such an absence. Or, perhaps as cats were often named in the same way, then maybe, cat-like, I had nine lives. If that were so, it would be by now far fewer than nine for all I've come through. I sighed, made sure the road was clear and turned the car around to head back in the right direction.

Scratching the match across his desktop, Bill touched the flame to the cigarette between his lip, then extinguished the tinder with a smoky puff and cast the cindered stick into an ashtray already growing full, despite the morning hour.

"How can you do that?" I felt compelled to ask.

"What, smoke? Tobacco is good for you." I recoiled.

"No, it isn't, and especially not for you."

"Rubbish. What does it matter, anyway?" Oh, right, he was dying, Lord help me. Perhaps if he couldn't breathe it all the way in, it wasn't doing him much harm, or maybe his lungs were beyond any further damage.

"Let me guess why you're here," I let him, "the monument thing, right?"

"Yes, Bill." I steeled myself, still uncertain what my line would be. In with both feet, then. "I've been doing some thinking, and," he stopped me cold, both in interruption and what he interrupted with.

"I'll go." I had to let that hang for a second or so. I hardly believed it; the two words flowed out among a bluish plume of breath. There was no way I had heard that right.

"Pardon?"

"You deaf? I said I'll go. You make the arrangements, have the bills sent here. Happy?"

"Suppose. What's changed your mind?" He didn't answer straight away, sent a cloud upward and stamped the butt out.

"I will tell you later. Right now, get going. I'm busy." I didn't fail to notice that the ashtray was the only item on his desk, but I wasn't going to contradict him. The discussion was far easier than I had thought it would be. Took a lot less of my time, too. With little else to do before swinging back to town to fetch my family at the school, I thought to get some fresh air from the funk of Bill's office with a wander through the vineyard. It wasn't the most pleasant of days and the scenery was stark; the rows of vines seemingly lifeless, gnarly twisted branches. I didn't mind that they lacked what splendour their mid-season potential would show as the field was solitary and quiet. Wind creaked through the lattice and training ties while distantly a locomotive passed in a whispered beat of clicks. It was a cool breeze, rising up above the calm in bursts, bringing with it a few large flakes of snow, forebears of a flurry which steely clouds were set to dispatch. I fussed my scarf so that it rested from my shoulders up beyond my jacket's collar to the bottoms of my ears and stuffed my hands into deep pockets. Moving along one row of vines to the next, each step packed the existing layer of snow down further with a small crunch.

I wouldn't label my cousin by any stretch of imagination as care-free or cavalier in his approach to life. Bill was rare to do anything without purpose behind it. Shrewd, calculating, there was little within him of whim or fancy, each decision made with the certainty of detailed consideration. He had never been considered by those who know him of being much fun. Uncle Isaac had been of the same cloth, so Bill came by it fairly enough, and perhaps as he was the elder of the two sons, Bill took on the mantle of becoming his father's successor, while Alec had been consistently in trouble for being flighty and irresponsible. It was a macabre thought exercise to imagine how the business might have fared had Eck been the only living heir. Bill's approach to life put us at odds, and I think that had a lot to do with how much I was like his brother and not like himself. Not to say this was a set of differences which caused us to fall out with each other; although that did happen sometimes. Rather, it was my nature of doing things in the moment it occurred to me to do them which differed greatly from his always steady judicious strides towards an end. I had fully expected our two waves to crash in my visit's purpose that morning, because I was me and he him. Stuff any satisfaction I had from getting what I had wanted. That had been shoved out of my brain by the big blank of what was setting his course in a tack away from where it had been the last time we had spoken on the subject. Through my experience I have come to know that men who had been a flickering moment from their own deaths and lived slotted themselves into categories of broadly different sorts of mentality. Some were those who had decided that as what happened to them had been insufficient to kill them, then perhaps nothing would. Others had the notion that Death had not finished what was started and only a matter of time remained before whatever forces governed the Universe noticed the error. Both types had overdrawn their accounts, and while one had impeccable credit, the other had brokered their lives on margin. Either way, that most base, most powerful fear which accompanies self-awareness; that of the knowledge of life's finality; was dismissed. Men unafraid of death were those who exercised the highest levels of courage or dangerous carelessness.

Bill had been neither of the two. He had been himself in a way that defied the fact he well should be dead. The man went on as if he'd never been shown the Gates, or that nothing in his life was out of the ordinary; going through his days mechanically and astutely performing his work without signal of how his near fatal episode had affected him. As it wasn't the type of reducing the fear of death that a near miss or close shave created; which was something I could speak towards from more occasions than perhaps were healthy, maybe it had taken a while to set in. Bill had opportunity to develop any philosophy of mortality over months of surgery and convalescence, and it appeared his resolution was to put it aside and get on with business. I don't deny it was commendable, just that it was out of place from all I knew on the subject; especially so with mind to how brutal his minuet with Death had been.

After coming over to England as a gunner with the First Contingent and being left back for want of guns, Bill eventually made it across to France when the 2nd Division had been formed; arriving a few months after Alec had disappeared. Despite having little opportunity for practice—guns and shells were immediately required at the Front and could hardly be spared for training— Bill was made a sergeant and put in command of an 18- pounder as part of a battery in the Canadian Field Artillery. They had been slamming away at some hill everybody seems to have forgotten about, not long after we had taken the Ridge. I don't think it was any huge fire plan; rather the daily consignment of shells intended to assure the Hun that we were still interested in seeing him off.

"We had to keep moving the guns forward," he had told me, year before last in a rare moment of candour. That we had been engaged in what we called 'quality control' at the time may have been an aid to bald frankness. It was a bit of a tradition, an end of season affair which had nothing but a sly wink to do with the integrity of Inchmarlo product. It couldn't be, as any true analysis had to already have been performed by Julian, Uncle Isaac's long serving expert vintner. In more recent times, Bill had kept this excuse to get tits-up exactly as his father had and now included my brothers in law, Chas and Hen; who at that particular moment Bill had sent out to the storehouse for more merlot. He must have felt at ease, the drink besides, it was just the two of us in the room.

"That's to do with your lot; we could barely keep up with all the ground you were getting hold of," he'd said, in a tone not too far from being accusatory; as if the infantry performing their jobs as expected—which is to say advancing upon and destroying the enemy—was somehow an inconvenience to him. Few times were as dynamic as the early weeks of spring, 1917. We were doing what had seemed impossible the year before. Taking the field as we did, we were gaining ground not only of great measure in distance; but strategically important ground at that. To this day, I still had doubts of any significance attached to a great deal of what I was participant in. No one had ever shared with me why such places like that lonely collection of buildings which we called Spoon Farm were so important to have spent lives to gain. I never doubted that our capture of the Ridge took away a critical piece of real estate from Fritz. They never got it back, either.

"Do you know how tough it is to move a field piece over rough ground at a pace in keeping with men on foot?"

"No, I don't."

"It's fucking well tough, Junior, let me tell you that. We did it, though," he had taken a voice somewhere between anger and pride. "It meant we had little time to mask the guns." Caution sacrificed for speed, the artillery spared themselves the work of putting up concealing screens and netting to hide the guns, particularly from the air, as Bill recounted. "Must have been a spotter plane. I never saw it, and there's no one else left to ask if they noticed. Only explanation of how accurate they were. Five rounds, big calibre stuff, high explosive. My gun was far right of the battery. I saw it all, in rapid succession—boom, boom, boom—" he pounded the desktop, jostling the empty bottles. "Each of our guns in turn, crushed by the force. I shouted at my men, a useless thing to do." He had been half-way between his gun and the ammunition limber, returning to his piece with a spare tool for setting fuses to replace that which one of his men had dropped and lost.

"Wouldn't have done any good. There was nowhere to go. I don't remember the hit. It seemed a great age of no time passing, my men frozen in the mechanics of loading the next round. I can even see the shimmer of sunlight bright off the brass case being shoved into the breach. Felix, I can see that one moment as sure as if I had a photograph of it. Everything of it all; my crew, sweaty, bare-chested, smeared with grease and mud, the hot steely smell of the gun and liquid carbon residue.

It's an enchanting smell, I don't know why. I see the whole of it as a mimed act, no sound at all penetrates that ringing of ears we suffered from the noise of our own guns." Bill paused, having painted such a picture that I could almost see it myself, looking one last time at his doomed crew.

"The next moment, I'm looking up at a bright, clear sky. I couldn't make any sense of it. Why was I lying down in the muck when I should be working? Memory of the moment snapped back to me. I tried to get up, I still had to bring that tool over. Something wasn't right, my body wasn't obeying my brain. No pain; none that I could recall, anyhow. My arm and leg, my whole right side was stiff and very, very hot. As clear as that instant before is to me, then as much as now, those minutes afterwards seemed muddled and sluggish, very confused." He tipped a bottle to my glass and his, but little dribbled out so he set it aside. "Slowly, I got over to my left, struggling to raise myself on the strength of one arm. I fell back again, but not before I had a chance to catch a quick look at my gun. It was nothing but flinders and twisted steel; it was what had been broken away in shards from the blast what hit me," he actually laughed at this, "I take that bloody gun with me wherever I go now." Then, his expression changed, a maudlin sadness, the accelerated switch of mood from high to low which drink could fuel.

"I only had one thought. I had to get away. Damn it, Felix, I didn't have a mind to check on my crew." I stopped him.

"They were dead anyway, Bill."

"To Hell with that; how did I know? All I did was try to save myself. I'd rolled over, which took some doing, and made towards the limbers. I had to get away; I knew what the Hun would do next and my respirator I had hung up by our ammo store." As if to illustrate his point without intention, he was seized and wracked by a fit of barking coughs. "Didn't make it very far. I heard those shells hit, thumping like duds into that muddy ground, then that terrible hiss." His eyes were damp. "Oh, those beautiful mares; such lovely beasts. One by one, still in trace, they tried to bolt, couldn't and without a whimper, fell over, twitched a bit and that was them. Oh, Felix, such bonny animals you never saw, choked to death. Nothing so cruel as that could ever be." Bill had fallen silent, the memory of his poisoned drive team seeming to rend him more than the loss of the men of his crew. I felt out of place, a curious observer to another man's grief and the quiet room sat heavy upon us. Something about horses tricked my soggy brain and without thought, I burst forth, rather loudly, I recall.

"Tae the Lairds of Convention 'twas Claverhouse spoke," which inspired Bill to join me next,

"If the King's crown goes doon thar'll be crowns tae be broke," and on we went banishing the past by belting out as best we could remember the words to "Bonnie Dundee." We were so lost in it, so raucous neither he nor I had noticed that some time through our recital the twins had returned, who set down the bottles brought back and applauded our effort. Bill was grinning when we'd finished.

"Hey, Chas, come fill up my cup," said Bill, which he and I found the peak of hilarity, and we both laughed darkness away, my brothers-in-law studying us with mirrored quizzical faces, no doubt thinking us to be mad men.

"Felix!" Carried over a cold breeze winding through the empty vines partnered with a light dance of snow was my sister's voice. Morrigan ran the Estate's domestic functions, more so now that Aunt Ruth and Ma were getting older. She managed the household staff, a small clutch of maids and cooks as well as the field hands' accommodations and payroll. My sister never strayed far from the estate; only having lived away for a short time during the brief interlude between being a wife and a widow. Her husband I had never met, a merchant sailor who had been sent to the bottom of the Atlantic by means of a German torpedo.

"Felix!" she called again, louder.

"Eh?"

"For goodness' sake, what have you been up to, standing out in the snow? It would be a fine thing for you to freeze to death ten yards from the house with you staring off into nothing. You'd best waken up your ideas. Adelaide called; have you not to be at the school?"

Surely it wasn't time to have been there. I pulled my watch, a much loved and much worn piece, from my jacket. Oh, damn. I must have been out for an age. Only then did I realise how cold it was. I started back over the field at a trot.

"Ring her back, will you, Morri? Tell her I'm on my way." I was having a rather bad time of going absent over the past few days, and now I was probably going to get an earful about it.

To say Adelaide was put out by my lateness was difficult. I truly believe she made the best efforts to understand my shortfalls. Absent-mindedness wasn't anything created by my experiences; it was an indelible trait I've always had and could never get rid of. Perhaps the frequency and severity which I experienced spells were influenced by the war, only if it was to that hard time in my life my mind wandered to the most. The snow had begun to come by in earnest when I got to the school, which had slowed my drive a bit. Our roads, paved or not were not really intended to be travelled upon in anything other than the fairest conditions. I apologised, of course, when I pulled up, for being late. Aidie brushed it off, yet another one of my quirks, and dismissed it without asking me for an excuse, perhaps because I would have none to offer. Excuses are just bullshit, anyway. I can't count any which wouldn't be a wormy plea for clemency in some way of trying to diminish an act—or failure to act—already done. Her mood didn't seem altogether terse, the whole thing not worth going over, maybe. Anyhow, dinner was as usual, if not pushed back for the time which had come to be lost.

It was one of my favourite times of day, encircled around the table with them all, I felt less lonely than I usually do. I was pleased that Hamish had shown a good deal of initiative in that when he came home he set the fires and furnace and filled the coal buckets. It's his job to do anyway, but it was nice he'd done so without needing to be told. That I might have clouped him if I came home to a cold house was likely his motivation didn't sit well with me. I learned a long time ago it was better an assigned task be performed with a mind towards responsibility rather than fear of punishment for shirking. I wish I knew how to conduct myself in one way more than the other with my children, in a benign and constructive fashion as I have with my time in the army. I might know better, but that knowledge does me little good when I have such a weakness over my emotions. I certainly lacked the requisite understanding and practical application to inspire divine cooperation in our children as Adelaide had. Catching them afoul of rules or instruction, all she had to do was point at them sternly and hiss "Confession!"

I did not grow up in a Catholic household, and I really had little idea how guilt-inducing the prospect was. For we three; Morrigan, myself and our younger brother James, it was violence or fear of such which was implemented to keep us in check. To say that my approach is no different from how I was raised doesn't cut ice with me.

Throughout the dinner hour, the snow had continued and was settling in quickly rising drifts over roads and foot paths which required my attention to clear off around the front walk and driveway. In about an hour or such, Hamish and I were nearly finished. It was getting easier to rope him into household chores as he'd begun to find "Antoine and Belfry" a little juvenile. We only had the one set, so from seven to eight every weeknight the radio was co-opted for the purpose of keeping track of the dimwits' continued adventures; which never removed far from a set formula. Antoine needed constant supervision. There was rarely a moment in which Belfry was required elsewhere which didn't result in his counterpart tearing a priceless painting or inadvertently releasing a supposedly dangerous animal they'd been minding. It begs the question as to who keeps putting those idiots in charge of such things. Damage done, and thus, plot advanced, Belfry would return and the pair would have a rote exchange.

"What have you done now, Antoine?"

"Why, nothing, Belfry, nothing at all."

"Nothing? Well, it sure is a whole lot of nothing, then." There would be several minutes of lunacy in which various, often ridiculous, solutions were attempted, only to find out that the wrecked artwork was actually counterfeit or the vicious animal was in reality trained for the circus and had drawn an appreciative audience as opposed to mauled victims. What rubbish. Despite my distaste for the show, which was immaterial as I was not the audience it played for, I could have scored huge points with my children if I ever let it be known that one of the actors, he who played 'Antoine', a man called Llewellyn Dewey had been one of my old platoon's runners. I didn't let on because of any modesty on my part. The reason I kept it a secret was that I felt it might ruin the fantasy of the show. Llew was nothing at all alike to the person he put voice to.

Well, he was diminutive and excessively gentle in temperament, but he was no buffoon and had not a mote of his alter-ego's cowardly bent. That trait was just a foil to the more brash and overbearing other half of the duo, the loud-mouthed 'Belfry.' Truly, Llew was exceptionally brave. Time and again, he had risked his life to carry messages and orders over deadly ground. His last act of the war had been deemed courageous enough for an award of the Distinguished Conduct Medal. That decoration singled him out as the highest recognised soldier of Six Platoon, a head above me, in fact. Not bad for a chap who'd never fired a shot in anger. I doubted it was possible to put Llew in a state of anger, anyhow. It didn't mean I had to like his work, although it pleased me he had done so well, and was the idol of children everywhere, including my own.

As Hamish and I were scraping the last of this light dusting, the front door was flung open, the hallway lamps silhouetting Adelaide in the frame.

"Sergeant Major Strachan!" she yelled, her habit of addressing me by title being a peculiar way of letting me know she was cross. Hamish picked up on that.

"Uh-oh, Dad," he whispered, "looks like you're about to catch Hell," to which I cuffed his ear, a light warning tap.

"I'll be having no more of that language from you, Hammy." A light warning tap, I scoffed at myself. I could call it a tickle, if the effort was to try to make myself feel better about doing something I knew hurt more that the blow itself. It made no difference how I labelled it and my son's sheepish look tore into me harder than any blow I could deliver. I have no idea where my temper comes from other than a place beyond my control. What does one do? Catalogue it with the other unanswerable items of my mood and move on to the next moment with no resolve other than to distance myself by a matter of seconds from my lesser qualities. To Aidie I called back,

"Yes, dear?"

"Don't you 'yes, dear' me, Felix. I would speak to you in the kitchen. Now." I've got a smart kid. Seems like I was about to catch Hell.

"Finish up here," I told Hamish, "and be ready with that shovel, your Mum might need you to dig my grave."

I had no notion as to what I could have done to vex her so. It's not within her to have guile enough to allow hours to pass, to sit through a chatty and fine meal only to haul me up for an earlier transgression. Adelaide delivered her feelings, of one sort or another, directly as they came to her. As such, this had nothing to do with leaving her too long at the school, I was sure. But what could it have been? I went inside to accept my fate. Jacket, hat, scarf and gloves set on pegs to drip over the thick mat we laid by the front door in winter, I stepped out of my boots and strode into the kitchen. Adelaide was sat in such a way to face the entrance from the hall, so I had a continual view of her usually soft, rosy expression set sternly, her jade eyes peering at me sharp enough to etch glass. She wasn't just upset; she was pissed off; though I'm not as stupid as to say that out loud. In times like these, it was better off to say nothing at all.

69

"That was Patrick on the telephone just now," she began, meaning Paddy—Major Thorncliffe. Aidie never shortened any Christian names. I remained standing in the kitchen doorway, keenly aware that my feet, in heavy wool socks were damp and chilled on the thick checkerboard tiles. I waited for her to continue. Not that I lack integrity to cop to anything I'm brought to account over, it was usually best to let her lay out the charges so I could avoid coming clean on the wrong issue.

"Do you mean to tell me he's offered you a position and you've not given him an answer?"

"Well," I started, no more than a sort collection of sound to fill empty air. A stall, noting else, as I had no ready response to give her. I couldn't have, if I'd not had one to give Paddy in the first place.

"There are people going hungry for want of a dollar, and you're turning your back on work?"

"Ah, but, we do alright. Nobody's hungry in this house. Except Malachi, maybe."

"No use in trying to charm me this minute. Sure, we meet our ends; we're certainly more fortunate than some others. That aside, it would keep you busy. Felix, you're forever at a loose end these days without enough to do."

"I'm plenty busy," I tried to put across. She had none of it. Her look soured further.

"Busy? You flit about from here to the Estate with little purpose. William has got all the help he needs without you."

70

"So what if I don't go along with what Paddy has asked? What's so important that I take work we don't have a need for me to do?" Adelaide's face changed again; less anger, more worried.

"Because, Kitten, one day you'll wander off into your mind and not come back to me." I came in and took the chair beside her. She was right. I might just get stuck in my own twisted path of overgrown memory. I worried about it, as I should, but it seemed to be something that gripped her in a real terror. I know what fear looks like played over a person's face, and I saw that in her, pupils black and wide; a deep tunnel without light to show her soul at the far end.

"Aw, Pet. I'm not going anywhere," which I wasn't sure wasn't a lie, but I took her hand in mine to prove my reassurance.

"I hope to God not. Having something to fill your days would keep your feet on the ground." I couldn't disagree, but I at least could tell her why I had put a response to the offer aside.

"Did Paddy say what the job was about?"

"No. He only mentioned that you'd put him off, which he was taking to mean you weren't interested. So?"

"He wants me to become an instructor with North Lake University's branch of the Canadian Officer Training Corps."

"What is that, exactly?"

"Preparatory work. Classes and drills for university students to give them the requirement to sit their exams for a certificate they can use to obtain a commission." A lesson from the Great War was that the need for junior officers could not be met by supply. This thing, which Paddy had charge of at his school, worked towards creating a surplus of qualified candidates ready to take a commission within days of any large military emergency.

"I don't understand," she said, "isn't that altogether similar to what you do with the Militia? Why can't you do that a few more days a week?" Similar, I could concede. Really, though, the Militia was only a farce of army work. We drilled and practiced field problems, when we could get the troops to turn out or get our hands on enough equipment. It was a bit more like a private club than any true military outfit. I was coming up on twenty-one years in the service, poised to turn out for a pension. At which point I would no longer have a hand in any of the army's affairs. Only more idle time, Adelaide might point out. Well, I could find other things to occupy myself, but not this scheme; not for what it would make my responsibility. As Company Sergeant Major my position was to ensure the Other Ranks were present and correct. Instructing Officer Cadets, as Paddy was trying to get me to do meant giving my knowledge and experience over to men who would be making—be required to make—sound and timely decisions in the most strenuous conditions. My own record in such matters was wildly insufficient, and I was not prepared to put more on my conscience my inabilities had already placed.

"I'm no good for it," I found myself saying. It was clear she didn't believe me, so I pressed on. "I mean it. I will—as I have done—make mistakes."

"We all-" I stopped her, let go her hand and slammed my open palm on the table, which startled her. My words were slow, determined.

"I make mistakes, and that's what gets men killed." I wasn't speaking of probabilities, there were a number of examples I could site where my influence on events had not been sufficient to keep my men safe and all of them crashed through my mind in that instant, the visions and sounds of each one of many incidents flowing into every other in a singular, awful collage.

"Felix, love," she replied gently, "you're much too hard on yourself. I happen to know that you're far smarter than you think you are." Oh, not this again. Saying something over and over doesn't add to truth. This wasn't anything to do with being smart, anyway. Whatever intelligence I possessed made no difference to the images chiseled into my memory. I didn't want to hear it, her reassurances, her compassion. I was too occupied unwillingly reviewing scenes I was hardly able to bear at the time when they'd occurred and could not bear them any more so no matter how often they reappeared.

"So you keep telling me."

"Would I," soft words, "if it wasn't so?" I felt a flush rise past my collar, my thoughts too busy with terrible things of long ago to remain in the present. It seemed madness might not be far off as I was quickly losing the grasp of my composure which was slight at the best of times. I wasn't angry at her; I had no reason to be. My anger was at myself, a long-standing feud to which I'd found no resolution straining at me constantly under the surface. I stood sharply, the chair spinning away from me, all that tumult within overboiling outward, bursting away from me in a venomous shout something I had kept from her in all the years we've known together.

"If I'm so bloody smart, how come your father is dead?" I left the room before I could clearly see the wounded expression which I had no right to cause.

France, April, 1917

It always seemed to be some sort of wooded glade we were brought to immediately after being relieved from the line. I'd never spent so much time in forests and such like than I did in France and Belgium. At first, I'd thought perhaps the brains at the top end hoped that surrounding us with nature would help soothe the nerves of those who'd recently been exposed to the hardships of the front line; like the way a busy banker would quit the city at the weekend for fresh country air. That was by no means the reason. Our bosses did care about our well-being, though I'm sure that concern didn't go so far as desire to provide us pastoral backgrounds in which to rid ourselves of the jagged funk we collected upon any duration on the line. Very simply, woods such as this anonymous collection of trunks and shrub were used for concealment, especially from eyes above, which was still a novel concept. Such a purpose's effect was doubtful as the trees hereabouts had yet to fully punch forward with new leaves. Only the tiniest specks of green were working through otherwise bare branches. We'd certainly be spotted by any airman who cared to look, finding bundles of animated serge through a natural lattice like a nosy neighbour peering past a fence. It had snowed rather unexpectedly a few days ago, the day of our attack, and the weather had remained cool. This had left slushy clumps of filthy melt in the crooks of tawny roots. Ground underfoot, lain with a rotten blanket of last autumn's leaves, worked between thaw and freeze; so where I sat was grubby, cold and damp. Mattered little, that. All of us were filthy from what we'd been doing. I don't believe the enormity of what we had accomplished had settled. I really didn't know what such a big deal it was until some months later when Ma sent along a clipping from the Falls Parish Register. In it the journalist—who was writing from nowhere near France, so a grain of salt was required—had reminded his readers that one hundred years ago a man could be absolved his misdeeds if he could correctly claim to have fought at Waterloo. Never minding the historical veracity of that, such was the prestige we had gained in conquering the Ridge. Tosh; absentee drivel. Not one of us gave a flying fuck about prestige; we were just thankful we were still alive. I was a great deal more polite than that in my return letter to my mother.

All it had been at its occurrence was another fight, another episode of instant madness in which things happened so brutally swift it took an age afterward to make sense of it all. Granted, of course, one be permitted such an age to ponder and sort the litany of input accumulated. I'd find it easy to believe there's plenty who were killed in one scrap who hadn't fully sussed the fine details of how it was they hadn't been killed in the scrap just prior. I can't adequately describe what it's like to be in the middle of such things. It's either too extreme on one account of sensation or another that it defies definition; or it is that all energies are so electrically focused on moving from one instant to the next intact that the brain has no room to catalogue everything. I remember the abstract, the noise especially, but fine details escape me, for the most part. Except, and I cannot put this too finely, the worst, most extreme snatches of events within events. Those are the things which penetrate deep within, hold fast and cannot be diluted or dissolved even over a long passage of time.

From where I had tucked it in my web belt, I brought the pistol out, turned it over in my hands. Tim must have seen me do so, for he walked over, and sat beside me with a squelch of fetid floor.

"Are you going to keep it?" There was a good question. It was a very fine weapon, a nearly new Colt automatic. Possession of a sidearm, no guarantee for non-officer types, particularly one of this kind made one the envy of others. Then, there was what misery this particular piece had caused; things which couldn't be undone whether or not I held on to it.

"I might, just. That is, if I don't give it away freely to the next German who passes by."

"You aren't blaming yourself, Catscratch?" He asked; a genuine, paternal tone of concern.

"How can I not?"

We had made our approach between two storms. The first was planned, perfected if not having been practically tested; the shielding creeping barrage moving point to point in a rigidly timed tide of hit, lift, shift and hit which when done well gave us a wall of spinning steel to walk just yards arrear from. It determined that Fritz could not mount his works to repel us until we were at the very edge of those works. The barrage would then clear off to allow us to take our prize and keep any hope of our enemy's retreat or relief slim by grinding down his rearward approaches.

The second storm was unexpected, and fortuitous. Thick and fast wind, moving in the same direction as our attack was pushing damp snow towards the German lines. Had the Hun not been forced low by our barrage, this blizzard would have stung and blinded him and its fullness shrouded our figures to anyone at distance. Throughout the war I was never not wholly unafraid, nor could I say that continued exposure made any difference to reducing fear. At most, there might have been gained some insight to what might be dismissed as a present threat. Gaining that insight was critical in determining when to lay still, when to move forward or backward or when, no matter action or inaction, moments were in no one's hands but God's. Besides coming to understand what needed my concern or merited ignoring was a bitter realisation that it was certain as time progressed and the war continued it grew measurably worse in superlative deadliness. What this signalled to me was that the longer I was present in this realm, the more peril I would be exposed to which diminished in measure the odds of my survival. So, while always there was a seam of fear, I could say that on this particular morning of shell fire and snow fall I felt the least amount of terror than any other time when moving towards the enemy.

The two storms together were not entirely ideal in concert. We had to move to the artillery fire plan in exact measure. Elsewise, we would either be without the advantage of protection it gave us, or underneath it ourselves. While the details of this plan had been inclusive of the infantry's capability to move at speed over the terrain we faced; I don't know if those planners had made any considerations for the terrain being less than ideal. The snow wasn't deep, and it was landing on ground still frozen from the chill. Even so, it was a slick surface; hard to gain purchase upon and we needed sure-footedness to cope with the final few yards of the assault being uphill. We could do it, we had to do it. I'd be damned, and quite rightly so if I was going to allow a spring squall to hold me back. This motivation to my task was far beyond anything of my prior experience. It was a drive which had been augmented by not only having been told what was to be accomplished but also by having made understood why it was important; that our participation fit into the wide scope of the entire operation. Knowing that taking our objective had real significance made a world of difference. We had a sense of having a stake in success which had been absent last autumn. As far as I'm aware, our orders for the attack on Spoon Farm had little to do with explaining effect of what we were being sent to cause. Quite possible the officers had been given such specifics which works out to six men in two hundred in a rifle company who'd any clear idea of our goal and how to achieve it. It hadn't occurred to me then what a daft idea that was. An ordinary private as I had been at the time had savvy enough to follow direction, and little more than that. Almost everything in the year we'd spent training before even getting to France had been incomplete of anything save the simplest of concepts with regard to field problems. Keeping things simple admittedly has its attractions. It saves a bunch on time to not have to teach beyond simplicity of the subject, or student, for that matter. Problem was that no-one had ever seen anything like this war, and none could have fathomed how much mechanisation changed war's behaviour, giving almost all advantage to the defender in pure numbers. That meant for us being set loose on Spoon Farm our methods, anything but advanced to begin with were outdated; a redundancy created whenever it had been first demonstrated that a company of 120 riflemen could be outgunned tenfold by a section of nine men operating three Maxims. Our work to reach the level of skill required to have any chance at success at the Ridge had needed to be remedial in some respects, revolutionary in others. One nagging and unavoidable concern was that we were on a tight schedule to have everything—old and new—up to snuff in time for the offensive. It was such a narrow time frame it seemed insufficient to learn all which had been missed, overlooked or recently developed.

Six months from our first trial had come and gone and perhaps half of that time had been dedicated to our becoming ready for this attack. For our part in the General Offensive of 1917, we'd first have to get beyond the rudimentary training we'd had and gain the proficiency of regulars while learning all the adjusted doctrine which had been developed to compensate for the realities of the modern battlefield. This became more an immersive process the closer it came to stepping past the Line of Departure. All of that went on as we still did our part in front line rotations. From just after the New Year, our position remained stable, making each trip to the firing line a practical application of the performance objectives within the updated, amended or new manuals and pamphlets printed by the War Office. One thing we had been tasked with in combining what we were learning and maintaining a static defense was to be in control of No-man's Land. We had to become familiar with the ground our eventual attack would cross, while ensuring the integrity of our section of the line and protecting the great deal of preparatory work, including what was being done by engineers and tunnelers. Constant patrols, observation posts and aggressive raids grew our confidence in arms and allowed us intimate knowledge of our environment. What we were doing was also keeping the enemy on their back foot. Our continual presence in the contested ground made outward travel on Fritz' end prohibitive. Knowing by reasonable inference what our activity signified, their priority became strengthening the positions from which to repel an attack. Already they had great advantage of the high ground, plus they'd had it in hand for several years of improvement and had defeated all previous attempts at it. Unless we were able to take our purpose seriously in all we did, our attack wouldn't stand a chance. All winter long we were kept busy in studying the landscape, in person where our patrols gathered first-hand intelligence and from higher headquarters in the form of aerial photographs, survey maps and a scale model of the whole axis of our advance in proper relief detailed to show all notable features.

Training began to consist of mock attacks over a hill which bore some resemblance to our objective so that we knew what it felt like to take a high feature by going directly up it. It came a point through all this applied learning I felt I could move to my specific objective blindfolded. I had certainly been over it several times in the dead dark of night. Given such detailed understanding of terrain our confidence in success became unshakeable. We worked the land in such a way as to stake our ownership of it and discourage any interloping. As there could be no serving of notice of eviction until everything was in place for the General Offensive, the best we could do was make clear to the Hun that his lease was shortly due to expire. What we did leading up to the attack when we were forward continued to keep the initiative in our favour by being a constant nuisance. The idea was to take the fight to the enemy without let and thus wear down their resolve. For months on end, raids against their works and outposts left them uncertain as to our intent. Because our work up included these practical elements, there were times we had to make allowances for losses prior to the main event. When one of those raids, which turned out to be both the largest and the last, claimed, among many others, Matt Norton, I had been bumped up to take over his command of One Section, Six Platoon. It was the men of this section I led towards the enemy that morning, in my second proper battle and the first time I had been put in charge of something, ever.

Our approach to the point of entry to the German trench had gone almost as well as we had practiced.

Mill bombs had scattered those defending the fire bay, in one turn of the word or another. There was nothing to stall our progress, that was the main thing. The models we had studied and the mock-ups we'd used in training had been very well done. I had never been in that trench, but I felt so familiar with it, thanks to those training aids, it was as if I had stood in that place a thousand times before. My leap over the parapet was a touch sprightlier than was cautious and I slipped a bit as I landed on the elevated wood floor below. In that, I lost a fraction of a second, but it was nearly enough to be my last. I barely had gained my feet when my eyes came against a shimmer of steel, a bayonet, being driven towards me be a Hun who'd just stepped beyond the traverse to my right and into the bay. I parried, automatically, instinctively and took a pace towards my adversary to deliver my riposte. I will never know if I would have made my thrust if I'd recognised him before I ripped into him with a lunge so hard, I took him off his feet, stuck so deep in his gut I had to put a boot on his shoulder to give me leverage to withdraw my point. Within the first seconds of gaining entry to the trench, leading my section to its objective of a machine gun casement, I had killed the only person on that gruesome tally of mine whose name I'd known. He was my enemy, and he may not have paused if he'd placed me, but nevertheless, writhing his last on the slatted wooden trench floor was Ulrich Ehrlingbacher.

Acquainted over a dead officer I had been sent into No-man's Land to retrieve sensitive documents from about six weeks before we attacked the Ridge; we'd spoken a handful of words. Ulrich's English was just good enough for his commander to send him to wait by the corpse in anticipation someone might come to find it. I believe they may have thought it might be a stretcher party, to fetch the body itself, and in a rare moment of decency decided to warn off such an attempt. This officer had been killed not twenty yards from the German parapet; the same one I would force my way across on the attack. Mucking about in shifting a body so close to enemy lines would only result in more casualties, so they sent Ulrich to wait. I hadn't been sure what to make of it, I had never been so close to a German I hadn't been in the process of killing; and here was one taking dictation to get the details in order to place the body in a marked grave. "A soldier's burial," is what Ulrich had promised. Never mind I gave him the wrong name, that was in itself a whole other affair, in which this officer had made his way to the front lines under false pretenses for a purpose he'd been stopped by his death from carrying out. Then, there was the pistol. The officer had it drawn when he had been shot and it lay in that bit of low ground in easy reach of both me and Ulrich. It had been very dark, that night in February, and I hadn't been able to determine if Ulrich had been armed. I had my rifle and a trench knife, so the advantage may have been mine. However, this was a tenuous truce which could be ruined by any sudden movement made by either one of us. So, in that moment I bought my safety by offering the Colt to him so long as he waited until I was well gone to snatch it up. That was that, and aside from being an extraordinary episode, I gave the whole thing very little thought and went on with the war.

So, it had come to that strangely snowy April morning where I had run into—run through—the only German in spitting distance who was likely to have a Colt .45 snugly wedged between wide leather belt and grey tunic. I was surprised, surprised to the boundary of shock, and that held me in place, I tarried a moment, then cut right to move towards the traverse my first men were charging. By the time I got there, the casement had been taken. My men were arranging themselves to either cover likely approaches of counter attack or to link up with Two Section who would be working down the same trench in the opposite direction, all exactly to plan and repetitive drills. I cannot describe the absolute thrill which coursed through me at the time, a genuine joyful surprise that things had gone so perfectly; which spoke towards how often I had come to expect things to place anywhere close to perfect. Our day's work, this moment which had consumed most of our active time since January, was done and dusted within the fifteen minutes we'd been allocated to do it.

There was one detail I had missed, an unforeseen, unpredictable variable I had overlooked. In my encounter with Ulrich at the first moments of gaining lodgement, I had hesitated, then moved on without following through. I had not stuck him a second time to make sure he was dead. I paid immediately for that, and the memory of it continues to extract a toll. While the elation of the feat we had just pulled off was just beginning to gel, pounding and powerful gunshots carried over from the direction I had come. I returned that way to encounter the wickedly horrid display my negligence had caused. Andy Ferguson, as my 2I/C had been last man in. His role being that of a wrangler, giving direction to the men I wasn't able to because of my position at the front of our file. He'd not made it any further than the fire step, where he had taken pause, quickly dying. There was no question of that. His farm boy frame had been passed through by several shots. A .45 at close range does not create straight channels through-and-through. Slugs tend to carve ever-widening paths as they travel beyond impact. It was impossible to tell how many times he'd been hit, exactly. The ratio of what had been removed by force from his body to what remained was nothing from which anyone could recover. As fatally hurt as he was, Andy had got a shot off from his rifle, which had been Ulrich's coup-de-grace. In between the two, Ulrich at the parados wall and Andy at the parapet side, a squat, rotund and mostly headless heap lay; a heavy fall having snapped the slats which made the raised floor of the trench. Kelley O'Leary was dead. Andy had time left for only a few words before he slumped over, death rarely being graceful, and for a moment I was by myself in a section of German trench, presided by these spiritless men. I had been privy to vulgar scenes fairly often by that point, but this was the first time such a display made me feel sick. It was a slaughter yard of incomplete figures, every surface of this small section of trench had one bit or another of the pieces which King's Horses and Men couldn't put together again. It wasn't that sight which sickened; my gut had plummeted and churned in witness of my most dreadful error.

Andy had been my friend since we had been in the queue next to one another to sign up for the service. It was he who first came up with the nickname "Catscratch," and had the lively nature to ensure it caught on with all our other mates. He and I had walked every step of this foul business together. Rarely was there a moment when one of us was given a tough job that the other didn't elect to come along. In that, he had saved my life, once. Twice, perhaps. I was not able, could never be able to say the same.

Kelley never said very much, not venturing beyond single words on the occasions which he did, which made him hard to figure. His sparseness of words gave him an impenetrable personality. Perhaps it was best to view him as a man of actions, and his had been to watch over his section mates with the diligence only a father could have. That was a vigilance which he applied even to me, which was a bit awkward seeing as I outranked him. I don't recall anything that he'd done which was directly to my salvation, but he, like Andy, had never come up short to any dangerous task; which certainly helped to keep many of us able to see the end of another day. Everything going on around me as I took in the scene before me, the crash of shell bursts, the whir of spinning ball bearings, tinny snaps of small arms fire, shouts of orders, screams of wounded, wail of bagpipes, had no effect on me. The world was noise and for a moment I stood apart from it all. It was Tim Tremaine who called me back into the urgency of the present.

Gently, he spoke to me upon sight of the gory surroundings, bringing my mind to remember there was still a lot left to do and I could not have the time to grieve over what I had caused. I would find that I would never have ample time for that. A small consolation was that I had not seen it happen. The image I was faced with was terrible enough, something which would not lose cohesion in the recess of memory. So much the better I didn't have a record of the actions which had taken place, leaving me without the material to have it play out on the stage of my mind again, and again, and again.

Once the business of securing our objective—consolidating as it's known—was complete there would be time to organise the mess which had been made. Lieutenant Thorncliffe oversaw the coordination of the platoon's efforts in turning the trench we'd captured from the way it had faced us that morning to facing it in the direction our fight was moving. As usual, the Lieutenant was at the forefront, certain, confident in his fashion which reassured us all. This behaviour was even more remarkable as he was sporting several ugly, deep cuts caused by a German grenade which had been thrown his way on the approach. The same bomb had killed Sweeny, his batman. All he said to me when I reported to him was

"I'm sorry, Felix," which was a rare and touching intimacy. "Let's keep looking forward." So that's what I tried to do, without any certainty that I could.

There was little worry about a counterattack where we were holding. Our new real estate had been the foremost German line; part of the system of trenches we'd called the 'Red Line.' This was the first of four such reporting lines; to be assaulted and captured each in turn in a kind of leap-frog method. We who had been first out at 'Zero Hour' took and held the Red Line only, which follow up units would pass through on their way to fight for the next bit of vital ground, the 'Black Line.' A lot of traffic came through as the day went forward, fortunately all of it going in one direction and not the other. With Tremaine's help, we placed the bodies to one side of the trench using Andy and Kelly's canvas kilt aprons to cover all three as best we could. The snow, still falling, rested in small batches in the creases and depths formed by the material resting over rough remains. For the course of the rest of the day, I spent my time moving from one traverse to another, those immediately left and right of that fatal fire bay. My section was split between the two opposite lengths and I had to do my duty to look after the living. There was nothing I could do for the dead.

The sun set, behind us, perhaps a little further away than was usual for the distance we had covered from the horizon. Fighting continued, though this had also outpaced us, with the occasional bright flash of a furious explosion to accompany the rumbling echo of constant artillery punctuated with sharp rasping pops and ticks of rifles and machine guns growing further estranged from us on the Red Line as the battle moved along. With nightfall, and that we were well away from the developing fray, word was passed along to us to stand-down fifty percent. This allowed half of the men to rest in place while the other half stood watch, switching over on a two hour bit. Tim said he'd remain on for the first turn. Allowed a moment to myself, I went back to that fire bay and sat with the departed. I had taken up the pistol from Ulrich's hand in the immediacy following that awful event. To the man's credit, he had managed to get the whole magazine, seven rounds, out, hitting two targets while he lay eviscerated on that wood floor. Such things are what posthumous awards are meant for, and a real pity that it added to the sheet of the wrong side. I didn't want to think about it, and distracted myself watching the Very flares ascending in daylight brightness, then returning, crackling, sparking as the fall of a dying star. Once spent, they winked, flickered and came back to earth; the trail of smoke from their burning spread on the wind, the burnt core landing and hissing lightly from snowflakes made to melt at a distance from contact by means of latent heat. Smaller flares, of fireworks colours and swishing rockets added to the sudden brightness of the Very illuminations; a radiance which gave the dark sky a festive touch not in keeping with setting. If I could ignore the purpose of those flares and rockets and care only for the way they danced with each other among the blowing snow and pitch coated sky, I could pretend to be far away from this space of desolation, wish myself back to the fields of my home. I could just about transport in my imagination to any place where such absolute things as life and death; of preserving one and causing the other had never been put to me as something of my concern or influence; anywhere but where I was, where I could not be forced to act as an agent of suffering—mine or anyone else's. These three objects, that's all they were, what had made them men; that intangible force of existence had gone, they were not the first I had seen. This was the first time I had been really responsible for the deaths of human beings, if only because it had always been simpler not to think of the enemy as such. That loader I had shot and killed at Spoon Farm had been nobody. These three with me here had been somebody. It made a good deal of difference in how I felt about being a contributor to their last moments. The more I tried not to think of it, the more I did, so I kept looking upward, counting the flares as they puffed and popped, my head back so that I couldn't tell if the dampness on my cheeks was falling snow or weeping tears.

"Hullo?" Came a voice from the sandbagged heights of what had been our way in. I turned, stood up.

"Yes?"

"Stretcher bearers, Corp. Time to bring out your dead." Was the fool smiling?

"Don't be so fucking cheerful, mate. These are friends of mine."

"Sorry," he replied, climbing down, his mates handing the folded objects of their profession over the wall to him. "It's a bloody awful job we got. Try to do it in such a way to keep mind off that. Sometimes forget our manners."

"Okay," I conceded.

"Right, so. Two going back?"

"Three."

"What, the fucking Kraut?"

"Yes, Private, the fucking Kraut."

"Just as soon leave him for all the effort it would take. Let him rot with the rest of them."

"Not your choice to make, as I'm not asking you, I'm telling you—or am I assuming too much that you know the difference between the two?"

"No, Corporal. Why, though?"

"The man deserves a soldier's burial." I didn't care if he understood, only that my order be obeyed. The graves team set each body on a stretcher and bore them, in turn over the bags. It was the last I saw of the worst mistake I ever made.

Canada, January, 1936

The fire had petered to nothing, long enough for the room to grow cool and slightly damp, the tiniest chill breeze passing downward from the flue. It must have been late, and I was only able to make a vague guess at how far the night had gone; long since it was past time for me to have wound the mantle clock, at least. We sat in that silence a moment, which wasn't complete with Malachi gently content in my lap, rumbling away in his sleep. Adelaide had sat on the rug at arm's length from my chair in that curiously chaste way of crossed ankles and touched knees which ladies adopt on resting directly upon a floor. Whole minutes may have passed since I had stopped talking. I was unable to suss what she might have felt, her face betrayed no height or low of expression. As much as I couldn't discern her feelings from outward appearance, I wasn't even sure as to what I felt. The details I'd just shared was the most I'd ever revealed about my war to anyone who hadn't been there, the particulars of which most concerned the audience of one I had played to whose opinion was the most important of any for me. It changed nothing about what had happened, how those circumstances came about, only one more person knew about them. Maybe it was that I didn't know what to feel because she hadn't given any indication of how what I'd shared affected her. Resolving my emotional limbo was reliant on her response alone. Malachi fidgeted, stretched out his lanky, soot-coloured paws, and settled back. It made me smile; his adorable ways never failed to. Then I caught myself, as what I had let go into the open and a grin, no matter how fine, were not matching. At last, she spoke.

"Was he in a state of grace?"

"Pardon?"

"Dad, before he died. Had he made confession?"

"Yes," I answered immediately. Kelley never failed in his devotion, even if it meant having his sins heard by our Regimental Chaplain, Reverend MacCowan, who was—as is traditional for Scots regiments—Presbyterian and not a Catholic priest. In the case of the fight at the Ridge, and that it was Easter, Colonel Sinclair had arranged for the few RC's in our ranks to attend Confession and Mass at the church of the French village we had been billeted in just before we moved up to take our starting positions.

"Good," she replied, letting out a slow breath. "That's all that matters." I was confused. Hadn't she heard me?

"I don't get it. I mean, his soul was looked after, that bit I understand. That's not as important as how he died, because of me."

"Now, that's what I don't understand. Who has ever blamed you for that?"

"No one," I admitted.

"You said both Timothy and Patrick didn't have words with you over it. Patrick would have had you in front of Colonel Sinclair in an instant if he thought you failing in duty." Aidie was right about that. Paddy was a good officer in that he never let any deed go

94

unrewarded or unpunished as the case may have required. He had been rather busy at the time, though.

"The man had a hole torn through his cheek; his arm a bleeding mess and had his batman shredded to nothing just prior. I'd say his mind was elsewhere." She shook her head.

"I think you want to blame yourself." My answer to her now echoed what I'd said to Tim while contemplating what to do with the offending weapon.

"I don't see how I couldn't." In one way of thinking about it, I was guilty twice over. First, by action—giving the pistol to Ulrich—and by inaction in not killing him straight away. Either one on its own wasn't altogether bad. Swaps of articles took place in chance encounters on neutral ground if both parties were more interested in getting back to friendly lines safely. It was far from normal practice, and tales of such things are told because of their outstanding rarity rather than frequency. Making a decision not to finish off a wounded enemy was something done in the heat of the moment, and not done too often, either. I'm certain that if it had not been someone I recognised, I would never have hesitated. Put together, both parts were incidents of my influence. That was always how I figured why the fault for Kelley and Andy's deaths was mine.

"Can you know the future?" What did that mean?

"No, of course not."

"it's my understanding that the only one who can was He who Dad was at peace with. You are a fine man, Felix, but you are not God to know what may come. Have you made a mistake like that since?" Oh, no, I had not. Any German I came into reach with afterward I damn well made sure was dead, dead, dead. I also never let the Colt out of my sight, which, not without irony, was put to use in assuring my enemy's death.

"Then there's nothing to it," and she meant it. For Adelaide, such things were as linear as that. I understood the process of her philosophy, even if I wasn't able to believe in it as fully as she. My experience had been that the ultimate acceptance of credit or blame for my influence on events was mine to take. Just as I couldn't take praise for something I didn't do; I couldn't avoid responsibility for everything I'd done. Without as deep a sense of faith as had Adelaide, I wasn't capable of abdicating my actions, even to God. I had to be able to forgive myself; which was a process still unknown to me for all the time gone between past and present. While it was a bold action to at last tell her the details of her father's death, I didn't think that would be sufficient for me to finally let go that part of my history or that her absolution of it might clear my conscience. I wasn't capable of separating my actions from their consequences, though it meant a great deal to me that she could, in her own way. That I hadn't the certainty Adelaide would have it within her to do so was a large part of why I had kept the whole truth of the event to myself. At least if I wasn't going to be washed clean by my admission, I no longer had the burden of carrying such a personally terrible secret; which was worth a relative measure of peace of mind.

"It was a very difficult time, when we had the telegram," she said, standing up and going over to the mantle. I was aware of this. Mother O'Leary, Irene, for whom our daughter is named, was consumptive. After years of wicked illness, she succumbed in the same Easter week her husband had breathed his last in France. The telegram gone to the O'Leary household arrived before the children had time to cope with the death of one parent and thus forced them into having to cope with so quickly becoming orphans. They were hardly waifs, though. Both Adelaide and the next eldest, Kelley the Younger were working and the twins, Charles and Henry, soon to be seven, Aidie had been looking after as Mother O'Leary wasn't able in her infirmity.

Adelaide took up the tiny white China teapot, a keepsake of hers, glazed with light blue whirls and curlicues meant to mimic the work of ancient artisans which rested undisturbed among the pictures on the shelf. Taking the top off, she reached inside with two fingers.

"We hadn't expected anything more, after that. Some weeks later, this letter came." She drew out a limp, heavily creased and yellowed page. "I only read it once, upon receiving it, and had to put it away. It felt strange. Dad was alive and well when he wrote it, as was Mother. Alive, at least, if not entirely well. Both had gone away and it was curiously queer to have something so paused in time." Crossing back to me in my chair, she handed the page to me. "I think there might be a bit in that which would be good for you to read just now." I unfolded the aged leaf; with care it didn't fall to bits in my hands. It was a piece of stationary with a YMCA letterhead, the Association having done a great deal for troop's comfort, including facilitating letters home. Beneath the heading, in blocky script were more words written down than I believe I had heard Kelley speak in all the time I had known him. It was addressed to Adelaide, which made sense as Mother O'Leary couldn't read at all. About halfway down the page of loose grammar and creative misspellings my eye landed on a familiar collection of letters; my own name.

"*A very fine young man,*" Kelley had written, "*without thinking of himself, he got two men away from danger and helped us all to keep fighting while the Germans was doing their best in killing us. None of us might be living without him. I will introduce you when I am home. You are certain to like him.*" He went on to describe me as being "*highly thought of,*" as well as "*all sorts of funny, smart and brave.*" I tingled reading it, these sentiments his taciturn nature prevented from voicing directly to me. Remembering him in the way he took such a paternal role with everyone in the section, what he had written felt as uplifting as they might have if they had been said by my own father. So I imagined, anyway, not really knowing what reflecting my father's pride actually felt like.

The letter had been dated the day before Good Friday, not but five days before he died.

"I put it away," she said again. "He wasn't going to be back home, and I didn't want to be reminded of that just then. And then, the letter you wrote came." That note I had sent, not knowing she was both illiterate and dead, to Kelley's widow. I'd written it with a mind to what Uncle Isaac and Aunt Ruth would never be able to receive with regards to Eck; those platitudes of a quick and painless death. "I knew from your concern of our feelings that Dad was right about you. It wasn't your mother on her own who brought us together." I had nothing to say.

"Dad believed in you; he was prepared to trust you with his life. I can tell you with certainty he would have known that while you would do everything to keep that trust, it wasn't ultimately up to you. He always knew that was beyond the ability of any man. There is no way he would ever blame you for something he always assigned to God's will, so neither can I, nor should you."

Again, I had no response.

"If Dad was right about you—your finer qualities," she went on, reaching out to scratch Malachi's ear, "which I know he was, because I know you, then it follows Patrick wouldn't ask you to help him now, if there were any doubts as to your ability."

"I suppose not." Her hand finished with the cat and rested on my knee, which she gave a little squeeze.

"Good. I'll not tell you what to do about this, but I would like you to put some thought towards it."

"I'll telephone Paddy in a few days."

"No need. His call wasn't just about work. He and Caroline want to take us to a night club in the city on Saturday."

"A night club?" I made a face, one of mild displeasure. I don't like going to night clubs. Crowds, especially lively crowds, set me on edge. My Saturday night in a loud smoky room, with me stuffed into my evening suit? "For Pete's sake, why?"

"Patrick wouldn't say. Told me it was a surprise, that you'd be sure to enjoy it. He said for me to tell you it would be fun." I don't think that assurance changed my expression much. Whenever Paddy had insisted something was going to be fun, he was using the word to mask an event nowhere near amusement. Going to a night club, for me at least, was in step with this habit.

"You can gurn all you want, Kitten. I accepted his invitation, so we are going. Don't you want to know the surprise?" I've had a rather bleak history of surprising things, and again, I saw no difference here. "Complain to Malachi, if you want. I'm away to bed. Don't forget to wind the clock."

Promising Adelaide I would think about it wasn't really much of a promise as I had already been thinking for some weeks now. Within that period, I had any number of things to insert into any process of thought to defer giving Paddy a definite answer. The holidays were top cover for the most part. I had more than enough to cope with at home with children positively incandescently anxious about Christmas. Morning of, rather, if not the late-night Mass Adelaide required them to attend on the Eve. Thank Christ He made me a 'Proddy' as I'm far too lazy for all the effort it takes to follow Aidie's piety. I maintain that I'm all correct with the Almighty; I had to be for getting through what I've experienced. With the New Year now beyond and the kids returned to school, there was very little I could offer to put off a response. I would have to decide, sooner rather than later, to what level I was going to participate in or at least be an influence upon, future events.

That was the entire nature of my trepidation with the COTC. To live with any of my failures, some of which had been very costly, was difficult enough. Preparing future leaders might mean any failure or oversight on my part could become drastically consequential. An officer is charged with an immense amount of responsibility to carry out their mission and because of that are endowed with a likewise immense authority. That is the nature of their commission; that which makes them officers. It is in a pure sense a mandate to act on behalf of a head of state in absentia. Hence the term "King's Commission." What that really means is, within stipulated limitations, an officer's word is law; their orders binding. An ill-prepared leader of a platoon or company might well be able to send dozens of men into certain death by means of poor judgement without any legal culpability. Moral responsibility would be another matter, and as far as I'm concerned wouldn't end with the person who made a deadly error but ultimately with those who prepared that person to take on a position of such grave authority in the first place. Deciding to be part of the development of future officers might not amount to much of anything in the usual case of affairs. Those students were being given opportunity to add a modicum of military leadership to their curricula vitae which might help in gaining a leg-up in civil business. I was of the opinion, however, that we might not be moving through a usual course of affairs.

In the very same country against which I had fought, a bombastic man had risen to power partly because he inspired the belief that the war, and most particularly the loss of that war had not been their fault. In some twist of logic light on fact, this philosophy concluded that in some sideways fashion, they hadn't actually lost the war. From that, the people of this country had been informed that the peace afterward was a short shrift which had robbed them of their rightful place at the forefront of civilisation. Nobody seemed enthusiastic about correcting this gross misapprehension, and the Germans themselves seemed all too enthusiastic about some imaginative restoration to greatness. Foreign affairs are well above my pay-grade—as much perhaps as they should also be for a bicycle messenger with a silly moustache—and as Adelaide pointed out, I cannot know the future with any certainty. My point of view was that all the best statesmen may try to make pacts and compromises to avoid war; but if one among that mix holds war as an immoveable eventual policy, there is nothing in those lofty levels of diplomacy other than brokering for time. Time in which, deluded that peace can be preserved, no preparation for war would be made except by those who want it. If jackboots started to march tomorrow, next week or next year, we would be in no fit state to stop them. It was my own memories which possessed the tragic details of lacking much in the way of readiness. Nothing spoke to that than the signal difference between the skirmish at Spoon Farm and our attack on the Ridge. Soldiering is a deceptively complex trade. I concede it is a trade which might be learned under the duress of experience; it still remains entirely reliant on sufficient time to get to grips with its finer points. Having to do so on the job could come at the cost of remaining effective. So much the better to have all of that sussed prior to shots being fired.

"I've done it again, Malachi," I told the furry lap warmer. "I've thought myself into a corner." He was too busy dreaming in a twitching animated fashion to give an answer. That's alright, I don't understand him anyway. It was true, tough. Should the world go dark again and we weren't prepared for it, disaster would follow. I could be one of two things. I might take this opportunity and be at best, even imperfectly, as much a part of the solution as it might be in my power to be. Or, I could demur and in a place of inaction would then be part of the problem. Seems I had been coming at this the wrong way. It wasn't about earnings or filling my empty days. The offer to assist in the Training Corps could not, by one matter of applied thought, be separated in any way from a sense of duty. In that light, it came to me that I really didn't have a choice; which strangely made me feel entirely more comfortable about the whole thing.

I came away from that evening let go of one of the darkest corners of my memory and with a satisfactory resignation to a path laid out before me. I slept dreamlessly well that night, for the first time in a long time.

I don't go into the city very much. I've no need to which is just as well because I'm not fond of cities. They are a lot to get used to for a fellow like me who spent a great deal of life in less hectic surroundings. At this point, much of what I know of things hectic is by nature associated to my time abroad. A reasonable desire to have less mayhem and more order is why I never go to a big city if I can avoid it. Adelaide, on the other hand, was at home in urban surroundings. Quite literally as she grew up, studied and had her first teaching job all within a cluster of crowded blocks in the heart of Toronto. I recall it was some effort to convince her to decamp for Inchmarlo. Buying our house in Falls Parish was a long fought-out compromise. Early on, it made sense to live at the Estate because Aidie had been firm in not giving up her career any more than she felt sufficient for the sake of raising the children. Inchmarlo, with my mother, aunt and sister was overstuffed with women willing to give me tutelage in the rearing of bairns and it was our good fortune that the busiest times in the vineyard coincided with Adelaide being away from school for the summer holidays. I didn't care that such an arrangement had meant taking on jobs more usual for a wife than a husband. What did it matter who did what? Knowing the vacancy an absent father creates in young folk, I wanted to miss nothing in our children's introduction to the world. From it I had been gifted such wonderful experiences made bittersweet that Da had not had such a chance. We took our house at Ontario Road within Falls Parish just as Philip became old enough to begin school. Adelaide had a set desire to making a home of our own when it became practicable to do so. I had no opposition to the idea; it was the execution which took some getting used to, never having lived on a street enclosed by other houses; and a counter-offer of building a cottage on the

Estate was rebuffed by her, and more importantly Bill who claimed he was not made of land for houses. Inchmarlo Estate was a holding of decent hectares among other large properties and as such, rather isolated. Adelaide liked it there, she said, because it was so different from where she had lived. I knew she also wished to live away from the Estate for the very same reason. All of that meant when there was the least excuse to spend any amount of time in the city, even with the required effort in getting there into account, Adelaide was for it. If, such as this evening, I was required by any slim reason to attend as well, there was no strategy I'd figured so far which would get me out of it. She knows me, my Aidie, and she's no' feart to make that her advantage. This time, having accepted the invitation on our behalf, she had secured her night out by knowing I could never, in good manner, renege. Smarter than I give myself due she tells me? I might be, but not smarter than her, not by a long shot.

"Stop fussing," she said, her hand on my cuff lowering my arm from neck to lap. My bowtie was trying to garrote me, and I kept sitting on the tails of my jacket which then tightened my shoulders. "You're very dashing," a mollification of flattery. Paint my nose orange and I'd be a puffin.

I leaned over so I could speak in Paddy's ear while he fought the road.

"So, come on, where are you taking us?" There was a crunch as he worked through too many gears at once.

"I've got the hottest tickets in town, you'll see."

"You realise I know your score on 'you'll see'?" He smiled, which from my side on point of view was as genial as these things get. Taken directly, his expressions were kept taut by the gouge of pinched flesh of where he'd been sewn shut on his left side.

"This one's got them all beat, Catscratch. At least I can promise you there'll be no one trying to kill us." Grand. His driving might do that first.

The city seemed to approach us more so we it; a great illuminated beast beckoning from surrounding darkness. Growing in dimension as distance closed it went from an object on the horizon to our entire surroundings. Majestic buildings towered over the crowded streetside properties as stone sentinels; constructed by and thus displaying in their construction the heart of the city; wealth and its power. For most of the way, we had been a solitary car on the road, the blanket of night held off by our headlamps alone. At once within reaching the limits we became one of a fleet, an armada of engines and horns moving in all directions ahead and abeam in a somewhat herded fashion of straight yielding to cross at one signal, then by opposites at the next. Falls Parish has no electric traffic signals, they were on nearly every corner here. Besides their purpose, all those switching lights were just that many more points of illumination to add to an artificial glow of streetlamps, storefronts and by the snap of fluorescence on hoardings. With buildings packed together like broken brick teeth, each lighted claim of business lunged outward to streetside, cleverly arranged at different heights to allow a block length to be read at once. That run up South Main at home having no two houses alike was incidentally charming. In the city, though, there were so many packed and cramped that the uninterrupted line of incongruity was stupefying. Anything beyond five floors rose above the streetlights and aside from the odd lamp from upper-level windows, they blurred into the night sky and furnace smoke, distant corners visible by the beacon of glaring billboards. Of these bright but silent appeals there were no shortages to help make mind up for what to eat, drink or smoke. For the fickle or undecided, this could be dizzying as no two streets consistently agreed on which was best and tried to convince by use of bigger letters, more colourful images, banks of lights and snappy slogans. All that was needed to ensure that competing brands already seen were forgotten and those yet to appear were not remembered. Some of the better ones were animated, blinking their message in repetitive flashes, mixing with the errant sparks of trolleys meeting joins in the cables above them. The tram wires ran among a network of overhead lines. Electric and telephone mains strung web-like were stanchioned at lengths all down every road by timber poles with great rookeries of breakers and switches weaved around their peaks. All this in placement and purpose made the whole scene what it was; busy. It wasn't a busyness of a directed, collective goal. Rather, it was one of individual intents—each car, tram or pedestrian striking out on their own errands, flowing by and passing through all others on theirs. The city's light, both functional and decorative, poorly mimicked day with many deep shadows and slim laneways untouched, nowhere was it of any radiance enough to lend more than a pale orange bath not entirely a different shade than a Very flare. It all reflected dismally upon banks of filthy slush; much saturated snow swept along with all the other dirt of the road's surface into lumpy piles where pavements met the street. With nothing left on display of seasonal joy, there was no warmth to this light, which not being of any real stellar brilliance anyway only gave a sallow depth to the tiredness of a long winter.

Thankfully, getting into this grid of streets forced Paddy to slow down, some. Turning off one road and onto another by the time we came to a stop, pulling up to the curb, I would not have been able to find my way out unassisted. That was another reason I don't like the city. I dread the panicked feeling of being lost. Aidie leaned across me to look out the window at the building beyond the sidewalk.

"Oh," she cooed, "it's very modern." So it was, all bright glass and shiny steel, dark grained wood between, lit throughout with dazzling neon tubes, and that was just the paneling beneath a hotly glowing marquee drawing to a single point of twin doors decked in buttoned leather inset with brass lined portholes.

"Take the girls in, Felix, while I find somewhere to park. Caroline, you've the tickets?" his wife nodded. I stepped out and helped the both alight.

"We could have taken the train in," said Caroline apologetically. "But you know Pat, he just loves to drive that car."

"All that practice he should be better at it," a quip I was sure I said only to my own amusement. Aidie heard me, though, and poked my side.

"Be nice," she cautioned. I turned my attention to where I had been brought. 'The Mint Leaf Club,' swimming twirls of lighted letters throwing the name into the night. Where, 'For One Night Only' it was presenting 'The Utilities Management Board.' There was a touch of something familiar about that, although I'm not really up on current musical acts. We went in, were shown our table and Paddy wasn't long in joining us.

"Left the car safely up a wall?"

"Shut it, Catscratch." The waiter came and went, returning with drinks. The room was lively, folks hustling about heavily clothed tables, causing that low rumble of chatter all mixing to one sound. I wanted to press Paddy for more information, thinking he'd be more forthcoming now that we'd arrived. It seemed, though, we'd arrived just on the dot for what was about to happen. The house lights faded, leaving the lamps upon each table seem afloat on a dark sea. With a click and hum, a spotlight played on the frosty green curtain which robed the stage beyond the two-toned polished wood dance floor. Into its glow leapt—actually gaining height leapt—a rakishly excitable looking fellow, our impresario, who reached into the curtains' central part for a microphone stand he placed in front of himself.

"Ladies and gentlemen," a pause, "La-dies and gen-tle-men." Here was a chap who really wanted to make sure he got his point across. "Welcome to the Mint Leaf Club," a small wait for a trickle of applause. "To-nite,

109

ladies and gentlemen, we here at the Mint Leaf Club have a little something extra to give you, you hep?" Slightly larger applause, he was building towards something, and the crowd was on his line. "I mean, we get some of the biggest names on our stage; shining stars north and south, east and west. Nothing, but nothing, no sir, nothing like what we got tonight. These fellahs only left Montreal because they burned that burg to the ground. Yeah, that's how hot they are." The audience nearly levitated with excitement. "Far and wide, these guys are known for laying down the most sizzling licks, the wildest, way-out heppest sounds ever to fill the human ear. Yes, we got 'em for you folks tonight, and only tonight—as they'll probably gonna hafta go on the lam for arson! Will you please welcome, to our stage, here to blow you out of your chairs, the Utilities Management Board, featuring the incomparable Mendel Ames!" There was riotous applause, cheers and whistles, but I was not paying attention. Had that chap said 'Mendel Ames'? The spotlight dimmed, and the stage lights rose with the curtains parting. Clapping and cat-calls continued, and indeed, Mendel Ames took centre stage at the microphone, clarinet in hand, his band mates arranged in a raked crescent behind him, in monogrammed pews.

"Good evening," he said, and everyone seemed to grow more hysterical. Paddy was whistling through his fingers in a call I've heard above gunfire it's that loud. Ames made no further effort to address the audience, exploding and spellbound in anticipation. He turned to face the band, raised an arm to count a beat, and then they tore the roof right off. I don't know much about popular music, which was why, as Paddy had promised, I had been surprised.

"I don't believe it," I told him in between the first and second set.

"I know. Damn good luck in getting tickets for this."

"Pat's forever listening to their albums at home," Caroline confided, "so nice we were able to come see them now."

"That's not what I meant. I don't know their music." Paddy looked shocked.

"How could you not? UTM is the name in jazz."

"What do I know about jazz?"

"Alright, so, you hadn't any notion of what Ames has done with himself?" I hadn't. I hadn't thought much about it, either. War's end became a rather lengthy process of waiting, moving slowly in stages from Belgium, where we waited some more, then France, with another turn of waiting, crossing over to England only for a spell of continued waiting. Finally, we boarded ship, sailed the Atlantic and entrained from Halifax to Toronto. Most men had done what soldiers returning from a long campaign have always done, which is to sink into the obscurity of the rest of their lives. As close as we all may have been at the face of it, once our papers were stamped and files closed at Exhibition Camp late spring of '19, we scattered as chaff from whence in this large country we had come.

"How did you get tickets, Patrick?" Aidie asked. I didn't give him leave to answer.

"I know," I said, "he sent them."

"Who?"

"Him," I pointed beyond Paddy's shoulder to the man who had just approached our table.

"So glad you could make it, sir," said Ames. Paddy stood to his feet in genuine enthusiasm, shaking hands with a musician he was so fond of who had once been a soldier he wasn't.

"You know I'm a big fan, Mendel. What a great set that was."

"Thank you. More to come, sir, just you wait." Paddy introduced Caroline who also had kind words for Ames' performance, then he came round the table to me. I stood to greet him.

"Good to see you, Mendel." He beamed.

"And you, Sergeant."

"You don't work for me anymore. Felix is just fine. Mendel, may I present my wife, Adelaide?"

"Enchanté, Madame," he charmed her with a slight bow as he took her hand.

"Pleasure, Mister Ames."

"Oh, no, Mrs. Strachan, that won't do, I'm Mendel. Let me tell you how much I was looking forward to this evening. I so rarely get a chance to play a small enough club that I can get out and kibbutz with the audience. I've had to wait a long time to say I'm sorry for the pain I was back then."

"That's very big of you, Mendel," I told him, "but I'd say you made up for it at the very last minute."

"You're too kind, Felix. Mrs. Strachan, you may not know this, but your husband took all of my nonsense in stride despite what was a real effort on my end to be aggravating. No man in the platoon was lesser than any other to him. Each one of us would have followed him through the gates of Hell." Adelaide didn't miss a beat, or an opportunity to reinforce a point.

"I do, Mendel. The only one who doesn't seem to know it is Felix himself."

"That so? Listen, Sarge, what you did that day spoke volumes of character." He turned to Adelaide. "He was prepared—gosh I'd say he was about to- sacrifice himself to get everyone out of the jam we were in. Where I'm from, such a person is a 'Mensch.' No finer compliment exists and I'm long overdue for paying it. Few men of his ilk, Mrs. Strachan."

"That's because the rest of them are dead," I said, a line which Aide glowered at. She has little truck with cynicism. Ames, though, he chuckled.

"Can't stay, this whole thing is going out live on radio—and those fellahs are as tight on time as the army. Enjoy the rest of the show." He left to put on the second act, melting into the crowd, accepting passing handshakes and admiring back slaps as he went. A penny dropped.

That phone call, days prior with the invitation and a word in Adelaide's ear about his job offer?

"You did this on purpose, Paddy." My old friend and boss knew how to butter me up to a task. This affair was an unmissable chance to twist my arm with adulation. Paddy smiled, in that half-moon way of his damaged face.

"Did it work?"

Some questions don't need answers.

PART II

"Age Shall Not Weary Them"

Canada, March, 1936

That evening at the Mint Leaf Club, Mendel Ames had certainly paid me flattering praise. It turned out, however, that the whole affair was a set-up well beyond what I termed coinciding events. What I had not considered was how influential Paddy remained with the men he had commanded. Along with that was his bullish streak of near obstinate stubbornness when it came to having things his way. My failure was to not heed that attitude of his in thinking about his offer. I should have known better that he wouldn't allow me to pass, because he wanted my participation and there was no length his contrivances wouldn't reach. Being a fan of Ames' music, Paddy had long been in touch with him, corresponding through the production company that made the band's recordings. It was always his desire to attend a live performance, and as such had been working to arrange one. Enter the question of me and a vacant position of COTC Instructor; Paddy was then throwing single stones at several birds. All he had to do was get the Utilities Management Board a Toronto gig to fulfill a yearning to hear them in person, and take me along because he knew Ames had wanted opportunity to speak to me apologetically for a dicey past. Thus, bolstered by flattery, my persuasion to Paddy's cause would be complete.

It wasn't as easy as it might seem at face value. Ames' band was very popular, making the cost of booking such a top act beyond all but the ritziest clubs in the city, and almost all of them wouldn't book a band led by a Polish Jew, no matter how famous they were. I don't see what the fucking problem was. Ames may have been a pain, a sullen conscript with a very outspoken desire against being compelled to war, which was the nature of his misbehaviour, although he did come to the fore when he was most needed. It matters to me in no way how he approaches the Almighty. I was born in Scotland, yet I am seen as Canadian. Ames had been born in Canada, but was often considered only a Pollock and a Jew. It turned my stomach that a person could put his life to risk, albeit unwillingly in Ames' case, and not be seen as belonging to the very country he was born to and sent halfway around the world to defend.

Such barriers did not deter Paddy, and he enlisted the help of another chap we knew who'd made a name in the performing arts. It had been Llewellyn Dewey, working with his program's sponsors, who had arranged to get a broadcast at the Mint Leaf, which was a smaller venue, but had no scruples to bigotry. I learned all of these details much after the fact; and have no problem in saying it was a masterful plan. Paddy's designs were not often anything less, and everything he engineered almost always ended with him getting exactly what he intended, as he had in this on all fronts. It all wound up with me in Paddy's university office one afternoon.

His academic seat was a tight room without windows. There was a transom above the door, and the door itself was set with a pane of pebbled glass within its walnut frame, but these did little to improve the stuffiness of still air or dispel floating particles of dust. What subjects he taught required possession of a great deal of books; thick, musty old volumes written in Latin or Greek or French. It was less a bureau and more of a closet in which to store writing everyone but one man had forgotten about. The only space even remotely clear of books was his desk, and that only because he couldn't open some of the larger tomes up to view their pages without ample surface area. Stacks of books were lain on top of the shoulder-high shelves which ran the length of all the walls, interrupted solely by the door jamb. These stacks, some impossibly high, were necessary as the shelves were bursting with other volumes. Most of the floor had been given over to towering piles of still more books, some dangerously constructed with a smaller title supporting those of more serious weight. Moving from door to desk required great skill to avoid causing a landslide of the printed word. I'd never seen so many books crammed into such a small space. Each time I paid him a visit here, which was seldom as the walls seemed to grow closer the longer I stayed, I was tempted to sarcasm by asking him if he had anything to read. Unlikely as it is for me to avoid a sarcastic joke, I held off only because it was near certain he'd miss that I was having fun and pull out some dense work from the muddle to give me a loan of, claiming it to be interesting or insightful or one of the most faithful modern translations of some bloke who popped his clogs long before Christ was a cowboy.

What was really remarkable about the state of Paddy's office was that its entire lack of order was really out of character for the neat and tidy, not fussy, just casually squared-away nature of his usual conduct. Although, my exposure of his conduct was nearly entirely limited to military affairs, and as far as I knew this higgledy-piggledy was precisely in keeping with him as the professor. I am not so professionally engaged as to require an office myself, but I dare say if I did, neither Paddy nor Bill set any standard I would emulate. He welcomed me in, asked me to excuse the mess, and invited me to take a seat. Which, in order to do so, required the removal of a handful of scattered titles and a whish of his palm across the chair's surface to chase off any dust. With the both of us supine, loomed over by his teetering literary columns, he at once launched into the nature of what he wanted my help to do.

"We are in the process of preparing young men to achieve the qualifications required to become commissioned officers. That is a fairly straightforward process. The syllabus is laid out in manuals with examinations for certification based directly upon it." He thumped a short stack of maroon booklets on his desk. "Certification allows the candidate to apply for a King's Commission." I didn't know for whose benefit he was saying all of this, I already knew these ins-and-outs. He picked up and held out a copy of the manual he had just referred to.

"Do you see anything amiss with this book, Sergeant Major?" Well, I hadn't read it, so I wasn't able to opine on the contents. reading it wouldn't have taken me long.

"It's awfully thin, sir." It was only the two of us, and the office door was shut, but we were both in uniform and we always played up properly whenever so.

"Correct. All I need do in my capacity as Officer Commanding, North Lake University Cadet Corps is follow this book, teach the lectures and instruct the drills as indicated and lo, we will have a crop of lads ready to be 'One-Pip Wonders.' I don't think that is sufficient."

"Nor do I, sir."

"Didn't think you would. And that, Sergeant Major, is why I need your help. You know me; I just can't be satisfied doing things by half, and this slim book doesn't get close to half, in my mind. We are going to follow it, because we have to, but we are going to develop a concurrent program of more in-depth and relevant instruction. No man shall pass out of this Corps who wouldn't be the equal of any office we knew in the war."

I liked this approach and told him so. There was a lot lacking in the quality of training and experience available in the Non-Permanent Active Militia, much of which was a gap between what theory espoused and what was practical to implement. On paper, the King's Own Canadian Scots was a regiment of a single battalion. These days, a battalion consisted of a Headquarters, to which was directly attached the HQ Company, the battalion's administrative body, and the

Support Company, an amalgam of heavy weapons. The core of the battalion was four Rifle Companies, the elements of which undertake the mission of closing with and destroying the enemy. It makes for a pretty formidable group, properly kitted out with all requisite weapons and transport, except that such a thing only exists on paper. Tight spending on defense limited our organisation to a skeleton headquarters, composed only of aspects required for administrative function and a single rifle company. I might be able to shrug my shoulders and rationalise that we hadn't need to be at full establishment and maintaining a smaller group was fitting both political and economic situations. At the same time, we never had anything like the requisite numbers turn up for a parade night or a weekend exercise, and were completely devoid of essential equipment, including most heavy weapons that weren't machine guns and an entire dearth of motor transport. Each year, a few more of the old boys turned in their kit, and hardly enough young fellows were coming up in their place; a net loss of numbers and experience. Without correct equipment or the wise counsel of veterans, it was incredibly difficult to take our drills seriously, and a lot of 'notional'-- which is to say things existing in name only—friendly units, A/T weapons, enemy legions all gave our manoeuvres too much in the way of imagination and often descended into a child's game of pretend. Vital skills such as marksmanship were still prioritised, but usually through an annual applied shoot for qualification, and little more. Rarely, if ever, did we practice cooperatively with other arms; artillery, armour or engineers, nor was any emphasis placed on working in combination with them in such a way as we did with success in the Great War. A dismal view was that we had men who could drill well and march a good distance, which is exactly the same state of affairs as was for us coming into France in the summer of 1916. Anything at all which was within our ability to overcome shortfalls in training that we chose not to put in play would only make us complicit in any failures in execution. I knew all too well that such failures would be measured in lives lost.

"There is a real danger," he said, "in relying too heavily on doctrine. It should dictate the framework of training and instruction, but nothing much beyond that."

"You'd rather not have us do things by the book."

"Exactly. I treat this manual as scripture and all we shall get are devotees incapable of doing anything beyond chapter and verse. It's going to take some doing as the resources we require will not be forthcoming. Your role, specifically, will be to get the candidates used to relying on the expertise of senior NCOs. You and I will work together in creating instructional periods and drills aimed towards the practicalities of fieldcraft and battlecraft. We will do a lot of 'Tactical Exercises Without Troops' which is a lot of make-believe, but as we haven't got troops, there's little else we can do. My other instructors, officers, some of whom are new themselves, will handle the prescribed syllabus. It will be up to them to turn the candidates into officers, while we, Sergeant Major, will make them into soldiers."

"Yes, sir."

"Good. Just one more thing I want from you. You are going to sit in on the syllabus classes."

"Why so, sir?"

"So you can teach them yourself, should need arise," he answered very quickly. More quickly than I could dismiss it may have been a prepared answer in place of what he really meant it for.

"Oh, boy," he said, dropping the book so he could rub his hands together in his way of nervous enjoyment, "this is going to be fun." I wish he would stop saying that. I've known him far too long to understand he has a very loose grasp on the definition of 'fun'.

France, June, 1917

There wasn't a lot of time left. I would never have thought that the long hours of daylight in summer could be anything other than pleasantly welcome. All things seemed to be backward here. Night was safely dark; day was dangerously light. Being perennially close to the enemy necessitated that we be more active at night than we were in daytime. This was rooted in the entire abandonment of the usual and expected. Not all nights were alike, though, and a cloudless sky showing a multitude of stars such as what I was contending with inspired me to move with a great deal more caution, making exaggerated strides to soften my footsteps and not draw any attention by sudden moves. Sense, when driven by fear, pulls against prudence and creates a strong desire to cover the distance of No-man's Land in one great rush. Only a few seconds of dash would see me safe back in our front line. I had to fight that urge. Attempting a run for home would almost certainly wind up in getting shot, and not necessarily by the opposing side. The moon was on the wane, which was good, for it didn't add anything to residual brightness and the ground I needed to cover was well broken. A little muddy from recent spells of wet weather, but none too bad it was fairly cratered with shell holes deep enough to keep below any eye line on what would erstwhile have been a wide plain of little feature.

Moving in such a fashion, concentrated, counterintuitive, was absolutely draining, the late-night air thickly humid not helping matters at all except for what may only be an assumption that damp air traps sound. Other side of that coin was that it wasn't humid enough to create any sort of hanging moisture thick enough to act as any sort of screen. It could not be too long before the first essence of dawn would tip over the horizon and I was fairly certain there was still a good deal of ground to cover. If daylight were to come before we made that distance, there might be nothing for it but to stay put, wait the day out. If, that is, Cunningham had that long, which he certainly had not.

"Am I dying, Corporal?" He was.

"What am I, a doctor? Keep quiet. We'll make another dash in a bit."

It wasn't so long ago that Lieutenant Thorncliffe had been telling the raiding party what fun we were all going to be having. He wasn't demented, his cheerfulness and joyful predictions were just the sort of bombast needed to quell any unease. A worried or nervous officer could transmit those qualities to his men as sure as a sneeze brings a cold. It was an officer's job to project certainty of completing any task with uninterrupted optimism. This was decently kept in check by his leading NCOs adopting a reasonable level of realistic cynicism.

"The Hun," he had told us, this small team he had assembled for this job, "has always been tiresomely predictable, and now he's added carelessness to the mix." Thorncliffe was addressing us from a striped canvas sling back beach chair he habitually held orders groups from, which gave him extra points for nonchalance. I did my part by standing nearby, leaning against the cement wall of the barn stall we crowded, my arms crossed; face expressionless. The barn appeared incomplete. Sections of its planked siding were missing, robbed for construction, furnishing or the fire, and there were holes of varied calibres torn through the roof gained over three years of occasional air bursts. Not entirely a protective structure, it hadn't much to it to even exclude the slightest breeze or drop of rain. As the days gone by had been wet and muggy, no easy comfort could be had in our stay here. The latent musky smell of generations of stock was only a tiny speck of the odious air, of which mouldy damp straw took front place. A consolation for the mean nature of our surroundings was that we were already damp and smelly to begin with.

It was good to have Mister Thorncliffe back. We had not seen him since our relief from the Ridge when, at that point only, he excused himself to seek medical attention. The worst of his injuries was the lacerations of his face, the peppering of iron shards had been mostly superficial, save for a through-and-through of his left cheek, which took with it everything on his upper plate from eye tooth on back. Six weeks of recouperation had been ample for him and he had wasted no time in getting back to business, in spite of what still looked like a delicate injury. Whatever technique had been used in closing the wound and his missing teeth sank and tightened the one side of his face, the deep and serrated scars showed as bright pinks and reds against his Celt-inherited pallor.

"Got a job from Captain McCormack, Catscratch. I need a solid Corporal. You game?" His flattery was kind, but unnecessary. True, these types of excursions were voluntary, so a compliment of my ability might perk up my enthusiasm. That would be a good strategy if my enthusiasm was the only thing keeping me from agreeing to go. He'd done more to secure my assent by asking me directly.

"Yes, sir. What sort of job?"

"A snatch. Get two more men, experienced raiders, from Six Platoon. Five Platoon is giving me four of theirs. Meet me in that barn in fifteen minutes with your volunteers, Corporal."

I had got Tommy Park and Lonnie Brentwood and we'd hustled into the stall, which would have little room once the whole crew were assembled, to get good spots for the O Group.

"Careless," he repeated. "Three nights running our Observation Posts and patrols have noted activity on this part of the line. Sounds of tool work and parties of men seen shifting material into the area, including what seem to be wood joists or railway ties."

We still held the very precisely built trenches we'd evicted Fritz from that spring. In light of that, he was forced to cope with second-rate networks having gone into disuse or had never been fully constructed before the line shifted when the trenches were first being established. Night after night they were making furious efforts to build upon and make improvements to these works. We had made this all the more frustrating by our artillery destroying as much of their effort as could be done with daytime shelling and by us in the infantry by going out at night to directly harass enemy working parties or to catalogue areas of interest for our big guns to smash. In essence, this was the same kind of work—that of ownership of No-man's Land—we'd engaged in before we attacked the Ridge. There was little at present to suggest that anything we had been doing was inclusive of preparing for another full go at Fritz. It was a means to an end, as we had been told and reminded of over the months following the abrupt wind-down of the General Offensive. Our activity of late lacked as clear a purpose of a definite objective such as the Ridge had been; so it made a great amount of sense that we had been kept informed as to how what we were doing fit into the progress of the war. Otherwise, it could appear as though our work was of little value. It was something called 'Active Defense' which isn't as contrary a term as it first seems. It was all very well, and perhaps entirely possible, to sit tight in a fortress of trenches until such a time another big advance could be made. In that way, all we could do is to prevent losing the war while we got things ready to win it, and was blindly optimistic to hope that the enemy would oblige us by doing the same. As consideration of victory required us to defeat, conclusively, the enemy's ability to continue fighting and that we were not in a position to achieve that, it would be by smaller actions of limited scope that we could cause the enemy to use up resources in men and materiel they would require to effectively defend against another dedicated offensive. Keeping pressure on the Hun with pocket attacks and ambuscades was our component of this stratagem, which also had the dual benefit of not weakening our defenses anywhere by having to concentrate forces as would be required in preparation of a big fight while preventing the Germans the freedom to shift their strength to any one area in anticipation of any such large-scale attack, whenever it was to come. What this added up to was little more than making pin-pricks, but when viewed from a broader perspective—a consideration which had been impressed upon us at the troop level more and more frequently and that in itself was a new concept—it was being done in such a way as Fritz couldn't scratch everywhere it itched all at once.

With a piece of charcoal, the Lieutenant sketched a diagram of the enemy front line which concerned us that evening.

"It's a fair bet they're putting in a dug-out on the forward edge of this section. The ground rises up a little right there. Prevailing wisdom would have it that building a reinforced structure at that point, where such a thing would have a superb line of sight on our trenches makes it ideal for an artillery spotter's post." It would have been a simple matter to dial in a few heavy shells on top of it, and that would have been that. Simple isn't always best. "We've been charitable in letting Fritz finish up. Perhaps he might think it safe enough to start operating from it. If so, we stand a good chance to grab some prisoners. Valuable ones." taking a clueless *Landser* who couldn't divulge time of day wasn't going to result in much useful intelligence. Snagging an artillery observer, who were usually officers and by nature of their job had to be well-informed could allow us to learn more about the enemy situation at large than the rank-and-file were aware of.

"I want this to go like lightning. You four from Five Platoon will be my blocking force. Boswell and Preston go right, Fielding and Cunningham left. Set your charges," he drew 'X's' on either side of his diagram, "and that will isolate the enemy post. The rest of us will jump that position and grab anything or anyone we can get our hands on. We want prisoners, so try not to kill everybody. Brentwood, you'll lay a charge on a long fuse right as we leave, and that will tell them we aren't taking kindly to these types of improvements in our neighbourhood. Five minutes in and out. Done right, the rest of them might think our blasting charges targeted shelling and keep low while we're back in time for tea." Thorncliffe then laid out our time and routes of departure and return, and the intensive schedule of rehearsal we'd undertake before leaving.

"Oh boy," he finished his orders with, "this is going to be fun." It wasn't, of course.

Very lights infrequently popped into being, cascading their glimmer over rough and broken ground. They were bright enough to curtail movement, but unpredictable in appearance. Most often, these flares were fired in response to perceived movement or sound, usually to give machine guns something to shoot at. Individual flares, going up overhead, swishing as they went were often followed by a ripping belch of automatic fire. Both sides were at that game, and if listened for carefully, one could discern distance from friendly or enemy lines by the subtle difference in sound between a Vickers or a Maxim. Protective as darkness was, it could also be my enemy. This blasted land, blown apart again and again by shelling made one piece as indistinguishable as the next. The craters made good points to aim for, keeping us out of sight during a bath of flares, but were not distinct enough to ensure I was headed in the right direction. I wasn't at all worried I had at any point become so disoriented as to be travelling back towards the German line. Rather, a shift in my heading too far left or right could have us wandering outside our unit's front-line positions and towards a neighbouring unit whose outposts would have a different password than the one we had arranged with our chaps. I could only retain my bearings when flares were alight. Keeping one eye closed to save my night vision, I did my best to pick out a single point to which I would move when next it was reasonable to do so. The dearth of singular points of any unique feature gave this exercise an air of futility; there were worse things to worry about, though. I also could not discount the possibility that there may be present, on this rough plain I had yet to cross, an enemy patrol. Even worse, there could be a patrol or raid from one of our friendly neighbours who might easily mistake two figures shuffling about in the dark of night for a pair of Fritzes.

A few moments of darkness came, except for the horizonal flashes of the big guns. I decided not to wait to chance a few moments more.

"Right, lad, we're moving," I told him. Cunningham obliged by bracing himself against me, arm over my shoulders while I grasped him around the waist, careful not to disturb the field bandages, sopping and filthy, which were the only things keeping his guts from spilling out.

After the raid, we had moved to our withdrawing point, two prisoners in tow, and a head count came up short.

"Did anyone see them?" Thorncliffe had asked. No one had. We were still on Fritz' turf. Those prisoners of ours could have, if they were prepared to die for it, call out to their mates, and the whole raid would be done for. We were on a time table, dictated entirely by the length of fuse on the charge Brentwood had set to cover our escape. We'd best not be anywhere nearby when it went off. Thorncliffe looked worried, which worried me, so uncommon was it to see such an expression on him. Perhaps it was the scarred and stiff side of his face making it hard to determine his feeling, but it deepened when a weak voice carried over from the direction the two absent men had gone.

"Help." The Hun were not beyond trying to trap us by shouting out pleas in English. Whether this was that sort of trick or not, any delay in our plan was purely to the enemy's advantage. Even if our raid had clipped this section of trenches apart from the rest of the system, experience had shown they had good capability of rapid recovery from these hits. That capacity for reaction was a factor in why our operations were so rigidly set to quick and immoveable timings. We had very few options to incorporate things not gone to plan, leaving the Lieutenant in the unenviable position of being obliged to his mission at the expense of abandoning men under his command.

"Go back, sir, I'll find them." Lord only knows what possessed me to volunteer myself. It might have only been my understanding that in not being bound to duty of the task at hand as he was, I could do what he most wanted to do himself if he had luxury of choice. I must have been on the right track, because Thorncliffe had authority to refute my offer, but instead he told me,

"Be quick, Catscratch. We'll be moving in relays, but we can't wait for you."

"Just have the tea ready, sir," I've got some sauce to me, sure, but it was just the kind of daft thing to say to convince all involved, especially myself, I wasn't going to come to any harm.

"How much time have I got, Lonnie?"

"Well less than ten minutes, now" Brentwood told me.

"Wouldn't have thought you East Coast boys could count to ten."

"Go fuck yourself, Catscratch."

"We'll see about that when I get home." He grinned. "Good luck, Corp."

"Ta. Here," I handed him my rifle; I might need two free hands. "Right, I'm off."

Regaining the German trench presented little difficulty. The blocks created by one half of the raiding party, using charges to deliberately collapse trench walls had severed our targeted section from the rest of the front line. Cunningham and Fielding had been assigned the left traverse, which of the two was furthest from our point of lodgement. These trenches were meagre affairs, certainly not constructed to the usual degree of precision the Germans were fond of. Patrols prior to our raid had reported deep, but narrow excavations, more 'V' shaped than 'U' in cross-section. Very few had raised floors or good drainage and almost none had revetments, which is material used—corrugated iron particularly—to shore up earthen walls and keep the trench from falling in upon itself. This in particular had worked to our raid's advantage. A couple of small charges at either end were sufficient to cause deep landslides and create our blocks. I never did figure out what exactly had gone wrong. Details don't matter much at some points. The charges set had stove in the trench walls, but more damage than intended had been done. Fielding was all over the place in a wicked smear of pulp. Cunningham was not much better off.

"Fine time to be laying about," I told him, hoping to sound cheery and that nothing in my voice or expression communicated the dire state he was in. Most of his chest was exposed. I can never fathom how it is that a man's body can be so ruined and yet still function.

"Is it bad?" he wheezed, while I tied his bandage and mine over the cavity.

"Not at all," I lied, "but let's get you out of this muck." I worked him into a sitting position. Even if I could get him back, there was little hope. "You're going to have to help me, Cunningham. I'm going to lift you up, and when I do, put your feet under you." He nodded, weakly. Cunningham had great force of will, and gave a heroic effort in getting up and out of that ditch when half of him was inside-out.

An hour, perhaps closer to two of a series of small jogs, I'd managed to shift him a little more than halfway back. The important thing was that I got the both of us away to a safe distance before Brentwood's charge blew apart the lumber and turf artillery observer's position. To move quickly, I did have to drag him a bit, though if he could manage forward under his own power, it saved me from pulling him through mud and murky puddles, which even in those circumstances seemed a touch undignified. We made another hop. A dash like a three-legged race brought us to the cover of a wide shell hole. We sloshed through the scummy filth six inches deep along the bottom, and I laid him down gently on the incline.

Somewhere distant, a machine gun rattled in a rapid set of bursts, more flares went aloft, forcing us to hold our ground. There was no good way to hurry this up when nervous idiots on both sides kept lighting the night with magnesium stars. I might have been able to make forward distance by crawling, clawing my way towards friendly lines and not break my body from the ground; Cunningham was in no shape for that.

"Alright?" I asked.

"I am," he started, which I thought was his answer, but he continued, "I am dying, Corporal."

"You might be," was as far as I was going to commit on the subject.

"Here's just as good a place as any." I had my doubts, but wasn't going to contradict him. "You can leave me, then." Without time enough to tell him what I was up to, I said,

"Can't, won't." I had it within my power to prevent something worse than death; which in itself was well beyond preventing. Any mourning over his loss, and with that all the unanswerable questions his people would carry forever after news of his passing, I was not going to allow them to not know where his body lay. A thought occurred.

"What's your name, Cunningham?"

"Niall," his breathing had slowed. Surprised he'd lasted this long, he wouldn't much longer.

"Niall, I'm Felix."

"Hi," he said, or so I thought I heard. It may have just been the sound of his last air escaping. I had seen men wounded in so many different ways and of all kinds of severity that it didn't bear exact counting. Of those, I hadn't been party to on so badly wounded, fatally wounded and aware of the mortal nature of those injuries who continued to drive himself right up to the moment of departure as he. Niall Cunningham made no complaint, not so much as a wince or a whimper. The Almighty as my witness, I could have no other feelings but admiration and envy for his courage. I was already resolved to my task of returning with him to our lines; to fail him after he had so nobly faced his fate would have been derelict and an insult to his superb effort.

It was a lot easier to carry him the rest of the way when I didn't have to worry about doing him further harm. Knowing what no knowing had done to my family, I had to make sure that he was not going to disappear into this sluice of war. Bringing him in guaranteed for one homestead their boy did not vanish to nothing. There was remarkably little else to give in consolation. It would have been a strenuous leap of logic to attach any reasonable meaning to his death, whether his actions were of any part to our advantage was outside anything but the broadest speculation. In that, he was by no means a minority. Far more men were killed in these luckless ways than directly in contact with the Hun. It was frustrating to think that a man could devote so much to a purpose only to buy it for nothing more than to have been standing in the wrong spot an instant too long on the night of a very minor action. For anyone at remove, those only loosely acquainted with how the war was to be won, a seemingly pointless death would likely be beyond easy comprehension. This was why we did our best to soften the impact for those at home, with those stock platitudes of a quick, painless death and so on, even if what we said couldn't be completely true. Of that, of all the kind-hearted lies I might tell of his last moments, one such would not be that Niall Cunningham was among friends when he died.

Canada, March, 1936

"Would you agree, Sergeant Major?" Grief, how long had he gone on talking for?

"I'm sorry, sir. My mind was elsewhere. What was the question?"

"Fun, Catscratch. What do you think?" Seems we were still on that.

"You know we differ on that notion, but in this case, it seems there might be some enjoyment. Not every day I get to ride herd on those who'll be my bosses."

"That's the idea. I'm not of mind to hold anyone's hand through the process. I'd rather a whole serial wash out than pass any unfit to hold a commission to the same standards as the Colonel." When Paddy said 'the Colonel' it was taken as writ he wasn't referring to Lieutenant Colonel Daventry, our current Regimental CO; but instead invoked the memory of Barclay Sinclair. Not to discount Daventry, a very fine gentleman and competent officer, having commanded 'A' Company throughout the war, but there was a lingering reverence the late Colonel still inspired. It could easily be said that any officer who served under him aspired to the example he set, mainly because he had always been explicit in that being the standard his officers would be held to, without fail. If Paddy was insistent those principles be upheld, we stood a good chance of creating fine officers and conscientious leaders. I hoped that would be enough, and tied to that was also the hope we would not need them. Funny thing about hope; it does alright until reality gets in the way.

"We don't start until the fall semester, but I'll have you on the books in the meantime while we work on our additions to the program. That we'll get done in time for you to take leave for your trip. Looking forward to it?"

"Yes, and no," I answered honestly, not being able to offer a response of any better clarity than that. To be certain either way, I would have to know what to expect and how closely that would match what I was expecting for myself. Knowing that was difficult when held up against my not being sure how I felt about being there the first time. I'd had no ambiguity in the whole process in that instance, and perhaps because the picture of what I imagined awaited me at the Front was so absolutely demolished by a reality beyond anything I could have conceived was reason enough to not commit a certain forecast on this upcoming trip. Having a sense that what I had been a part of had any real or lasting consequences might be of some help, but twenty years of thinking about it had not revealed anything of that sort. All that had mattered then was survival, and not particularly applied to the war on the whole. In some cases, it had come down to getting from one instant to the next. Placing too much faith in the future when it might not exist would have been a waste of energy. Absolute focus on the moment at hand prevented distractions from the unknowns of fear and hope. It was entirely practical, even required, as extremity of emotion reduced ability to think critically and act without hesitation. Once achieved, it's a difficult mindset to move beyond. The unforeseen problem with such a complete self-denial was that it was temporary and everything I had willed myself to not dwell upon for the sake of survival had returned as soon as my survival was no longer in doubt.

I came home that afternoon with those thoughts very much on my mind. Not that they were ever absent, but as time wore closer to my journey to France, it seemed I was becoming ever more occupied with animate visions of my past. I went directly from passing through the front door, down the hall and out the kitchen to the back yard, treading lightly all along the way so as to not alert Adelaide I'd gone through the house with my boots on. After spending time in Paddy's enclosure of airless dust and musty clutter I was starved for the freshness of an open space. There had been a recent spell of mild weather which led to the hope that soon would come the first rush of spring. That afternoon wasn't anything of bright cheerfulness, the sky's colour muted by a solid cover of light grey. It didn't seem to discourage the birds who were calling out claims on territory to which they had only recently returned. Their interwoven songs lilted over the disyncopation of melt dripping from eaves and trickling through downspouts. I breathed healthy, moist air sprinkled with the heavy earthen tones of thawed ground. Receding snow was in its worst form, lumpy, isolated piles specked with mud, the debris of small

141

stones, withered leaves and dead pine needles accumulated on the gradual withdrawal. The uncovered lawn was struggling with the melt, its lowest points entirely sunk in puddles. Some of the turf was only patchy spots of whispy straw coloured grass which hadn't borne up over winter's depth. This year had more snow than others of recent memory and as it continued to thaw, it was keeping too much bottom ground saturated for too long. Without interference, the immediate result wasn't much of a concern, but was more to do with recognising the power such a gently unassuming thing as water had to damage something as solid and strong as concrete over a process of patient years. I considered that I might need to dig down for a weeping tile to shunt overflow away from the house's foundation. Just another hole in the ground to add to the many I have had to dig. At least, I reminded myself, I wasn't going to live in this particular ditch. I called Hamish out, he was just at the kitchen table, near to where the back door let into the yard, going through his home lessons.

"Yes, Dad?"

"I'll need your help over next weekend, Hammy," I told him, not for the first time noticing I didn't have to look so much downward to address him eye to eye. Another year, I'll probably have to look up the way. The boy was on track to be tall and lean, more so in that was a Strachan than an O'Leary; although his mother's gifts were apparent in his brightly green eyes and a wave of rusty hair. I suppose it was the fashion to wear it as he did, grown long up top in wavy fronds and held in place with some sort of industrial fixative.

"We'll go along to Massey's Hardware and order some crushed stone. Then, we're going to dig down along the lounge side of the house, at the fence, there."

"What, like a drainage ditch?" I couldn't help to smile. the lad was bright. More O'Leary than Strachan, as I suppose things like that are meant to even out.

"Exactly."

"I guess you had to do a lot of that in the war, huh, Dad?" The question may have come from no other association of what little he knew about the Great War, and that I had not changed from my uniform since I had come directly from my meeting with Paddy. I have little doubt my children have a curiosity about these things in general and my personal experience specifically. It was rare to be asked a direct question such as Hamish had asked. When he was younger, as Irene and Philip still were, it was far easier to construct overly simple answers. It worked because the capacity to understand in youth was equal to my capacity to explain, which in turn was based upon the fact that even as a grown man, having gone through it first-hand, I lacked the capacity to understand a great deal of it myself. Smaller minds, the blank slate of innocence in youth, can only comprehend things beyond the immediate in an abstract fashion. Hamish was growing into adolescence which brought on a capability for analytical thought and I could no longer condescend to him with a simplicity I still had a few years left in stock for his siblings. Fine, I thought, the boy deserves a straight answer, if for no other reason than he was old enough to see through patronising parental bullshit. I had to be careful, though. Giving Hamish benefit of the doubt in his ability to comprehend might still be overstepped by being too direct, too frank. I let out a long, slow breath.

"A little bit, but not quite the same. Our lot were forever working on keeping trenches in a decent condition, and even the meanest of them were far more substantial than the yard work you and I are going to do. All in all, the effort we put into trenches was in the most part to keep them in good enough shape to give us protection from the Hu—the enemy. More complex things—drainage is a good example—all the work required to make trenches liveable, that was for the engineers to handle. We had other work needing done."

"What was it like?" Damn. That was a question I must have known would come at some point, but I'd not taken any time in all those years to have an answer prepared.

"Hmm?"

"The war. What was it like?" What could I say? I will not lie to my child, all the same I might not have the words, never mind the desire, to tell the whole truth.   It was simple enough to explain the technicalities. All the things of a soldier's life, for an outstanding majority of it, are not much different than life in any other place or occupation. Largely, our time was spent in a routine which had no more deprivation than a common labourer. At times, such a comparison was direct, as we were sometimes seconded to build rail lines which the logistics of the war required. Those hardships which were comparable, hard physical work, poor and inadequate food, no escape from nature's elements, separation from family and meagre pay may have made the overwhelmingly greater percentage like-to-like. A smaller, but far more critical aspect of life was absent in a peace-time job which was ever present in war; the sole and dedicated business of a warrior. Our time at the Front was pinned to that. No matter what we were doing, all efforts boiled down to what we had come to the war to do. In simplest terms, that purpose was as ever it had been: To close with and destroy the enemy. I wouldn't think to minimise what such a thing entailed; it was all horrible stuff.

On the whole, the war consisted of extremes. All things contained within it were superlative, all the time and seemingly all at once. Fear, gut-crunching, animalistically base terror was the underscore of everything, counterbalanced by numbing, passion-draining boredom and a fatigue which no period of rest could truly slake; a permanent condition of feeling neither entirely awake nor completely asleep, an awareness of certain periods of blankness upon which no memory was made record of and mundane actions performed automatically without input of physical will. Only seldom did this constant brew get suddenly thrown aside in manic instances with the speed and ferocity of an explosive rocket, flashes of exhilaration which might be minutes as much as days in length, where perception of time is perverted to be either more quick or slow than the Universe's meter, and again, in a snap, as striking a solid body at a dizzying velocity, reverting to the irregular regularity of being tired, bored and afraid in a warped solution of too much of all of them, and no end in sight. None of any of that occurred in a vacuum. Appended to these perpetual strains were environmental absolutes of cold or heat, the dryness of a desert or the dampness of a bog. Most times, it would be one or the other with periods of violent swings of several climates at quick succession, but usually it was interminable spells of singular types of discomfort.

The din and discord of battle is what most folk understand about war, or thought they did, as much as I might understand the life of an Eskimo. I know they live hard lives in a harsh environment, but unless I trek up to the Northwest and live among them, I can never authentically understand what such a life is like. Point being, it is the fighting of battles which become the by-and-large, although heavily sanitised notions, of the war as seen by a removed public. What fails to be realised is that a pitched battle, no matter how accurately visualised was a most rare exception of events. Grand victories, such as we had at the Ridge, were a minority of what life and death was in the war. The vast majority of deaths did not occur in some fantastic, heroic campaign of measurable results toward eventual victory. Most men went in small fracases that amounted to very little significance, or in a slow but constant drip of a few a day brought low in the process known as 'trench wastage.' This callous term coolly described any death by any cause while simply existing day—to-day in a combat area which was not directly attributed to combat; which in fact is the rule; dying in a mortal struggle in close contact with the enemy an exception of the whole. Mainly, this was because our time was largely just that, existing day-to-day, which far better describes life in the war.

If properly administered, we spent far more time out of the forward lines than in them. No more than three or four days in the firing line at one stretch, and that within ten days, or thereabouts of a rotation between firing, support and reserve trenches as our triple depth of static lines were usually organised. The balance of time was spent 'in the rear' where we were employed as working parties, engaged in training or properly 'at rest.' Taken into consideration, that might mean a thumbed scale of one third of our lives was spent 'up front', and that time was by no means spent exclusively in making concerted efforts against the enemy. A fraction of a fraction was occupied in that. What tended to happen for the most part was not without danger, but was really quite distant and detached from the tiny share of time we had any sort of direct action. Engagements were a brief blink of total experience that only seemed more pertinent for their intensity. It was being in the midst of these slivers of time where it was most apparent that the human condition had been entirely reduced to bottom line of will to live which sometimes became very intimate and completely personal.

France, August, 1917

Rain pattered down upon exposed ground in tiny splashes, further encouraging the muddying of ochre clay. Every surface, the clinging earth, soaked burlap sandbags, soggy and slick wood and iron trench construction being struck by fat drops gave out different tones, dull and sharp across a broad register of trebles and basses with constant, rapid uneven beats; small noises piping over the grumbling of distant guns. All this water ran downward and collected in craters made ponds, the ground so abused by our machinations having lost all ability to regulate what was already a pretty high water table. For a few days running, it had been more wet than dry, and such consistent rains falling on our heavily travelled battleground was churning it all together into a swampy brick red morass. It was an unforgiving mud, a sludge with glue-like fastness which fouled moving parts on weapons, required a driving strength to move feet forward in and out of its sucking grasp and it coated everything, fibres of clothing, hair and skin to a single bland shade. The entire sky was hidden behind low and dark roaming clouds whose thickness obscured the least light from a weak sliver of moon and the grains of far-away stars. Days which the rain had left alone had been brutally hot; the sun baking the land dry with all the damp collected sitting heavy on breezeless air, a steamy, oppressive oven which drained strength merely by being within it. The only movement on such sultry days seemed to be the minimum required to prevent providing an immobile surface for flies to land upon. All the rotten things about invited thick swarms of the pests whose buzzing was a constant hum heard between shell bursts carried on a rancid air of decaying waste and human compost so vile, it stung and burned to breathe it. Some odours, fair as well as foul, the nose gains accustom to, but not this note which just seemed to grow in strength as time allowed the sources of the pong to putrefy.

   Idle hours under a bleaching sun in thirsty discomfort of little relief, brains slow-cooking inside steel helmets, parched gullets pinched by high, tight-fastened woolen collars, was exactly opposite to a night of returned rain. Emptying clouds slammed the humid air back to the ground in near solid sheets, exposing all to anguishing wet chill so rapid and complete within moments everything was soaked through, allowing the cold to drive right to the bone. Soggy clay grasped in wodging chunks to squelching boots, all surfaces quickly slick and slippery with fetid liquid muck. Every bit of that, as miserable as it might seem was to my advantage precisely because it was miserable.   Night's darkness and rain's constant splash obscured sight and sound. The elements couldn't have been more cooperative had I the power to ask them to be. As it was, I was able to use my whole environment to screen my careful approach. What I was working toward required all of my energy dedicated to a single purpose; that of remaining invisible. Our senses have had the advantage of unknown thousands of years to become fairly attuned to instantly perceive anything which might threaten survival. I was taking such exactness in my placement of body, every fibre and sinew measuring inches and feet of infinitesimal gains such that I might defeat something as deeply seated as human instinct. Only by being inseparable from the ground, creating no unnatural outlines, contrast or silhouette I could become part of the landscape, blended and indistinguishable where even breathing felt too obviously motive. Little grabs of distance, requiring patience to overrule ambition took all I had in devotion and concentration. Even the tiniest twitch caught at the corner of vision would be enough to draw unwanted attention. I only had a slight distance to cover to place myself in the best position for the job I had to do, not much more than three times my own length. At last reaching my goal, my muscles burned with the strain of such intensely focused energy, but getting this far was only the beginning.

Darkness and wet weather were more than just conditions to assist me in my move into position; this most dour and drizzly of a dreach evening was likely to have a deeper, emotive affect and that was something I planned to exploit as well. Alone with his thoughts, wet, cold, presumably tired and quite possibly hungry, a sentry might not be putting his all in his task. the mind wanders, flits from a disturbed but unchanging landscape. Eyes grow bored of looking over the same bumps and muddy folds. Damp skin puckers and the body convulses in an icy shiver. Dreaminess takes hold, thoughts move away from the misery of the moment to visions of warmth, comfort and home. I can't reach inside a man's head, but I can project those qualities easily because it was natural. I was wet, cold, tired and homesick too. It was not that I was miserable which was advantageous, but that he was miserable.

The post overlooked a sea of shimmering twists of wire. That was foolish, we'd never come that way. Starting only inches below the parapet, the wire trap cascaded down and outward to a depth of twenty yards or so. Coiled bands strung between pickets at varying heights had been woven through with straight lengths of cross-hatched concertina creating a tangled wall that while flexing in the breeze and twitching under the rain was perfectly impassible. I had made my approach from a defile, where the land sloped away at an angle from the left edge of the advanced position he occupied. Less work had been done here to construct entanglements. The area had been kept under fire to discourage any efforts to build or repair, specifically to the benefit on this excursion and I had been able to close distance without being impeded by barbed hedgerows or the noise of snapping through thick steel strands. I waited.

Having taken such pains to approach, I had to be certain of my next move. It would be quick and it could not suffer any error in timing or placement. How well I did it, either perfect or not at all was going to be the measure of success or failure; quite possibly fatal failure of this whole scheme. The party I was with was reliant on how I acted in the next few seconds. A misstep would all but ruin all we had laid out in getting to this point.   Loss of stomach for my immediately subsequent task was something best not examined either.

I could see him in profile, not much more than a shadow of head and shoulders peeking above a layer of sandbags, his features most defined by the rounded top and angled edges of his helmet. Remaining still a while longer, my patience was rewarded. Very subtly, but certainly, his head dipped, forward and down. I leapt.

Body to body, closer than a dance, I wrapped my left arm under his jaw and forced his head back, exposing a taught neck. One move; swift, a single cut, I ran my blade from just below the left mandible and brought the chiv across throat and pulled away an equal distance on the right-hand side from my first strike. It was, so I had instructed, the same type of cut to bleed a deer. I wouldn't know; I couldn't bear to hunt deer. The worst part, but the part which let me know I had done it thoroughly enough was the crack of steel and cartilage as I tore through the windpipe. The continuous sweep of my knife, side to side, was all that was required. I'd opened vessels which now emptied into his lungs, snapping vocal cords along the way. I let him drop, allowing him to die in a few moments of silent panic as he drowned in his own blood on the floor of his outpost which the downpour had made into an ankle-deep reservoir of murky filth. His mate I almost overlooked. Curled up in a rain cape, asleep on a double-wide stack of sandbags, at first glance he appeared no more than a lumpy feature piled into the far corner. Had I come in through the other side, triple aprons of wire notwithstanding, I would have landed right on top of him. Before he could stir, I stove his head in with two or three overhand blows from the studded leaden-tipped coche I had brought along snugged in my belt. Death for him was instant.

With no one to raise the alarm, my men followed me into the trench, moving precisely as we had practiced, each of them casting Mills bombs around traverses and down dug-outs. They knew the layout of this spur line from the good reports made by reconnaissance both on the ground and by air. Each man was well-rehearsed in which direction to move and to which spots their grenades were to go. We'd had the previous day to run through our movements on a mock-up constructed of thick tape laid out upon the ground to the exact dimensions of our target. After neutralising the sentry, I was to hold the position, guard our exfiltration point and call the withdrawal at the appointed time. I almost didn't need a watch; I could count cadence by the bursting of Mills bombs. Thirty seconds in, two muffled thuds, explosions contained within a dugout, left centre. Forty seconds, the same, two successive thumps, dugout, right crook. Forty-five, several more bombs gone off, louder, as the right traverse was cleared, and just at the first minute the noise of securing the left traverse. The seconds in-between were increasingly filled with shouts, foreign voices I didn't understand verbally, but knew from tone and timbre the context, of surprise, confusion and panic. It would have seemed to them the havoc all around was furious and random, a period of madness, not disproved by the lads having decided to smear their face with war paint and make Hellish whoops and cries like Indians. It had been Brant's idea, and that being he was of the Six Nations Band, he came by such things honestly. He had equated this type of raid to his people's warrior history; it being common to commit an act to frighten the enemy and keep him from any sense of safety, even within the walls of his own fortress.

Even though I knew precisely what was going on beyond the sentry post, their ghastly racket frightened me. That being the case, I was inclined to think we'd made a success of it, and despite the seemingly sudden randomness of it all, we were in complete control; entirely concerted, and before we got too carried away, I would call the retire at five minutes. That was five minutes in which, while bedlam was underway, I was left to my own thoughts all that time being watched by the widely shocked lifeless eyes of the man I had bled, whose face had settled in a pained grimace. The rain and the cold weren't much of a bother to him anymore. His was an ignoble end lacking anything of civility. Strange, that. We were supposed to have been at this contest to ensure the survival of civilisation, never minding for the moment any difference of opinion he and I may have had on what that fairly broad notion meant in any detail. Yet, here we were; trying to champion a cause by acting in ways supremely contradictory to what we were fighting to preserve, gain or restore, depending on which lens the whole thing was viewed through. I couldn't doubt that very many of us—we or they—lacked at least some grasp of morality. Presuming the enemy to be wicked, we'd had to temper our actions against them which required us to forego any moral sensibility. A great deal of control and moderation exerted by the disciplined structure of military authority had been applied—not always as well or completely as may have been needed—to keep us from descending too far into a permanently base state. In that respect, this dead German and myself were quite similar. I had to reassure myself that if the shoe had been on the other foot, it would be me, glassy-eyed in a puddle of scummy rainwater and blood; that this corpse would have shown the same zeal and dedication to his work as I.

From that, I wished to know something. It was a rhetorical thought, and remained so as I did not have nearly enough information to forward a satisfactory answer. As things unfolded in this place, I gained more reason to chew this notion over. The act of crushing a man's skull after slitting another man's throat was a fairly good example. It was this: If a tame animal is put into the wild, where wild they must learn to act in order to survive, can it be expected of that animal to go back to being tame once brought out of the wilderness? My inclination was to believe that such an animal would have to be taught to reverse their regression. Man is no mere animal, I don't give that any doubt, the difference being our intellect. Our own construction of tame and wild is reflected in how we define morality. Which, to me, makes the idea of going from one to the other and back again just that more complex. Because, and this being the crux of this particular thought, for all the conditioning and encouragement to selectively abandon ethics in the one direction, as in war, I was not aware of any like effort in the way of undoing all of that when we were at last given leave to move in the other direction, back to being tame, as it were. It would be simple, perhaps, to attempt dismissal of immoral acts wholly on the basis that some of these were permissible—even necessary—in war. Simple, but not easy.

I shuddered, partly from the thought that continuing to act in a sanguinary fashion might have no reverse and partly from the soaking weather. This drenching helped to bring my mind back to what was on hand. I was still standing guard at the raid's point of entry, mindful of both time and the danger of letting my thoughts wander, even for a moment. It was enough to be taken by surprise, exactly how I had taken that chap now somewhat more submerged by continued rain and his dead weight pressing down upon wet clay. Those eyes still seemed fixed on me and I was tempted to give his head a slight punt to point his empty gaze in another direction, but oddly enough, that act seemed a little unnecessarily cruel. I pulled my whistle out, five minutes nearly gone by. I could allow no flexibility in that. We were a small party, roaming a section of the enemy's front line. Any dalliance could let Fritz recover from the shock of the raid and overwhelm us. Plus, at half-past the hour, less than fifteen minutes away, a snap barrage would be fired to cover our return and I preferred to not be under it. I blew one solid long note, then two short pips, and the lads were back to me in good order. I patted each man on the shoulder as he passed me up onto the firestep and over the bags to ensure I had everyone. Brant told me "Last man," as he passed, leaping to the outpost's parapet. He stood his full height, thumped his chest with his fist, and howled.

"I am David Foster Brant!" He called out, "I am a warrior from the Six Nations Band of Brantford! I have raided your works, and taken the lives of your comrades! You are not safe; you are all going to die!" Then, shouting another bloody whoop, he flung a hatchet so that it stuck fast in a sandbag. Before the raid, he'd carved our Regiment's initials on the handle and decorated it with a strip of cloth bearing our tartan tied around the choke between grip and blade head. It was, he said, tradition to boast to one's enemy who it was that had mounted the raid, but he hadn't told me it would involve such performance. Rather wish he'd done it after I'd left; his brash display made quite the target. Either we had wrecked the place so thoroughly, or that anyone left was too dismayed to respond, allowing Brant to make a clear get-away. With Brant gone by, I had the correct number and I got ready to leave. I had a moment to meet the glare on the coupon of the German I had killed. There's no question the act was pure, cold-blooded slaughter; but

158

that wasn't how things worked here. I wasn't much bothered by it, which in itself was disturbing. Except for a permanent tingling charge of fear, there was a great emptiness where usually rested everything of pity or remorse. If I had more time to mull it all over, I might have been worried about such a void. There wasn't ever any of that kind of time. I unpinned a Mills bomb and bowled it along the communication trench which led from outpost to main line, one final act to discourage anyone trying to follow us out. Before it went off, I hauled myself over the parapet to disappear into the depth of night.

Canada, March, 1936

"What was it like?" That was a very understandable question to be asked. Unfortunately, it was flawed. It inferred that a response be comparative; so that it might be relatable to the inquisitor. No easy task that, when the experience being asked about has no comparison. Best I could manage would be to say that it was nothing at all as to what I might have thought it would be. Hardly satisfactory, as things are not defined on the basis of what they are not. There was also the problem of all the parts of my experience which I could not disclose because of how unnatural it had sometimes been. In finally telling Adelaide about how her father died, I intentionally omitted the detail on what I had felt when I ran through Ulrich with my bayonet. Up to that moment, from days prior to the attack, all I had been concerned about was that I was gripped with a fierce terror. It was beyond what it usually meant to be afraid; more a sensation of dread which became a heavy emptiness unsettling body and mind to the brink of both collapsing into paralysis. That operation had been our first all-out effort since we'd advanced against Spoon Farm. The memory of our struggle there was continually present with me during our preparations for the battle at the Ridge; principally my desire never to go through such a thing again. I had begun to worry that I wasn't capable of going into the same thing a second time. Perversely, my fear wasn't about what I might have to face, but that fear would prevent me from facing whatever was to come. The very moment I struck home with my point, that fear gave way to a lively sense of powerfulness, a strangely placed but strong notion of satisfaction. I hadn't found any reasonable way to explain that to myself, let alone to anyone else. Such things are too far removed from simple absolutes of good and evil. Being a participant in the violence can perhaps be reconciled as merely an aspect of the whole event. How it feels to enact such violence is not so easily understood as it potentially paints the actors in monstrous colours, blurring benevolence and the bestial. There had been such a disconnect from natural law that I could never admit my true feelings without irrevocable damage to how my character was perceived by others.

What was it like? It was exactly like getting away with murder. It was learning that taking life can be made easy once it's known how doing so reduces the heaviness of fear for one's own life and lack of control over it by placing an empowering level of control over the life of someone else. It was queerly narcotic and because of that, very dangerous. The extremity of war, the unnatural nature of war, the reduction of humanity of war, try as I might, cannot be made relatable to the uninitiated, as it requires an understanding only attainable through experience. If I felt anything about the war, it was that a small amount of my own reasoning felt bad for not feeling bad about it. Twisted logic such as that was hard enough for me to find the leading ends to un-work them for myself, to say nothing about being able to do so to aid in someone else's comprehension. From whatever I could choose to say, at least I didn't have the glaikit look of that feckless chap from that guilt-inducing recruitment poster obviously having no answer to his children's questions on the war. My silence wasn't from having nothing to say, it was that I had too much to be heard. Hamish stood waiting for an answer.

"It was," I ventured, pausing to fall upon the right word, "inhuman." That was most certainly understating things but only because there are many things that defy mere statements. In a flash of my mind's eye, I saw a familiarity in his look. A slender face with a narrow nose, he has little of his Mum's Dad, but his eyes, when he was held in a thought was exactly like Kelley. It was a gentleness, a silent air of a compassionate soul. I saw him there, my late father-in-law looking out at me through my son's eyes. It was too much. I felt myself welling up. I went so far; with all the ugliness I had committed locked away in memory as to make a personal admission.

"I was inhuman." He hugged me. He's a kind boy.

"'salright, Dad. You're no monster." I held my son's embrace so he might not see me shaking, trembling with the vastness of so many emotions all at once. I'm no monster, perhaps, but only if I might be permitted to live the rest of my days without ever letting on how close I have come, with my deeds past to being so defined. I wasn't always certain that in having outlived the war my humanity remained intact or undisturbed. In not allowing an iota of a fractured

162

morality to cloud any assessment of who I am, I was obliged to take excruciating efforts to keep my past within, at times as if I was leaning my weight against a canal lock braced tight on the sewaged assortment of all the things I had perpetrated. I daren't give way as the volume of my deeds would burst over me in a flood with such force to not only carry me off, but to destroy everything in its path.

"You feel better?" he asked. I gave him another hug. What a decent young man I've got.

"Yes, ta."

"Say, can I get back to my homework? Mum will need the table soon."

"Aye, Laddie." He went back in and I stood a moment longer by myself in the backyard, struck through with an uplifting pride. I didn't care that for those moments just gone roles had reversed and it had been son consoling father. Not one bit, for I saw in him there the measure of the man he would become. I daubed my eyes with my handkerchief, a rather old, somewhat threaded cloth I had kept for many years. It had been well used and was dimmed by countless washings which could never fully remove the tint of old dirt. Part of a set, I'd received this hanky in one of the first parcels Adelaide had sent me after we had begun to exchange letters. She'd asked if there was anything I was in need of. My reply requesting handkerchiefs had come after much consideration of what I might ask for which would be of some practical use, but not overly presumptive as to the nature of our acquaintance. Her return just left me with more questions of presumption. I'd been sent six immaculate white cotton handkerchiefs upon each in green thread she had embroidered my initials, 'FDS.' She did very good needlework. Twenty years on the letters were still apparent, if not as vibrant. Not all my memories of the war are terrifying.

"Dad?" Hamish called from the kitchen. "Telephone call for you; Major Thorncliffe." I went in and picked up the call.

"You still dressed, Sergeant Major?" I said that I was. "Good. Be ready at your front door, Caroline's going to swing by to fetch you to the barracks."

"What's going on?" I asked, but the line was vacant.

Within the hour, I was once again seated opposite Paddy with his desk between us, although this was his office at Sinclair Barracks, no simple conference this. It was hard to make anything of what it might be. We appeared to be the only ones present, aside from his office, no other rooms were lit and the wide space of the building's open interior of parade square at ground level and gantry above was absent of activity. The Major's telephone call was spare of any detail save for an unspoken urgency. My legs itched. I detested the new battle dress and the rules limiting wearing of kilts to formal occasions. Wool trousers braised my thighs raw and aflame. I've had lice that were gentler. A constant effort was required on my part to not shift about in my chair with discomfort which might be mistaken for nervousness. From what he had just told me, the news was not good.

"He's done what?" I asked, after first hearing, forgetting just briefly the proprieties of office.

"Occupied the Rhineland." My stomach got in the elevator and pressed the button for a non-stop descent to the basement. This wasn't supposed to have happened; it wasn't even supposed to be possible. The peace treaty which had resolved the war had greatly restricted Germany's armed forces. These provisions had been blithely ignored and the response to the violation was equally ignorant. No one seemed to mind that our old enemy was laying keels, building aeroplanes and conscripting troops over maximum allowance. The prevailing thinking appeared to be that if the Germans weren't doing anything with them, there was no harm in having the stuff they weren't supposed to have. I would need someone to explain that to me as any sense of such an attitude escaped my ken. What bloody use is a treaty made to secure peace if one side turned a blind eye to the other's flaunting of terms? Alright, so now it was they had done something with their new toys. With one violation, another had been made.

Created as a buffer between Germany and its Western neighbours, the Rhineland was a broad stretch of territory which was to have been strictly off-limits to any encroachments by German armed forces. The Allies had occupied it after the war as a security measure, and had been set to do so, according to the same treaty, for several years beyond. Except that an early withdrawal had been negotiated. All that seems to have done was to leave the door open.

"The distinguished leaders of Europe," Thorncliffe said, "are allowing the situation to be dictated to them through the ramblings of a non-combatant corporal." He swiveled his chair to the cabinet behind him, producing a decanter and two diamond-patterned etched crystal tumbles. A good measure was poured out.

"Irish whiskey, I'm afraid, Sergeant Major," he said apologetically, as if he felt I might be insulted by the offer.

"Gift horse, sir." We touched glasses and sank the drop. The Major poured another.

"So far," he began, "no one knows what to make of it, much less what to do about it. The *Gefreiter* is telling everybody that the move is 'purely symbolic'."

"What the Hell does that even mean?"

"I'm pretty sure he doesn't really know. That asshat talks a lot of rubbish." It did seem that way, from how he appeared in newsreels. Manically extemporising, it was fun to imagine, and not too difficult with his exaggerated expressions and furiously animated gestures that his audience didn't understand his Austrian accent and were merely being polite in enthusiastically applauding his efforts. It was all too clear, though, that his words, his whole message, was comprehended. I don't know too much of politics, but it looked to me that one does best in that field by offering simple solutions to complex problems. The bigger the problem, the more basic the solution. It never seemed to make any difference how obviously impractical or unrelated to the problem such a solution appeared to be. It was bought, wholesale and ravenously. I'm certainly not disposed to give Germans much credit, but I would have thought them better than to be taken in by a bunch of smartly dressed medicine show salesmen. A real problem was that state of affairs was not an isolated case, and not the first of its kind. There was that preening thrust-jawed jumped-up newspaper boy in Italy, and a shrimpish man in Spain who appeared like a heavily decorated ski instructor. All the while, the rest of the world admired the accomplishments of men dedicated to purpose while pretending not to notice what that purpose was or how, precisely, it had been accomplished.

"It's being said that German troops are under orders to withdraw if opposed by force."

"Well, good. So, what do the French plan on doing?"

"Nothing, thus far. A lot of chatting between Paris and London, but no one's made a move." A third drink was poured. "I don't put any stock in the notion of the Germans going back the way they came if we start shooting at them. Old habits die hard." I was inclined to agree. "I spoke with the District Commander, just before I called you. With Colonel Daventry still away on his holidays, I'm acting CO. If that telephone rings, it might mean the worst, and we'll be put on Active Service. So, drink up before we have to be good boys for the King."

"Very good, sir. What's our plan for mobilisation?"

"We don't have one." Ah. I took my turn to pour. Should the balloon go up, the immediacy would be madness. We would be obligated to go wherever we were sent and do what we were told to do, without anyone issuing those orders having an established framework to organise everything required to respond to a national emergency. By this far along, I should really be used to how the army operates. Largely it was tediously bureaucratic, stymied in stuffy redundancies and inflexible procedure, which without notice could shift to an alternate mode of pure reactionism, moving moment to moment on the fly with incautious improvisation. All of us caught up in that sort of proclivity to work between stoic pro forma and undiluted freneticism had not only to be versed in both modes of operation, realising there was little median between one extreme and the other, but also blessed with the insight to know which method was in fashion, realising it could change over with absolutely no notice. The worst disasters occurred when there was no agreement on which way things were being run at a particular time, which was actually what tended to happen the majority of the time. There's no simple way to adequately explain how tremendously maddening it could be, particularly from the centre of the storm, nor can I find reason as to why working within it thrilled me so much. I loved the scattered puzzle of it all, tumbling through it, upside-down and backward at breakneck speed putting pieces together in order to see the whole thing coalesce.

"There might not be anything pigeon-holed," the Major said, "and maybe something like this will create an urgency to that end. Not holding my breath on that one. However, do you think that our government would make expenditures it didn't expect a return on?"

"What do you mean?"

"Okay," he gently patted the telephone which had remained quiet, "we might not be marching tonight. Doesn't mean we won't tomorrow, next week or next year. What I'm saying is that the COTC wouldn't be getting a dime if the folk in Ottawa didn't have cause to have a bushel of junior officers ready to go. This thing isn't playing up at uniformed recreation." He dipped into his leather valise which was leaned against his desk and brought forth another of those maroon booklets. "See," he indicated a section of paragraphs, "provision for students in professional degrees. Streaming for candidates towards the Medical Corps, Engineers, Signals, all trades, essentially." I read along, though the words weren't retained all too well what with my brain swimming in whiskey. "If I didn't know any better, I'd say we were building an army."

"Albeit, sir one of officers with no men for them to lead."

"Any worry we'd be short of volunteers when the time comes?" I shook my head. Of course there wouldn't be. There never is. "So much the better to have leadership in place. Might not be a lot in the way of overt planning, but a good foundation is some kind of start. That includes you."

"I can see why you want my help with this, sir. Give the cadets the benefit of experience."

"That's part of it. The other part is that I want to put that experience of yours to use in the most effective way I can. You're going to write for your own certificate."

"Awa'," I scoffed, the liquor superseding the correct deferential manners, "I'm no officer type."

"Who is?"

"I've not got the schooling." I never finished secondary school, having gone off to war instead.

"You realise I'm faculty at the university, Sergeant Major? I can get you enrolled in a snap."

I brought my tumbler up close to my eye, tilted it to see past the robust amber spirit, half-way pretending to be wary of him having placed the King's shilling at the bottom of the glass. That's an old recruitment trick. The coin was a soldier's daily pay, and accepting it was considered a binding contract. If recruitment men were having difficulty in rallying their set quota of new enlistments, they would sometimes contrive to underhand methods. Gather village lads at the pub, standing them drinks and telling inflated stories might influence a few. Get some of them half-bagged, slip a shilling in their mug and collar them for taking it up when they fished it out would nab the still reluctant. I really don't know if there's any truth to that ever happening, notwithstanding we don't even use shillings in Canada.

"You're not ordering me to do this, are you, sir?"

"Not in my power to. No, I'm requesting; enthusiastically suggesting, giving counsel to an old friend." Call it what he liked; I didn't feel there was any leeway. I'm nowhere used to an officer's words being subject to broad discretion. "You're due to muster out soon. The only practical way of retaining you would be to push for a commission. Let's say we have to go up against the Hun in any kind of near future. COTC will provide us with plenty of qualified individuals, but none who've really been put to the test."

The other shoe dropped. It was nice to think he'd gone out of his way, call in some favours from Ames and Dewey, get Adelaide to give me an earful, just to convince me to take on some extra days' work in an instructional role. His effort might seem to outdistance reward, except that Patrick Desmond Thorncliffe spared nothing in pursuit of his goal. It was my mistake in thinking he'd set his bar for accomplishment as low as that. He was a man of maximum effort towards maximum result; always has been. If I knew him as well as all that, then I'd do him a disservice to not think he knew me equally as well. My tenure with the army had been a large part of my life, and was by its nature restrictive to many aspects of self-determination. Much of what had been asked of me within the institution was obligatory. Sometimes, even the few things presented with a veneer of choice were not as they seemed. Ostensibly, remaining with the Militia after the war instead of de-mobbing like most everyone else was up to me to accept or refuse.

Except it had been Colonel Sinclair who had asked me. While that didn't change the request to an order, such was my respect for the man, I could not ever turn aside anything he asked of me. With Paddy, it was much the same. He had always demonstrated a perfect emulation of the Colonel's admirable qualities, the kind of cheery and determined self-assuredness which compels men to follow. A personality like that was absolutely essential to possess when to follow might well mean being led to death. He topped up our glasses, having revealed his full purpose behind his machinations, and spoke with a touching sincerity.

"Felix, you're standing in your own way. What do you imagine you'll do when your cousin retires or, forbid, passes?"

"Take over the Estate."

"Why?"

"It's the family business."

"Do you want to run a vineyard?" He held a hand up before I could answer, had I been ready with an answer, which I wasn't. "I know you really don't want to. Your problem is that you have it in your head that such a thing is fixed. That is just all too convenient for not displaying courage enough to take strides to find what you would do otherwise. 'Och, aye, ne'er finished thae school' is just another poor excuse for never having to try."

"I don't sound like that."

"You don't hear yourself. I can't force you to stay in the army, or to take a commission, and I don't want you to do either just from any sense of loyalty.

Likewise, I can't push you into enrolling for a degree. I am only doing one thing: Giving you the opportunity to find what you're really capable of; to find something that will enable you to define yourself rather than letting yourself get defined by something." I poured another drink, if nothing else than to shut him up about it. Perception skewed by what I'd swallowed thus far let me believe that he was trying to trick me by making sentimental appeals into doing what he wanted of me.

"What would you have me study?" I asked, fully expecting a response of recommending a degree best fitting for a collateral infantry commission.

"Me? Nothing. You're not getting it, are you? It would be entirely up to you." That hit me with more force than the amount of drink I'd taken in. Which was saying something, as the Major and I had drunk rather a lot. As far as that went, it was a daunting procedure to operate the telephone in order to call my wife to fetch me home.

No matter how much effort is placed into trying to appear sober, I can't see myself from the outside.

"Look at the state of you," said Adelaide when she pulled up. I stumbled in my attempt to mount the passenger seat. It must have been very late; she had her night dress on under her coat. We, that is, Paddy and I, may have overdone things. I recall we had emptied the decanter.

"Was this just an excuse to get knees up?"

"War," the word slipped from my mouth. It was mumbled, my head in my chest, eyes down. I wasn't able to look out the windscreen because the road was bleary and weaving.

"Pardon?"

I held up thumb and finger, spaced narrowly apart.

"This close, very close, almost happened."

"What are you on about?" It might not have helped my case that I suddenly remembered a joke Paddy and I had come up with.

"Their houses are too small."

"Eh?"

"Last time, Fritz wanted a 'Place in the Sun.' Should have built a conservatory."

"This is nonsense. too much in excess—for you— that's the problem."

"Now, they want 'Living Room.' Why don't they just extend the lounge?"

"You're setting no fine example, talking absolute malarkey. It'll be no use speaking to you now. Don't say another word, there's a reek coming off you." It's just as well I don't drink all that often. Strange thing to say for a man with a good-sized stake in a winery, and it's not because of Adelaide scolding me for 'living in excess' as she puts it, although I never avoid a sharp tongue when I do. I don't get bent out of shape against any moral aversion, mine or hers. I avoid it because I'm barely in any real control of my emotions as it is, and a gross infusion of alcohol only seems to magnify the foremost feeling I might be working with at the time. Right enough if I was jolly, I could carry on making jokes and singing auld songs and be delighted with everything. Fact was, I was rarely jolly. I'm more prone, I'm afraid, to melancholy or anger, and that's bad enough without adding any fuel to those fires. Leaving the armoury that night was a completely new, and very different case in point.

I felt numb.

I reached the kitchen the following morning in a delicate shape of misery, after having been summoned by my wife via proxy of Philip sent to wake me, which he'd thought the most efficient method of doing so would be to poke me repeatedly on the forehead with his chubby fingers.

"Ow," I said, upon receiving such treatment, "stop that." Philip, young as he was, had enough good sense to cease jabbing at me when I told him; and then he delivered his message.

"Mummy wants you downstairs."

"Ta, son. Tell her I'll be down shortly."

"Okay," he said, "you sick, Daddy?"

"Not really."

"You smell funny," he remarked, and pulled a face. I suppose he was still at the age when mouth and brain are directly connected, without shunt of propriety.

"Go on and tell Mummy I'm on my way." Philip left, and I lurched into the upstairs hallway, over to the bath where I ran the cold tap into the sink and tried to smack life into my face with the shock of scooped palm-fulls of icy water. It did little to improve me, my reflection showing a pallid and drained face. I hoped there wouldn't be a row upcoming. I was in no state to make any defense.

"I would like you to tell me," Adelaide began, in a light tone, with no current of aggravation. Or, none I could detect, "what you and Partick got up to last night." That was simple enough. I told her we had started on a dram or two to fortify ourselves against what the news from Europe could mean. We had continued drinking to relieve our nerves when no orders came. Then, we had carried on drinking because we were already drunk and neither of us could see any harm in carrying on. It was the sort of decision made by the drink itself causing us to forget what the morning following would be like.

"The papers aren't making a fuss about it," she said. "Look," pointing at the columns of broadsheet on the table. "Westminster isn't condemning it and the German Chancellor is stating that their territorial ambitions are satisfied. There won't be any war over this." I took a moment to read, the very exercise of using my eyes making it seem they were clamped in tightening vices. Sure enough, there they were, the House of Lords shrugging its shoulders; the Germans were only 'going into their back garden.' Following that was a quote from the barking Wiener himself about the land grab being the end of things. Except, his statement as printed was in direct contradiction to other claims on territory he'd previously made. Doing nothing now to check these ambitions of his was only giving leave for another, larger stunt.

"Not this time," I said to her, "but this isn't the end of it. That wee man can't be taken at his word."

"I don't trust him either, he's as shifty as they come. I'm not after starting arguments over politics at this table."

"No argument, Aidie. I don't like at all what this points toward. He'll be thinking to do as he pleases. The longer that goes on, with us kidding that all's well, him and his lot will keep gathering strength to the point that when something is needed to be done about it, all the advantage will be his."

"You're that certain?" I felt that the designs were plain. One major pillar of the current German government was their view that the Treaty of Versailles was invalid. Not that certain clauses were unfair or open to interpretation; they believed the whole thing had been negotiated in bad faith by an illegitimate legislature, and as such was entirely without merit. A way of putting interpretation to that point of view could be that if one of the main signatories no longer recognised the document which drew the peace, the opposite state of affairs was in existence. Such as that, we were already at war, had never stopped being at war, despite decades of hiatus without open hostilities. Not looking at it in that relief meant we on the one side might allow the other to finish the Great War on their terms without the supposed victors having done anything about it.

"I can't think of it as anything but inevitable." I really couldn't, no matter how objectively I tried to push the thing through the sieve of reason. A great deal of future events, most of them, I would think, have too much about them in variable factors to be anything beyond imaginative speculation. This, however, was different. There remained a great deal in the shadowy realm of the indeterminate; the exacting methods or timing, which could only be guessed at, but not the direction these present events were moving in and what they were moving towards. Any attempt I made to evaluate the situation never escaped that there was nothing to be done to avoid another war. Such being the case, I would much prefer it would occur sooner rather than later, and not just to save the suspense of a long delay. Sooner begun is sooner finished, and for very sound reasons, I would like to get the ordeal out of the way before too much time were to pass. Hamish was fourteen. Once he was old enough to make his own decisions about it, I would have no grounds to refuse him should he wish to volunteer for service. I've little stomach for hypocrisy, but there was nothing more I wished to contradict myself on than that. It's a line of work which hasn't gone altogether well in our family. The boy's full name is Hamish Kelley Strachan, which remembers his grandfathers, both of whom were buried under foreign soil they had been fighting to gain. My father had been taken away by the most common of deaths in South Africa, the type of fever brought on by living in unsanitary conditions. In comparison, Kelly O'Leary's death, shot at close range, was a surprisingly rare occurrence. In the Great War, neither disease nor hand-to-hand combat were near as common a cause of casualties as was artillery, to which Bill could attest both given and received. It was entirely likely artillery fire which was complicit in Alec's mysterious end. Of mysterious ends, there was also Hamish's uncle to consider, Kelley the Younger. Not of age to have taken part in the Great War, the middle O'leary child had spent those years working as a meat packer. It was important work to be involved with, critical to the war effort. I don't think Kel saw it in the same way, and would rather have contributed more directly, but we finished up before he could have the opportunity. That blind desire is most likely what inspired him to run off, in the words of the note he left, to 'fight for Ireland.' What happened to him was anyone's guess, nothing more had been heard from him. We didn't even know which side of Ireland he intended to fight for. His scarper towards adventure was Adelaide's motives for apprenticing her youngest brothers, the twins, to the Estate to keep them from following along into a very ugly war. With Hamish, the lad had not shown any inclination towards the military; but that meant very little as neither had I, before the war began. Like me, it would be war which would change that for him, and only because I knew that my case was by no means a rarity. I would have no honest way to prevent him from rallying to the colours as any argument I could make against it was one which I had already rebutted when I went off against Ma's entreaties for me not to go. I wondered how much, if any, of that Aidie was considering, as she had just as much at stake, if not more.

"What would happen if it were to go that way?" I knew what she meant. It wasn't a broad question pertaining to what our response as a nation might entail; which was a good thing as I had no clear answer to provide on that. Her question was plain; meaning, what would happen to me?

"I would be liable for Active Service."

"They can't expect you to go fight another war."

"You know well it doesn't work like that." Adelaide was certainly not naïve. Any refusal to concede my observations as probably correct had more to do with not wanting to believe what these events might have in store for us.

"You have a family."

"Your Dad,"

"Stop. That's different."

"How? Did he not do what he felt was all he could to protect you? Why should I not do the same?"

"He hadn't already been through a war. No one's got any business to have you go through such a thing again. I can see plain what the first one has done to you." Through my dismal condition, I could palpably sense she was deeply worried about this. I took her hand.

"I'm not able to make a choice on this."

"Does it have to mean going in harm's way? Can't you stay to train, like with the cadet program?"

"It's up to the army to decide how to make best use of me. Besides, I couldn't live with myself if I stayed out. Me doing so would only mean someone else would take the place of wherever else I might be."

Everything of my experience in war disallowed any stretch of thought which would have anyone take upon hardships which should be upon me.

"Even if it meant you wouldn't come back to me?"

"Even so." We sat in silence of words for a moment, enrobed by the idle and active sounds of our home. From the garden, being cast in the light of the morning's sun were the cheeps and tweets of birds returned to nest, the gentle creaks of the house surrounding us settling against warming ground or being tickled by wind, and a slightly aggravating continual thump of our children bounding up and down the staircase for some unknown reason. I don't relish the anticipation of going to war. I have no desire to see such things or perform such acts as of the memories I can hardly abide. It will come or not regardless of my hopes. Any desire I might have, in whatever circumstance, to do all I have in my power to do to preserve what I could see and hear all around me as imperfectly ideal as it all was inclusive of having to relive the savagery of war, even if it killed me.

"William called before you came downstairs," Adelaide informed me, breaking away from the subject. "He wants you to call by the Estate to see him when you can."

"Did he say why?"

"No." Good, I thought. No need to treat it as urgent, then.

"I'll drive out to see him after taking you to school Monday."

As I approached his desk, Bill shook a sheaf of receipts in my face.

"When I told you to make the arrangements and have the bills sent here, I was not expecting you to bankrupt me."

"Ah, Bill," was as far as my rebuttal went.

"First class to Halifax? A state room on the crossing? Do you think I'm made of money?" I might have taken liberty, but what price comfort? It agitated him so much he lost his breath in shouting and coughed in sharp raspy hacks for a full minute or more. He caught up with himself and, arguably daft, lit up.

"You're not made of money, but you may as well be the way you hang on to it. I'd thought that since you didn't want to go in the first place, maybe going in style would suit you best." He jabbed a rude finger toward me, speaking through the cigarette clamped in his lips.

"There's your problem, Felix, thinking. I've half a mind not to go."

"You wouldn't," I said. I may have sent him the final reckoning, but the deposits on our reservations had come out of my pocket.

"No. I'd said I would go, and I won't reverse myself." Bill still hadn't told me why he'd switched tune in the first place. I reminded him.

"I will tell you later."

"That's what you said the last time."

"It's still not 'later', then, is it?" Remember what happened to the cat vis-à-vis curiosity, Felix." He

182

secured the offending receipts in a desk drawer. "That's that settled."

"You had me come up here to yell at me?" An eyebrow raised.

"What? No, don't be silly, for five minutes, at least. These costs are a side issue. There's to be a meeting this week. Local business and some of the town council, at Falls Parish Presbyterian Church."

"To what end?"

"It was your man, Reverend Galbraith what called me about it." Bill made no effort to hide an air of animosity. My cousin has absolutely no mind toward religion of any sort, claiming a practical agnosticism and an antipathy to miracles. My spiritual leanings might well be the plumb line between Adelaide's strict faith and Bill's complete lack of pious devotion. I couldn't have come see him here yesterday, as Adelaide won't have me drive the car on the Sabbath if it can at all be avoided to give an example of how these things mixed into one another. A philosophical question could be raised as to which one of us, if any, was correct. My mind told me we all were. God wouldn't be much of a supreme being if He couldn't appear to each individual in the way they perceive the reality they inhabit. All explained by science, was Bill's point of view; even if we hadn't yet figured the science of some things and had only the slightest grasp on what might explain the workings of the Universe.

Reverend Galbraith, my man, as Bill put it—he was the Regimental Chaplain as well as his civil ministry— had engaged my cousin in some winded debates on the subject of faith. Unfortunately, both men were firmly encamped on their hills and no ground could be made between them. This mutual immobility brought Bill to the boil and often ended any discussion with the harshness his temper allowed. For his part, the Reverend received Bill in a humility fitting his vocation. I think they'd get on rather well if fundamental and volatile subjects be avoided.

"He's asking community leaders to discuss problems and solutions to current economic difficulties."

"No, thanks. I'll go home and stare at the wallpaper for a livelier evening."

"I need you there to represent Inchmarlo." I hadn't been overly facetious in my objection to attending. There was no guessing it would be dull and pointless.

"Oh, come one, Bill. These things are nothing but a waste. Bunch of old men yelling at each other for things out of everyone's hands."

"I don't disagree, but the mayor will be there."

"So?"

"So, I'm putting it to you to impress him on what the Estate needs," he pushed a sheet of paper across his desk towards me. "All written down so you don't forget it." I took it up. It had one word on it: 'Roads.'

"Very funny. What about roads?" He took a few minutes to explain, a fairly sensible notion once made clear and made with a mind to keeping our property a going concern. I could easily understand Bill's desire to maintain his business. What I had failed to understand, about myself, was that while I had every hope Inchmarlo Estates would flourish, I never much thought about it being up to me, as it may well be once Bill was no longer at the helm.

The Estate was, for most of my youth, the entirety of existence. School, church and the occasional trip into town would be the extent of my travels, and none of those were altogether at great distances from my home. Not until I left for the army had I been away from the place for more than a few hours at a time, not since first coming to stay there from the town of my birth, Banchory, Aberdeenshire. Inchmarlo Estates was all I knew of Canada. A bit strange, perhaps, that I'm further travelled in other countries than my adopted home, but that's purely down to circumstance. It was, however, quite natural that when I was so far away, comforting thoughts centred around the pictures in my mind of the hewn grey flagstone house standing proudly above rolling hills of wily grape vines in strictly spaced and seemingly endless rows. This was the home to which I had dreamed of returning, had prayed for deliverance to. Those prayers, my petitions to God were the usual sort of bargains of me forever being on my best behaviour if only I could be allowed to put my feet upon my home again. God had held up His end, and I believe I had mine, only to have the result be an aggravating irony. What I had envisioned as my salvation, a future of quiet, decent and fulfilling labour was not as I had hoped. It was the same place, the same work which I had before the war. the difference was me, that was plain. I struggled with what could be done about it. I knew nothing else, and set as firm as the house's stone was the inevitability of the whole thing becoming mine. Paddy had been right, I didn't want it, but I also didn't know what it was that I did. That realisation, though, only made me feel that in not having any desire for any such endowment I was being callously ungracious to both my family and my Creator. I'm certain there's worse places to be, and many folk less fortunate than I. All the same, that didn't make my feelings less valid, even if I had little understanding of what those were, exactly, or what constructive steps I might take to address them.

"Now," Bill said, "for all else left to arrange for this trip; not one penny is to be promised before you check with me. Clear?" I nodded. "Out," he demanded, and out I went.

He's got no sense in how to have a good time, our Bill. Not that my choices of booking were really about having luxury for the enjoyment of it. It's a long way from Falls Parish to Le Havre via Halifax and I was certain that would be easiest to keep Bill's condition in mind. I had decided not to use that reasoning to counter any protests he might make about expense. The only result of making a reminder of his frailties would have been him throwing me out of his office five minutes earlier than he did. Fortunately for me, and far more important than my cousin's pride or tight purse strings was Adelaide understood my motives and the fact that the outrageous cost was being worked through the Estate. I would have no way of justifying such lavishness to her with our own money. Thinking of the cost strictly in terms of being beneficial to Bill's condition also helped me to justify to myself laying out expenditures which were beyond the means of most folk. My family was in an advantageous position to have not been too deeply affected by the financial crisis. It was likewise so for many of the properties beyond town. Some had even grown in size in being able to buy out smaller holdings which hadn't margin for depressed profits. It places a lot of curiosity about how such things are led to happen and why some get what seems more of a raw deal than others. If cause and effect were made clear, well, that would be one less timeless question on the Universe's secrets to contend with. Leaving me, all of us, I suppose, without ability to comprehend the big unknowable 'why' events unfold as they do. Why, through no personal failing, a man can lose everything, be ruined and reduced while the next fellow sails by no bother at all. And, hang that curiosity as far as financial success or failure are concerned, when this wondering can also fit more finite circumstances.

France, September, 1917

The men were loaded down like coolies with all manner of defensive stores. Some, working pairs, used bunches of corkscrew pickets as litters to balance tight spools of barbed wire over their shoulders. Others not so burdened hefted pre-made sections of duckboard or carried bales of sandbags, shovels, picks and an unlucky few were having to contend with awkward-sized sections of corry iron, which weren't all that heavy, but had rough edges fine enough to slice a hand open. Strapped about our persons in addition to all of that was as much small arms ammunition and Mills bombs we could manage and still be able to move forward. Two other platoons of 'B' Company were similarly laden, snaking in a long line of progress behind us. Six Platoon, being first in order of march was followed by Seven and Eight, all of us under the strain of these trench-building wares destined to take positions along a hump of middling prominence noted as 'Bell Hill' on our maps. We were on our way to relieve a company from the West Prairie Rifles—or, more precisely, what remained of it—who had secured the place earlier in the day. Five Platoon, assigned to 'Company Support' were at the tail end of our party. Not required outright to aid in what would be a rampant effort of construction. Five was not loaded as we, but instead had boxes and crates of ammunition as immediate reserve to what the rest of us were bringing forward. Somewhere in all of that was not one, but two of our battalion's Vickers MG's. this brought to mind the typical meanness of quartermasters. It was sardonically apocryphal that we were never given more, and often barely enough, in the way of stores items than was required. A general rule was to always request of the QM twice as much of what was needed as it was certain they'd only issue half of what was asked for. I could surmise we wouldn't have been given all this wumph if we weren't going to be in immediate need of it. To have so much easily given out did not bode well that we could be expected to have leave to keep Bell Hill without a lot of bother. It could be worse, I thought, in the moment forgetting that it could always be worse. If we weren't moving up to prepare a defense of this hill, we would have been going in to relieve the West P's to take the hill ourselves. That was what we had been preparing to do in the days prior to returning to the line.

Our battalion had remained in the rear for a good fortnight or so. It was a decently lengthy period of time to try and put what we had gone through during our last stint on the front out of our mind. Length of time was not the tonic it might seem, as some things were just not likely to ever go out of mind. Unless, that is, the memory of one tour up front were to be superseded by a fresher memory of equal or greater harshness. I don't give the fates enough credit sometimes that no matter what has gone by, no matter how horrible, cannot be overruled in the seat of reason by something more horrible yet. At least, this period of rest—the word only being a shade of its definition as such things go—had allowed us to receive replacements. While I had been given two new men for my section, I was still short-handed. During the summer months I had never had a full complement of troops. Indeed, I only had such in the first fifteen minutes of the Ridge when my numbers were reduced by the deaths of Ferguson and O'Leary. Men had come and gone in the time in-between. Most recently, in the span of one stint on the line, I had lost four men; one dead, two wounded and one missing. There was little hope that Taverly would show up. 'Missing' really meant 'Disappeared', as in ceasing to exist on as fine a level as the atomic. Things of our trade were capable of such eradication. A thread of solace I might have taken was that the laying down of life would have some significance attached to it. That thread had unravelled a fair bit as days, weeks and months went on and on with no tangible gain. These bits of ground, here and there, taken at great cost were not of any wide influence to pushing the balance of winning or losing to our favor. If I were to have been struck dead in this instant of filing along towards Bell Hill, a prospect not outside of all possibility, my life as far as being a part of the war would have no more effect on the outcome of it than Taverly's mysterious end or Plumrose's dismemberment under a misplaced friendly shrapnel burst. Tav and Bumnose had given their all for nothing of substance. They were two among many deaths incurred in a lengthy grappling match over ground disputed in a similar campaign the year before, which in part had included our sashay against Spoon Farm. It was difficult to see what the point might be in all of this, seemingly chewing over the same bits of turf without end. Difficult, perhaps, but not altogether impossible. The reasoning had been explained to us that to support operations in the North, it was necessary we maintain constant pressure locally; denying the enemy freedom of movement to re-deploy their reserves against our main effort through Flanders. All this wasn't a mere extension of the active defense of months earlier, the difference being the scale and intensity. Gamely poking at the Germans would hardly attract enough attention. We were making cheeky wee grabs at this bit of land or another. Not knowing if we here would be required to commit to a coordinated offensive, the targets in our portfolio were intended to give us the best kick-off position for such a thing, although I could easily envision us going one place or the next, up or down the length of Front under British control as the months unfolded to do what had been set for us to only wind up here yet again, the year following. It stood a good question to ask who among us now would be there, then, as we were few here now who had been present the year before. I'd never had any cause to think of my demise at any time in my life as anything besides the most certain but least likely event. Despite evidence pointing at the possibility of my end being sooner than I might have hoped, I had been able to retain my formed notions on the subject without change through the first year or so of my life as a soldier. Will to live is really just conceit of self-awareness. All this death going about was something happening to other people.

But, says the will, not me, it won't happen to me. Except I was failing to acknowledge that everyone is 'me' to themselves. There was nothing about me which was any more special to any one enough to guarantee stay of execution. There was nothing about myself which made me more deserving to live. That was a difficult realisation to come across as it pushed self-awareness against the ego to erode the notion that the world outside my inward identity owed me any preferred treatment towards my self-preservation. Once that bare truth comes to be realised, the next step was to figure out the best way to avoid an unavoidable thing. That mere impossibility summed up how I had approached the past two weeks in preparing my new men for the Front and it was hardly sufficient time to cover all of everything that may come. There was too much out there in the way of dangerous things to remember what precisely to do or not do in each case. These things comprised a list of such length no uninitiated mind could digest all at once. Nor was it possible to prepare a new man for a front-line tour entirely by theory alone. I was required to distill all pertinent information into the most concentrated spirit possible:

"Don't step in a place anyone ahead of you hasn't stepped. Never raise your head above the trench-line. Touch nothing you haven't been explicitly instructed to touch. Never be more than an arm's length from your rifle, respirator or web gear. Don't eat, drink or smoke at any time without permission. Stay within my sight at all times." By this point, I may as well have that printed on a card. "None of that will guarantee your survival, but it might just prevent a pointless death, and as those things go, that's the worst kind," was an *ad endum* I had incorporated to drive the point home. Really, not much of that would matter, as being clever or alert or quick had no influence on things beyond ability to control. Best I could do with replacements was to try to remember their names and prevent them from doing more harm to us than the Hun. That would be a serious enough consideration if this trip had been a routine occupation of an established position, or if we had been going ahead to doing what we had been rehearsing to do rather than throwing that to the wind for something else entirely.

Most of my attention was focused on remaining upright. I reckoned I had upon me enough weight to make me twice as heavy as I would be if I were dressed as Adam. A mis-step would not only tip my balance over and the landing with ballast would really hurt; I didn't think I'd be able to raise myself under my own power alone. The company was being led overland, crossing trench lines by means of pallet-board bridges lain from parados to parapet, and along the open ground in-between. Three years of war had pulverised the countryside to a desert. No-man's Land was aptly named, as not a thing appeared to be living here. Everything of vibrancy which had been upon this surface had been scraped away, blasted to oblivion or buried again and again as huge hosts of men used great destructive force in repeated attempts to seize a few more yards of dust and debris. I had to wonder just how much of France was left that had any more than purely figurative value to fight over.

Laiden men cursed and groaned while stumbling over dips and divots, slippy patches of mud still remaining from heavy rains of days just past. I was uncertain whether or not I was glad that the rain held off. While it made the going easier over terrain which would have been swampy otherwise, a clear, dry day beat the sweat out of us, soaking through our clothes in every respect like rain, from the inside out. Aside from brief daily ablutions, we'd had no wash and all together we were sending off a powerful stench of collected weeks living dirty. Urged by our officers stating and re-stating the need for us to move quickly, the tinker and rattle of swaying equipment was chorused by heavy, dry pants of open mouths and exertion. The line of men toting awkward loads, huffing and wheezing under the burden and a scorching white sun was somewhat like a living locomotive. This was madness; sheer, unadulterated folly. Moving above the trenches was wildly reckless. Doing so under a clear and bright sky invited catastrophe should even one German aeroplane be aloft. Somewhere, somebody was probably staking his reputation that throwing caution to the wind in having us do as we were doing. I hoped, and certainly not for that fellow's sake, whoever he may be, that he had been right. The world as seen from outside a trench's enclosure always seemed wider and more open than it may actually be. A trench's purpose was entirely protective, and after having become used to the method of living in one, to be without it was not unlike foregoing a pedestrian subway to cross a busy street streaming with cars, carts and trams; but that was no apt comparison. Here, standing taller than any other feature we could only move as fast as two-legged pack animals could and the traffic which might strike us would be invisible.

All the day had been approached at a rush, in the frantic and sometimes bizarrely aimless fashion of the army. Usually, the army excelled at putting order into chaos even if it might not seem so at first blush, or that some chaos appears to be of its own manufacture. A cynic, such as I can be from time to time, will only note where the institution falls short of that balance. I needn't look far to find example, without once considering how it is able to keep men attuned to purpose while all around is one step from madness. I might have been feeling a bit cynical on the way to Bell Hill. That morning, we had just been about to begin to set up for another course of training exercises. These were to be our final runs-though. Perfecting working as platoons in the days prior, we were going to practice cooperating as a full company in the morning, and then all four companies together in battalion formation that afternoon. After sundown, off we would go towards pre-arranged start points to put rehearsal into reality. Instead, the shouting started in a howling mass of voices. It was a disjointed aria of officers and sergeant majors flowing outward from Battalion HQ with a rapid slew of sudden instruction.

"Stop! God dammit, stop! You, fetch that platoon in. No, not that platoon, <u>that</u> one! 'B' Company? You—you with 'B' Company? Jesus wept, lad, if you ain't, why'd you answer? Never mind, now. Looking for 'B' Company. Yes, I said 'B'. Find your OC and tell him you're first in order of march. Form fours, by platoon, on that road, clear? Which road? That fucking road, son, the only road we got hereabouts. Company 2 I/C's to Battalion HQ for orders. Now, dammit!" This sort of rampaging, folded over and blended with other bellows some of which were contradictory or quickly countermanded somehow worked in getting us scattered from playing pretend and shook out onto the track leading up to the Front. No one seemed to know what was going on and anyone who did know wasn't present to tell us. Through the morning we marched at a quick pace to a dump where stores had been piled. The various needs of building a defensive structure were shared out and divided, and without much pause we were shoved back on the road, hoisting the different loads up in preparation to carry forward. Shouting started again; to drop everything in place, to go from one side of the depot to the other, double quick, as someone had realised we hadn't been issued any ammunition. With that minor trifle out of the way, back we went to where we had shed our construction kit and were at last on the move, making haste for lost time. We still hadn't been told what was expected of us when we got to where we were going. With everything we had been preparing to do so ungraciously chucked aside, the reason had probably something in the way of a major disruption of operations at large about it. For most of us, our battalion was the upper extent of our familiarity with military structure and it could sometimes be forgiven that the interdependent links of higher formations weren't much considered. I knew enough to infer that we were responding to an upset plan at the brigade level, but was perhaps embittered by experience to have not considered it was because things had gone better than expected. Even if I had, I wouldn't have felt any better about proceeding forward in daylight. Reliefs on the line were normally conducted at night to obscure our movement. Although, darkness didn't ever seem to matter all that much. Fritz was uncanny in knowing when a change of shift was going in, and would plaster our routes with artillery fire. It was an economical use of resources. A bombardment of usual intensity and duration fired during a relief process had potential to hit two times as many men as would usually be along the lines of communication at one time. Everything about this particular move was unnerving. The abrupt manner in which we went from a rigidly scheduled day to incautious uncertainty without anything by way of explanation was not indicative of a situation well in hand. Moving openly, over rather than through, our front-line system at the height of daylight without purpose being made clear only went towards me feeling even less easy about taking new men up the line for the first time than was usual. I'd had Kipling and McManus only over a week, just. I'm wary of new men, as a general rule. It had begun to seem as though each subsequent allotment of replacements we got were less well instructed than those received on the prior occasion. On top of that, I'd only had the balance of our time behind the lines to incorporate them into working with the rest of the section. A section, mind, which had just come out the other end of a tough and costly tour up front was in need of careful and considerate administration and throwing enthusiastic newcomers into the mix took my attention away from that task. Difficult enough to gain a balance of preparing the veteran to return and the novice to initiation on the job we had been supposed to be going to do; I was in no position to ensure preparation for what it was we were now going to do, not least because I had no idea what that was.

By the time we reached Bell Hill, the afternoon was at its worst in still, stifling heat and the sun at zenith in a dazzling brightness making it difficult to see. The works as we were brought up to them were German fire trenches dug around the waist of the hill. Not of any forbidding height, Bell Hill was the most elevated of a serration of rises from an otherwise level field, and the only one robust enough for a tiered defensive position to be set. Our friends from the West Prairie Rifles had taken these trenches with great assistance from our artillery and the works were thoroughly smashed. Revetments had been blown in, their debris, a mixture of peeled and crumpled iron sheets and shredded timber lay broken and flung about in splinters; sandbag walls with nothing solid to keep them set were nothing more than clumps of canvas-bound earth. Our infantry had added to all that the enemy dead who remained where they had fallen, whole and incomplete, some partially buried by the collapses here and there of unrestrained trench walls. Bell Hill had proven to be not as substantial a position as reckoned. Its lack of expected grandeur was in part why our battalion's role had changed; the fight for this feature had been less difficult than initially thought. The Hun had kept such a tight grip on the trench system the hill overlooked, it was assumed they would try to retain any ground with the same tenacity. That they hadn't was concerning. When the enemy acted in a way contrary to usual practice, it almost certainly meant they were doing so to keep the advantage. It had taken a couple of hours at a dog's pace to get there and we were all thankful when the halt was called. We were well forward, and despite being in the shadow of the hill, very exposed. Heavy boxes and oversized loads were immediately dropped, beating up clouds of sandy dust. Coughing and spitting, men bent double to try and catch wind back, the drain of physical effort in getting to this place pushing aside appreciation that we were at the business end of things.

"One Section, take a knee, eyes front, rifles at the ready," I snapped out between shallow, arid breaths to re-establish that we were more than a carrying party. "Weapons safe," I added, suddenly remembering I had no instruction as to what might be ahead of us. I caught Mr. Thorncliffe by eye as he came up from a group of company officers. He tagged each section commander on his way through our line and we gathered around.

"Very quickly," he began, "the West P's were not supposed to advance this far, only to those last ditches just behind us. We can thank them for doing what was supposed to be our job. They paid for it. This is the absolute tip of the spear. Our flanks are not secure, but that's already being worked on. 'A' and 'C' Companies will be moving up on our left, two companies from the Fort La Salle Regiment on our right. 'B' Company will hold this hill. Our platoon is the left edge of the position. Leave the heavy stores here; we'll occupy first and send work parties back to this point to pick up what we need as we dig in. Order of march, One, Three, Four, Two. Liaise with the party you're relieving, assess your position and be ready to report when I come through on my inspection. Shake your men out, follow me."

The West Prairie Rifles had sewn a bit of confusion. When their attack that morning had met resistance lighter than expected, rather than holding firm on their objective as plans had dictated, an immediate grab for Bell Hill had been given the go-ahead from Brigade HQ. The risk of having the West P's fight through their original stopping point was in opening up our flanks, but this had been taken as acceptable rather than allowing time to pass idle while waiting for us in the King's Own to take it on as was the original design; which was time the enemy could have used to reinforce his lines on the hill. Instead, and as the Lieutenant had pointed out, with thanks to the West P's, the very opposite was taking place. The opportunity to seize the initiative and momentum of the situation was given precedence over maintaining a congruent frontage of our Brigade's three forward battalions. Of course, now that we had it, they were going to want it back. Such was the usual logic of this type of small-scale positional warfare.

Thorncliffe led us around the edge of the hill by way of a trench switching from the forward line to positions which had been a secondary line on the reverse side, and now represented our primary defensive position. The going wasn't easy, moving both uphill and over or around the debris of ruined trenches, scrambling at points by hand and foot and glad that we'd dropped our extraneous stores before proceeding. What we came to were pits, really, not in good states of repair, either. This wasn't so much from anything we had done to them; quite simply they had not finished being built; if by not finished I meant barely started. The construction of a series of trench lines works from front to rear in priority and often support and reserve lines are not given the same effort in building as a firing line. Many turn out to be little more than scrapes. Some, including the one I was about to take over, were not even man-deep. This required approaching our new post in a crouch and having to keep bent low to remain heads-down from the trench lip.

"Who's in charge here?" I asked as I came to the four West P's manning the post. My first job was to find my counterpart of the section I was relieving to get the gen, and there wasn't an NCO among them.

"Suppose that's me," one of them said, "no one else left. Our lieutenant and sergeant both caught a packet. Platoon's being led by my section's corporal." He had two men working with entrenching tools in an effort to gain some depth and one keeping an eye on the plain extending below our position. "Damned hard fight," the Rifleman continued. His jacket was torn, held closed by one remaining button. Grime coated his face collected in the hollows under his eyes and sallow cheeks. The dark grit defining sunken features painted his look somewhat like a bare skull.

"Care to orient me?" I requested, handing over my water bottle. He took a swig, gave it back.

"Thanks, Corp. See those broken trees?" He pointed to a sparse crop of shattered wood, well to our left and about two dozen yards distant. It had been a small stand of elderly trees, the thickness of their stumps and circumference of the intersected piles of raggedly cleaved trunks told a story of another old thing ruined by our machinations. I indicated that I saw them.

"That's 'Timber', your left of arc." He swung his eyes right, and drew my attention to a clump of earth, nearly man height about twice as distant as Timber. It was maybe ten yards in length, thereabouts, and seemed a bit too finely shaped to be a natural feature. My inclination was that it may have been an earthen screen to conceal enemy movement.

"Mudpie," he told me was the feature's nickname and thus was established the extent, left and right, of my area of responsibility. In between these extremities the ground seemed rather open, except that it folded in little rises and depths as it played out from the base of Bell Hill. It was a bit of a disappointment to have possession of high ground which did not lend any advantage to lines of sight. the view was far better on the other side of the hill, where it overlooked a lengthy stretch of flatly laid ground. Bell Hill, it seemed, marked the edge of that flat expanse which was actually a broad plateau, dropping away on the side we were holding into a series of rises and dips, like waves caught in mid-break, an undulating surface of highs and lows with the disturbing feature of not being able to see the low ground from the rises.

"You can't see it, but beyond those markers, running left to right is a sunken cutting and beyond that, an old road." I brought out my map.

"Show me," I asked. He studied it quickly and ran a finger along the hidden ground.

"There," he said, and I traced the line with a red China pencil.

"Any trade since you took up position?"

"Came at us 'bout half hour after we'd driven them off. Nothing much since then. Some shelling, a little MG fire, but that was coming well right of Mudpie. That's about it."

"Alright," I said. The fellow was shifting about, casting looks at the field below us throughout his speech.

"Listen, buddy, we done here?"

"Nothing else you need to tell me?"

"No."

"Well, I suppose-"

"Good," he chirped, not letting me finish. He finger-whistled to his men. "Section up, we're moving," which they did as fast as they could manage and without further comment to me.

"Good luck to you, too," I breathed out to the backs of the Riflemen receding away from this forward edge through the shallow communication lines back the way we had just come, probably anxious to get as distant as they might be allowed before what might happen next. After a few hours of, according to that chap's report, token resistance what was going to happen was as near to certain as anything could be. The Hun would be massing, using the ground not visible to us and filtering through it forward into positions from which to spring a dedicated counter-attack. If they had withdrawn no further than the cutting beyond Timber and Mudpie, there wasn't a lot of distance to close, and a lot of dead ground in between in which to do it. I reckoned they would gather up and move into place at nightfall, perhaps even jumping us without benefit of a preparatory bombardment. It's what we would do, and I don't disallow them the same amount of horse sense.

"Lance Corporal Tremaine," I called Tim over. "Go along to Platoon HQ, ask Mister Thorncliffe to come our way at his earliest convenience. Try very hard to sell him on the idea of having Company send us one of the Vickers."

"You got it," and he was off. The Lieutenant would have been by as a matter of routine, I saw no harm in impressing on him that my need for him to see what was in front of me required urgent attention. We were not blessed with a lot of remaining daylight and my post was in no shape to be considered defensible.

"Lonnie!" I shouted for Brentwood.

"Yeah?"

"You and Brant on watch. Anything moving out there doesn't belong to us. Don't open fire without my say-so. the rest of you, keep digging. We may not have long and this mess ain't no better than half a grave. Dig like you'll find gold." Two men keeping an eye out made four of us to break into teams of one man on shovel, the other taking the spoil into sandbags and placing them, alternating running and facing, exactly as brick in layers along the parapet. In such a way, moving earth from bottom to top each bag-full added almost double to the depth of the hole. Working quickly, our efforts were greatly aided by the ground in which we were plying our shovels. I'd have never thought, even with my experience in working the vineyard, that I would come to have such an appreciation for something as plain and unassuming as dirt. An appreciation of the sort which might term me a connoisseur. Ground can be many things, and of them, quite frequently, it was too much of one or another. This was important because of the many things it could be; ground was everything to the infantryman. If it was too dry, half of what was dug would slide back and would need immediate and strong revetments before any good depth could be made. Too wet, and it would clump in big, sticky masses, holding tight onto shovels and picks, sitting damply heavy in sandbags and make every action require twice the effort. With that, it could be too rocky, or have too much clay or chalk, or too many roots and stumps of trees no longer entirely there. Bell Hill was composed of good, rich soil which had taken the heavy storms of the past weeks and drained most of the wetness through. It came up easy and stayed in place. A week earlier, we'd have been neck-deep in muck. A week later, if the weather were to stay calm, it might be like trying to shift a beach.

We'd made about a foot in depth—that being six inches down and six up—along our length by the time Tremaine returned with the Lieutenant. I handed my shovel off to Tim so he could keep working with Kipling while I talked to the Sir.

"I've just come from an orders group with Captain McCormack," he said. "Consulting with the other platoon commanders, we agree that this entire position," he paused, about to say something in the way of a negative comment an officer ought not to in front of a subordinate, so he chose more diplomatic words, "is less than ideal."

"It's shite, sir." I was not so constrained as he. Put my way or his, our opinions reflected the obvious. Bell Hill was a high feature, but the way the ground it dominated rose and fell left a great deal concealed from view. Timber and Mudpie were by far the worst in this regard, certainly in daylight, but in between those two features were plenty of places a man could hide and close up to us here. We'd been watching that ground and not a thing gave us any indication of German intentions. A counterattack in broad daylight was becoming less likely as the day moved on, which only bought us a handful of hours to strengthen our position against a strong night time push.

"Indeed," he said by way of agreement, "there's far too much in the way of a clear view down there. Tremor tells me you want a machine gun."

"Yes, sir. I'd like to have something that could keep that ground supressed. They're probably three-deep in that cutting just beyond, and if they've dug from there to Mudpie, they might well gather up there and be fifty yards distant waiting for the off."

"I'll have to talk to Captain McCormack, it's up to him where he wants to deploy those Vickers. You'll have it your way if I can convince him. In the meantime—let's see that shovel for a sec, Tremor—push a sap forward, here." With his borrowed tool, he bit into a slice of our parapet. "Ten yards, no further. If we get a gun sent this way, they'll place their pit at the forward edge of the sap. Better fields of fire." He tossed the shovel back to Tim who kept right on digging. "Before I go, do you want good news or bad news?"

"Given the choice? Good news, sir."

"Well, then, that is I can tell you the colour sequence for our SOS rockets." These were pyrotechnics not unlike ordinary fireworks, to be sent aloft should we come under heavy attack. Lit

207

according to an arranged sequence, it was a visual code for our artillery to fire Hell-bent-for-leather along our frontage. "It's green, red, green."

Good to know. If I saw that display overhead, I'd know to get everyone to ground.

"The bad news," he went on.

"Oh, there is bad news?"

"Isn't there always? The bad news, Catscratch, is that the guns aren't up on line yet." Fabulous. That meant we could come under pressure and just get a nice show of coloured light. "They're working on it, but I've not been told anything of progress. We are not moving back, regardless. Our orders are to hold. Should be fun." Oh, Christ. "I'll be back around as I can. Get that sap dug." I nodded, but I'm not sure he saw me, as he'd started to crawl off before he finished speaking. I switched out Brant and Brentwood, allowing fresh workers to keep pushing the trench floor down, putting Sloane and Tremain on sentry. That left me with Kipling and McManus to work on the sap Thorncliffe had asked for. I set the three of us up in a relay, one man digging, the next holding the sandbag to be filled, passing it to the third man to place it out of the way.

We'd managed good progress, working non-stop and by twilight we'd carved out a sap to the Lieutenant's desired length. It was a passage just substantial enough to move single file, but only at a crawl to not expose body above shallow depth. Repairs to the trench were really coming along as well, although we were required to suspend all work for the evening stand-to. It was after sundown, and thus we had resumed construction when Thorncliffe came by on his inspection tour, and it was getting on to full dark. Soon we would have to send for the material we had come with and had stacked at the base of the hill to our rear. Especially we would need the corrugated iron revetting to hold our walls steady. Even good soil as this was could not stand up without bracing. The deeper we went without retention, the more we risked collapse.

"Still no word on arty," he told me, our field guns not yet in place. "The Captain is holding one Vickers at Company HQ, the other is going in place with Seven Platoon, to your right, the centre of our position overall. Keep working on that sap, though. If need be, I'd like to have it as a place to move an MG to in a pinch. Finish it off with a 'T' gallery." One of a few standard and simple constructions, such a gallery was created by digging a square pit and building a wall of earth or sandbags in such a shape as the letter to give a raised platform for an emplaced weapon with room for its crew move around the perpendicular. Done well, it can permit a machine gun to traverse through 180 degrees while keeping the operators in cover. He handed me a Very pistol and some flares.

"Keep your eyes peeled, and try not to use these unless you're positive to catch them in the open." Thus far, we'd not seen anything to indicate any sort of counterattack. Might be Fritz had decided to let well enough alone. If that were true, it would be a first. Still, one can hope.

"How sure are we he's fixing to come over?"

"Nothing's certain, Catscratch. The Hun is a sore loser. I'd say," he mused, "if he's not come on in strength by now, he's probably going to hit with probing assaults, look for weaknesses." On that note, he moved off to check in with his other sections.

"Kipling, McManus, here's what we're doing," I brought them close so I could illustrate my instructions using my hands. The concept was straightforward; dig a square hole at the face of the sap. Method was not so straightforward, as to keep working without breaking cover required a difficult and not intuitive physical positioning. I did my best to explain the notion.

"The man up front will pass the spoil back. I know it might be easier or faster to just cast a shovel over top, but the Hun will be watching for that. He can hear us working," I warned them, "so best not give the game away by showing him where. Pass everything, in bags, behind you. We'll clear that away. Understood?" Both men nodded assent and went down toward the sap face to begin work. I had thought I was clear; I'd hoped for no mistakes in comprehending both meaning and importance of my instructions. Whether from ill-communication, inattentiveness or obstinance from how I told them to work, perhaps harder than seemed logical to them, whatever the reason, it matters little to the result. Sloane, who was on watch, crouched almost right beside me where I was gathering empty sandbags to bring down the sap, tugged at my sleeve.

"Dammit, Catscratch, will you look at 'em?" I followed his gaze, at my two men, both digging for all they were worth, dirt flying everywhere, working like maniacs at building the gallery and doing so, as it was more efficient, if not entirely incautious while kneeling, fully half exposed above the sap line.

"Keep down!" I hissed, and in the moment I did so, their attention turned towards me, failing to see a burling mass spring forward, catching one of them with a heavy swing of a German trench spade. My man howled, and I tossed myself down the sap, worming my way along, firing a Very light upward as I went, stuffed the flare gun in my belt and I laid hands on my knife and my Colt.

"Contact!" I heard Sloane call out from behind me, as soon as the flare popped in a bright flash of hotly orange light. I chanced a quick look over top the sap. the Hun, weirdly aglow, of form flickering with shadow under the flare were crawling about the heights like termites. I ducked back down, paused.

"One Section! Targets front, rapid rate!" I shouted, which singled me out as to where I was and that I was important enough to give orders, and I had barely finished yelling out before being clubbed. The blow only struck glancing against my helmet, but the force behind it still managed to scramble my egg a bit. I rolled onto my back to see my assailant, straddling the sap, fetching up for another strike. My men were pouring our fire, air lively with the snap and buzz of rifles cracking out fifteen rounds a minute. From a distance I could hear the rattle of Lewis guns and the gross thumps of Mills bombs. The arm was coming down, the thick truncheon whipping towards me. I thumbed the safety and let him have it. He collapsed on top of me, the dead weight taking my wind. I was about to shift him off, bloody heavy brute had fallen in such a way as to pin me. As I tried to push free, with my eyes skyward and the flare's light dimming, I saw three rockets go up, green, red, green. Then, nothing.

Canada, March, 1936

I fussed the covers off and fell out of bed entirely. The quilt and blankets had me trapped, having stopped being what they were for a moment to instead become several feet of French dirt layered on top of and all around me. The drop from bed to floor had me land in a smack. I sat up, slowly, and looked overtop the mattress. Adelaide seemed not to have been disturbed. I knew myself better than to try and get back to sleep. According to long habit, I went downstairs to put the coffee on. The kitchen was cool, but not cold. Certainly, it was warmer than it was outside and with a light rain tapping at the panes, it was most assuredly drier. I had very little in my memory of my time abroad of such simple and civilising comforts as those I could now easily take for granted. There's no mistake in thinking that I went months in France without a proper roof overhead or sheltered within four walls. Sitting at the kitchen table, eyes closed, I listened with concentration to the hiss of the gas flame on the hob and the breeze brushing against the window sash which caused a tiny stuttering rattle. These noises, subtle sounds of unmistakeable domesticity served to reinforce that I was in fact where I was and not where I had been. Some things of the war stood out more than others, and the events my mind had just played for me are without question among the most prominent. What had happened at Bell Hill was arguably the closest I came to death, and having survived it gave me more cause to wonder what it was that had kept me alive while the same event killed others. Kipling and McManus had not been more than a few yards from me and yet, here I was nearly two decades after the fact, upright and well while those two men remained entombed within a nothing little hill in France.

There was nothing at all within my power which might have allowed for any other outcome. The enemy attack was responded to by our SOS rockets which signalled our artillery to fire, who had not ranged properly, causing their shells to hit closer to our lines than intended, and one such struck the sap we had been working on. I didn't harbour any guilt for their demise. What I felt about such things like that was a hollowness of spirit that I don't fully understand. Whatever my ambitions for life might have been; regardless of my knowing what those were or whether even such desires would suit me or even be possible to attain, one critical factor stood in the way, which of course was that I needed to live long enough to pursue any ambition. Life is anything but certain, and at times much less so than others. My war was just over two years of consistent uncertainty and I don't recall having done much in the way of proselytizing on long term life goals through any of it other than what imaginings might bring a moment's comfort. Always, the hope wasn't for anything specific with the exception that I might remain alive to seek out the objects of any ambition. In that regard, I wasn't in any way any different than most others. Some men did develop a fatalism, which was at times eerily prescient;

214

but they were few. The majority of us sought to get through at least well enough to get on with the rest of our lives. That leaves me with the great mystery as to what forces exist which set me and my ambiguous ambitions aside while so many others were not so spared. Certainly, I can't claim that what I had asked fate to provide should I see the war through was any more noble, just or important than that of anyone else. I can't state with any authority that some unknowable force preserved me and not others for some kind of moral reasoning. Being as that may, it could well suggest there were among the war's dead those who desires were as deserving as mine of fulfillment; if not all of them, equally. It was massively unfair, and often, instead of gratitude for everything my life has given me, despite all I had around me, that I was here and others not, I was as empty as this early morning.

I might not ever be permitted a peek past the curtains to the inner workings of it all, so it seems undeniably cruel to be endowed with the desire to do just that. It might be perfectly reasonable to be asking "why me" and at the same time just as unreasonable to expect an answer. In the absence of such revelations, I might develop my own. As they would have to be based upon insufficient information, any I might come to could not with certainty be correct. Then, there it lays where practical understanding blurs into faith. Which in such circumstances would require me to believe that God plays favourites, which seems an odd thing for Him to do. Most of the time, I conclude that if there is a reasoning to events, my preservation indicates some purpose I'm meant to fulfill. If I knew why things transpire as they do, it would make reckoning of that purpose a good deal simpler. Simpler than that would be that there was no method or grand design to the Universe at large, letting me off the hook, purpose-wise. That would require me to pull myself from my core belief that all of existence must have some meaning, if only that it would otherwise seem a tremendous waste of energy.

Malachi was not long in joining me. I do like to think he does so to keep me company on these journeys from late night into early morning, though it's probably his instinct to follow into the kitchen anyone capable of opening the cupboard where his food was kept. To this end, he vocally expressed his demands.

"Wheesht!" I scolded him. "It's of no hour for your breakfast." What hour was it? Not long past midnight was my best guess. Regardless of what time it happened to be, my day always began when I got out of bed. I seem to have developed a type of alertness which applied itself the moment I woke. A trait to the benefit of my survival, maybe, even if its application in the present was imperfect. Some mornings were worse than others, my mind deciding alertness wasn't enough and that a sense of alarm was more prudent, and I could spend a tense few moments before my higher reasoning awoke and sorted out that there was nothing trying to kill me. During the war, I went from point to point under a heavy cloak of exhaustion. It was the feeling of a tiredness so complete that reality took on a fuzzy, cloudy edge, a distortion of distancing mind to body not entirely unlike a very lively dream. A surreal quality enveloped everything and nothing, not even physical survival, could out-match a desire for sleep. Quite the difference to where I find myself, in a warm house along a quiet street, worlds of time and distance from the fresh Hell of my youth. I don't have cause to keep myself awake and functioning for days on end. Of all the things I might have fantasised about for lacking them, the prospect of sleep was one I didn't ever seem to be able to meet in a reality I could have only hoped for and now seem to have gained.

"To really be a cat, Malachi. You drop off whenever it suits you." His reply, as usual, was of no help. He just restated his demand for food. I dropped a little cream in his dish while dressing my coffee, enough to shut him up for a few minutes, at least. Perhaps Adelaide was right, that I didn't have enough to occupy myself in my waking hours and that allowed me leave to live inside my own thoughts, doing nothing to tire me sufficiently for a good ling stretch on the rack. That might not entirely be the case, as living inside my own thoughts in opposition to what was going on beyond them in the physical world was not a new phenomenon. Such habits predated the war by as many years I had lived to that point. the only difference now was the severity and volume of thoughts collected in that brief period overseas and which continue to live with me. At one time, while I was in the process of that collection, I had posited that I might, given a decent enough interval, find these extreme experiences fading in such a way as my

217

memory of my first home in Banchory was nothing but an abstract and incomplete vision. That they had not, and remained at times as fresh as the first time I lived through them might credit for my survival not to God, but to His nemesis. Sure, you shall live, Satan might have told me, but only if you live all your past with your present. It would seem to suit his bag of tricks and I am absolutely certain that if such a contract had been on offer then, I would have signed it without a moment's pause. The only thing that mattered back then was the idea of getting through intact. Which was to be read as intact of life, if not necessarily of body, as one can still live without the presence of a limb. It never once occurred to me to consider that what cannot be lived without is an intact mind.

Such a thing was more insidious than death or physical injury as it's much harder to perceive unless it was an overt and total moral collapse; which was in fact, rare. What really happened was events stuck fast within the web of memory in an entirely subtle compilation to such a degree of gradual increments that any change in attitude or thinking seemed to be nothing unusual. Not that the mind becomes accustomed to difficult experiences rather than it doesn't remember what 'normal' used to be. As the goings on inside a man's skull need not be brought to outside attention, any descent from a clear and uncluttered mind is invisible, delicate and highly personal. Attempts to estimate any kind of degradation of spirit of reason required comparison with others undergoing the same conditions. By and large, it appeared my companions were able to manage all we were faced with and despite sometimes feeling I might have reached my own limit of what I could withstand, I would never allow myself to show I was less able than they. I was required by the nature of my obligations, duties and position to be equal to—at least if not actually better than—the continued ability of the men I led. I could not let them down by any failure to cope with the same things they had to. My feeling was that it was a debt I owed to them. From the moment I had been placed into a position of authority, it was made apparent that obedience was a conditional element. The army is by necessity so rigidly structured to make verbal or written orders legally binding; but that's actually just the bedrock of proper functioning. One who follows only because he must can only be led so far. Someone who allows himself to be led because he wants to follow those in authority over him is capable of achieving—or attempting to achieve—any task put to him. This, I was told, was entirely the obligation of the one in a position of leadership, to be worthy of the obedience of their subordinates. If, under the most strenuous conditions, my men persevered, then so must I, even if I never found the secret of what it was they were doing to maintain themselves through the same maddening things I was certain were driving me to irrevocable madness. There was no such secret or magic formula. I had failed to consider that in the unexpressed depths of their minds, they were all putting themselves to the same challenge of not letting anyone down by a failure to cope. Our silence on the subject, an unspoken collective belief that failure to measure up would be not a personal shortfall but a betrayal of compatriots was alone a great part of how we all continued to function altogether able if not individually insane.

Pulling into the church's parking lot, I couldn't help but feel a bit strange about attending a meeting on the effects of the Depression while having first class travel plans for a lengthy overseas sojourn. We were among the fortunate, a group of large stakeholders which comprised the agricultural base of the municipality of Falls Parish Township. The land remained productive and there had not been so harsh a length of seasons as had been experienced in the West. Most of the holdings hereabouts were commercial farms; fruit trees, dairy and wine, mostly. I can't pretend that economics at large had not impacted local business, all the same, the majority of them remained open thus far through such uncertain times, if not as vibrant as they had been. The cost, most unfortunately, had been in limiting production for reduced demand which had lessened the requirement for hands, which had added to a wider problem. The whole countryside was awash with men wandering loosely in search of the dignity of a day's wage. Occasionally, we had such call upon the Estate. Bill had not had the cold-heartedness of hanging a "No Work Here" sign at the gate. This, though, had meant needing to turn them away in person. Ma, Aunt Ruth or Morrigan would sometimes provide a meal or at the very least sandwiches and fruit for the men to take away with them. The appearance of men seeking work was not something I could lightly bear. From the look of these men, they had quite often the deeply set eyes of those who had seen too much and the way in which they left, in a silent, dropped shouldered stoic resignation told me they had come through the same trial of fire as I. Thankfully, I had not yet seen a face I recognised among the destitute. Seeing such hardship and worry on a stranger's face was bad enough. Turning an old comrade away empty would break my heart.

However, my impression was that landowners such as Harris, Balfour or Stephenson and my cousin were concerned tangentially by such a surplus of labour. Their minds were occupied by the worry that less production through lowered demand would overturn a critical balance between cost of working the land and profitable results, thus collapsing the local economy. Failure in one aspect of the township invited sympathetic failure of others; yet what was held to be most important was solely the self-interest of the stakeholders individually rather than realising that preservation was a collective issue. Eventually, the realisation would have to be reached that to thrive, the whole township needed to work to a common purpose.

"I've not seen you at services too recently," the Reverend said in greeting. I'd not yet put foot inside the church for this meeting and already I was getting grief.

"Ah, no, Padre," I hedged. I couldn't lie. He wasn't just the minister here; he was also regimental

Chaplain. Being dishonest would be akin to a double indemnity as by proxy I would be fibbing to both God and the King.

"Hard to get started on an early morning, hey? Not so bad for me, you know, just having the one a week." He winked, finally releasing my hand from the vise of his welcoming grip. I'll never quite fathom why all clergy had rock-crushing handshakes.

"I could make a better effort," I offered.

"You could," he nodded, "but don't put a face on it for my account. This might be His house, I warrant, though seeing as He is in all places at all times just come by to visit every now and again. Come awa' in."

"Yes, sir."

"All equals within these walls, Felix. Douglas, if you please."

"Alright." We stepped through the vestibule and into the chapel full of sleepy heat and the fine waxy smell of deeply polished pews. "Bill sends his regrets; it's hard for him to get about sometimes."

"That, and he's none too fond of me."

"Not you personally, Douglas. He's not found much use for religion."

"Ah, well. Believe or don't, we all go the same way in the end." He brought me round and introduced me to the other men present, most of whom I knew; local farmers, shopkeepers, members of the town council, and Mister Cosburn, the mayor. The Reverend checked his watch.

"I suppose we shall begin."

I really had no idea what was intended to be accomplished. Not one of us in the room had any real ability to affect change on a grand scale. The conversation was mostly an indictment of the federal government on behalf of the farmers whose accusations were floated towards Mayor Cosburn and his councillors, though they were, of course, not responsible for any failing at higher levels of governance. It descended into a bit of a bun fight which the Reverend made halting attempts to moderate. I hadn't said anything one way or the next and began to feel my time wasted. I stood to leave.

"One moment, Felix," Douglas called, "when I spoke with your cousin, he assured me we would hear from you this evening. Gentlemen, Felix Strachan of Inchmarlo Estates." All eyes turned to me. The Padre had certainly put me on the spot.

"I'll speak freely," I cautioned.

"I expect you to."

"Right, then. All I'm hearing is a lot of whinging over nothing anyone here can change; about what's to be done for our benefit and security. Shameful, that. It's tight times, sure, but there's none of us here on relief. Hasn't anyone thought to ask *them* what's needed, or are we too busy making sure we have dinner on our tables or coal in our stoves?"

"Do you have anything in mind, Mister Strachan?"

"Indeed I do, Mister Cosburn. I'd like to know why the town hasn't yet lain paved roads well beyond the main square. Instead of paying men on relief, pay them to work. Put pavement down on the concession roads out to the properties represented by the gentlemen here. The easier it's made for heavy traffic, the better our produce can get to market."

"We've been wanting roads for years, but that lot says we've to pay for them," said Balfour, a man of tremendous acreage of fruit trees. Breakfast tables across Canada were adorned with Bafour Jams.

"Surely you don't expect to get something for nothing, Mister Balfour? If we can agree to civic improvements that benefit our business, we would see that expenditure come back to us in revenue. In the case of Inchmarlo, my cousin tells me every shipment must have loss of product due to rough travel accounted for, or having delay in delivery penalties when we can't get stock over roads in bad weather. Bill estimates hard roads would almost eliminate these losses, without calculating for how much more we could ship with the kind of heavy lorries we could have on reliable roads. Besides, these things aren't about you, or me, or Town Hall, it's that the works be undertaken to give dignity to the unemployed."

"We do budget for such things," the Mayor said, "but it's beyond our means to do such wide-scale improvements."

"You do have the ability to apply for monies set aside by Ottawa and the Province for public works, correct?"

"Yes, Mister Strachan, but it's a lengthy process. I don't see having that sort of funding made available for months."

"Alright," I paused for thought, having run out of the items Bill had prepared me with. "Let's say we do get that money. Could it be used to recompense money laid out privately in trust to the Township?"

"What do you suggest?"

"I propose we collectively invest some of our operating capital as a loan to the corporation of Falls Parish to be repaid on receipt of a public works grant."

"How is this any different from paying to have it done ourselves?"

"Because, Mister Harris, you'd be getting that money back."

"Only to get taxed more to pay for that money at the back end. Paying twice is what you'll have us doing."

"What? No. Invest money to start construction, get that paid back. Taxes may well increase, but we'll be gaining in revenue from the roads, so as you'd be paying from a thicker bottom line." I turned to Cosburn. "Would the council agree to a moratorium on increasing property taxes for a period of time after construction is completed?"

"It would have to pass in chamber, but, yes."

"How much would we have to pay?"

"I would need to figure that," I answered, not entirely sure I knew how. "What if we could work it out so that our total expenditure is what we'd pay in a tax increase to get new roads with the understanding that money comes back to us when the loan comes due? What it costs to us is hardly the point, anyhow. Do we not have to turn men away who want to work when we've got none to give? I say, give them the work

225

we want done to improve our business, to the point we'll be needing to hire more hands in turn of how well we'll be doing because of those improvements, and damn to Hell with the cost in the here and now. Sorry, Padre."

"I use the words myself, sometimes, Felix. Occupationally, that is." There was a little laughter at that, but what surprised me was the applause and agreement my ideas received. It was nothing if not off the cuff, once I ran through Bill's script. Mr. Cosburn took me aside.

"Well done, Mister Strachan. Please call by my office and make a presentation which I can put in front of the entire town council."

"I'm afraid I wouldn't know how to do that. I was only bringing things up as they came to me."

"We'll figure out the details; it's the idea that's sound, young man. The sooner we get people working the better for all, wouldn't you say?"

"Gentlemen," the Reverend called out, "shall we close with a prayer?" That ended the meeting, but it was a start of something else for me. Certainly nothing I had envisioned. I had mostly been put out by men of means and influence arguing over their interests without consideration for those really faced with hardship. I might not often attend services at this church, but I know a thing or two about looking after others.

The day ahead was a straightforward enough notion of getting on with my work in the yard. It should have been clear to me by now, after all this time, that any notion of how I might conduct my day is never straightforward. It seemed massively unfair. Overseas, I stood to all my duties, followed my orders; I had been twice decorated "For Bravery in the Field." With all that in account, it was impossible to reckon as to why I seemed unable to undertake a simple project on the land of my own house. I went inside, placing my hat on an upright of one of the ladder-back chairs encircling the kitchen table. Pulling the seat away, I collapsed my bottom half upon it, upper half over the table top, burying my head in crossed arms. The ghastly images receded, urged on their way as Aidie gently ran her fingers through my hair.

"Are you alright, Kitten?"

"I don't know," I answered; third time in a row I provided such a blank response.

I had been standing in my yard, having arranged for a small load of crushed stone to be delivered, my sleeves rolled, shovel in hand. A fine, early spring day of a light breeze and warm sun painted the sky with specked tiny whispers of cloud a deeply bright blue. Neither too hot or cold, there was just the right balance for making a day of outdoor labour tolerable, if not enjoyable. The ground was still very wet, but there was no avoiding that. It having remained so was the reason I had set about this task in the first place. Except, I was still standing on the flagstone set upon the back of the house abutting the kitchen door. The shovel, still clean, I held at the short trail--length parallel to the ground-- in my left hand. I only had to walk a short distance to the edge of the yard and pry up the first bit of soil. All I had to do was something I had done countless times before. Hamish had correctly pointed out I'd done a lot of this sort of thing in the war, and that appeared to be part of the problem. My work, in essence, was to push a sap forward, there. Ten yards, no further. I didn't seem to be able to do it. Those instructions weren't mine; they had been given to me by Paddy Thorncliffe for our defense of Bell Hill. I couldn't be afraid that my life was in danger, I was aware of my true placement in space and time, away from the war. What I was having trouble with, despite knowing how nonsensical the idea, was a vision, as real and clear as the blue sky above that as soon as I turned the first spade full, I would uncover the putrid remains of Kipling and McManus. I closed my eyes in a hard blink, admonishing myself, to no use. I reminded myself where I was stood; what date it was. My mind remained fixed on other memories, actual examples of the times where in digging to provide protection for the living, we disturbed the dead.

The first time I uncovered a corpse, it had frightened me, as I suppose was quite natural. In due course, it became just another abnormal thing become normal. I'd like to be able to say that upon a disinterment we acted with the gravity and respect usually accorded the departed. I can't. We did not, most times, have enough liberty of situation. Dead is dead. It can't get worse for someone who is no longer alive, and it can always get worse for someone who is.

We were engaged in doing what we could to remain on the positive side of that balance. Waxen lumps of runny tallow robed in rotten wool—and it made no difference if that cloth was field grey, khaki serge or horizon blue—were given all the concern of any other shovel load of dirt.

There are no corpses in my back garden, I tried telling myself. I would get set to my task, almost step forward, and my mind would play another scene of legs and arms and filthy, rotting guts just waiting below the surface. Of a lawn, I rebutted directly against my disturbed imagination, in Falls Parish, Ontario. Full of the casualties left behind, my brain returned, to sit and decay in foul sludge reeking of shit and spoiled meat.

I have had it with this fucking nonsense!

"Felix!" I jumped. Adelaide had called me from the window above the kitchen sink. "What are you about with such language?" I may have said that last thought out loud; I hadn't realised.

"I don't know."

"Why did you do that just now?"

"Do what?"

"Fling the shovel across the yard." My left hand was empty, the tool standing upright, javelin-like, at the fence edge.

"I don't know."

"Perhaps," she soothed, "you'd best come in for a bit." I would like that, my love, but there's bits of me that might never come in.

PART III

"Nor the Years Condemn"

France, July, 1936

I was surprised how lushly green the countryside appeared. A memory of a profoundly disturbed landscape trumped the notion that the ground would recover its vitality. I also seemed to remember it without colour at all, as most of my recollections are prompted, so far beyond the years in which I first laid eyes upon this place, by photographs in monochromatic tones of slate greys or murky sepia. What I recall most vividly was that in actuality it was quite colourless; ground so abused it was thrown together in a single, lifeless hue. It may have been silly to retain a notion of what I might find here after a space of time might resemble my memories. The land over which much of the war had been fought had been productive, of one type of industry or another, there being little sense to make a contest over ground which had no such value; yet I was still bemused that it had, by and large, reverted to the purposes of livelihood after the contest was abandoned. There was a quality in seeing something I remembered so much in one fashion appearing to me in the present as another. It was as if I knew it, had an intimate familiarity with it, and yet at the same time completely alien to me. My senses recorded what lay in front of me in the half-way real feeling of recognising a place as seen in the twisted perception of a dream. The shift of resurrection, of the land claiming life after death, was neither entirely complete nor seamless.

Where fighting had been most sustained and fierce, a blanket of new growth had been tossed over top a worn and lumpy mattress which years of continued shellfire had beaten into uneven and unnatural rises and folds. Decades of rain collected in the largest of these man-made craters making hilltop ponds. Up and down the length of the land, the scars and stitched closures of trenches and tracks could still be discerned, the eye able to trace the path of a war which didn't move all that much in four years. Some ground, strangely, had actually been re-dug. In some notion that we had to be reminded of the system of works we had lived in and fought over; part of this network was reconstructed to an approximation of as it had been. It was farcical, as accurate to life as a stone sculpture. Ground was permanently retained by concrete made to look like sandbags, the floor a mockery in cement duckboards. It was annoyingly ironic. As lifeless and cold as No-man's Land had been, were these false trenches and now that former desolate territory was as full of life as the real trenches had been. What I saw, presented to me in this portion of the Monument was sterile, bare, and delivered nothing to me of my time spent in the genuine article which these manufactured scrapes strove to imitate. I hated it on sight. A few of the subways and tunnels we had used in the attack had been preserved. These were truer things as what had been constructed in the war remained intact and even a part of that system belonged to catacombs of centuries' age; the work to keep them open for public viewing was conservatory rather than some type of facsimile. I can't speak toward how authentic they remained, as I did not go down them. I have since my first time here developed an anathema to tight spaces and I worried I might be consumed by an unreasonable fright should I make a visit below.

What land could be worked had been put back to work, despite the farmers having to constantly reap a crop of what had been left behind. Munitions which had failed to do the only thing they were made to do, that is, explode, were extracted by the French and Belgians in quantities measuring hundreds of tons a year, in what was called, with passive, Gallic indifference to severity or danger the "Iron Harvest." That was not the only new yield the countryside gave. Acres upon acres of carefully tended grounds had been planted with simple greyish-white, arch-topped stones. All identical in size and shape save for any inscription made, these plain markers were purposefully making the statement that in death, we were all the same.

The crossing had been mainly uneventful. Bill seemed to have no interest in anything on offer as far as entertainments, perfectly content to sit in a lounge chair and fill our state room with smoke. He'd never been all that energetic, and his condition suited him being sedentary, but I had thought he would have made more of an effort to get above deck, take the air, seem in some way to be enjoying himself. I wouldn't say he was poor company, but he was not much out of form from his usually prickly self. For all the complaint he had made to me about the expense he'd had to outlay for my booking of first-class digs, his complete void of enthusiasm for anything such a stretch to luxury entailed was cause enough to wonder why he parted ways with the money instead of demanding I reduce our berth. I could well ask, again, why he had come at all if he wasn't doing anything more than what he would be doing had he not left home, if I wasn't certain he'd deliver some put-off as he had maintained since he'd told me he'd changed his mind about coming. Certainly, we weren't on a pleasure cruise, there was no celebratory nature to our voyage. All the same, it was a trifle annoying that Bill did little to not make it appear as though he was just that much removed from having been brought against his will. At least I was used to his manner, disappointed though I may have been that he didn't take opportunity to brighten up any for going abroad. It was downright embarrassing when his brusqueness was inflicted upon the unsuspecting, chief among those being Trevelyan, the valet assigned to us from having booked a state room.

Shortly after the ship cast off, a gentle knock on our door revealed an impeccably dressed, towering beanstalk of a man with a slim, sallow and joyless face of impenetrable expression punctuated with cool grey eyes, trim finger-width moustache and brilianteened hair. He carried a blazingly polished steel ice bucket in which was rooted a bottle of champagne.

"Good evening, sir," he said, gliding past me holding the door open allowing his ingress, "my name is Trevelyan; your valet." He set the bucket on its stand. "Messer's Strachan, is that correct?" No, not quite. He'd given the wrong pronunciation, Englishmen often do. It didn't start him off right with Bill.

"It's 'Stra-wn,' Trevelyan, and only I am 'Mister.' My cousin is 'Sergeant Major' correctly." Trevelyan remained composed, not even blinking.

"Very good, sir."

"And what the Hell have you brought us?" Bill pointed to the bucket in a gesture of undisguised contempt.

"Champagne, sir. With the complements of the Captain."

"Take it away. If the Captain wants to compliment me, you can return with a bottle of Inchmarlo, chardonnay '33."

"Very good, sir." Still unphased, he gathered his bucket and refused bottle making his way out. I followed, shutting the door behind me.

"A moment, if you please, Trevelyan."

"Yes, Sergeant Major?"

"I'll ask you to forgive my cousin. Mister Strachan is, well, abrupt at the best of times, and he was rather reluctant at the prospect of this trip in the first place."

"Very good, Sergeant Major."

"We're also not accustomed to such deference. It makes me a little uneasy, to be honest."

"I understand. Most clients I attend expect me to comport myself in the fashion to which they are most familiar. Social status as it was, you see."

"Aye. So, what is it you do for us?"

"Make myself available for your comfort and convenience. I shall keep your rooms, attend at table, run messages and procure from the purser, lay out your clothes, polish your shoes."

"I do that last one myself."

"Really?" He reacted as if I told him I cobbled a fresh pair on the daily.

"It will be Mister Strachan who'll require most of that, though he won't admit it. I'd advise you to do such things in a way which won't call into question his limitations."

"Very good, Sergeant Major."

"One more thing, Trevelyan. Does this ship have an inventory of Inchmarlo wines?"

"Indeed it does. Polaris Lines has a contract of exclusivity with that label, since the war. Very difficult to get French wines, as I'm certain you can appreciate."

"Is that so? What do you think of it, as far as quality?" For the first time, his face betrayed an expression, a very slight, razor thin smile.

"It is a young label," he began, "but despite that, it is my opinion, Sergeant Major, that your family produces a very comparable vintage." Clever man, he.

"Excellent. I'll let you get on."

"Very good, Sergeant Major." Ten days of 'Very good, Sergeant Major,' was not nearly long enough to get used to it.

This was the fourth time I had crossed this ocean, in one direction or the other. The first I don't remember much at all; I would have been younger than Philip is now. It wouldn't have been altogether too long after receiving word that Da had gone. We would not have been travelling in the lap of luxury, but certainly better attended than my next two crossings. The Atlantic was a dangerous place, then. Many people, including myself, sometimes prejudice thinking of the war being nothing other than the Western Front. No question that it was the main theatre of operations, but men, equipment and munitions didn't spontaneously appear. These things had to come from somewhere, and the longer the war continued, the more that somewhere was across the ocean. Now, the term 'war of attrition' has one meaning; the more often considered notion of reducing the enemy's manpower to a state of such inferiority as to no longer be able to continue making war. Another idea of attrition is not focused on the lives of soldiers so much as the availability of the means to make war. A man in the field who hasn't enough to eat and no bullets or shells to hurl across the way is about as useful in a fight as one who is dead. Strategy on both sides reflected this in attempts to strangle the flow of resources to such a degree as to cause a material collapse in the field. It wasn't, of course, all one thing or the other but rather application of both which was the path to victory in a cruelly stalemated war. We won, perhaps, for no other reason than that we had more stuff than the Germans.

Twenty years ago, I was just one very tiny, singular portion of all that stuff and it would have been far more economic for Germany to be rid of me and the thousands with me in one fell swoop of hulling a transport mid-crossing rather than doing so piecemeal on the battlefield over the course of years. I'm not informed enough to know how hard they tried in my case, but the threat was very real. Our ship had been a liner, much like this one, but any recognition between a passenger steamer and a troop transport wasn't even skin deep. Absolutely anything which could ignite in flames had been removed, including paint on surfaces, all the fixtures and accents of wood. Maximizing space for carrying capacity also necessitated stripping the interior to a sparse minimum. What may have been a finely appointed ship for the well-to-do was bare, naked, cold steel crammed length, breadth and height with men and tangled jungles of hammocks. Not that we expected to go over in the tops of fashion or comfort, our minds were most assuredly locked on what lay ahead in ignorant anticipation absent any real understanding of fear. Young, fit and keen, we were all adventurers with a mindset so devoid of reality only exposure to experience would cure. The journey in the other direction was absent that energy. Still outfitted as for Active Service, the ship was sparse and characterless as had been the vessel we'd boarded coming over to war. Our mood was not anything near the excitation which could be reasonably expected of men returning home after a long and difficult absence. We had all shifted into a state of absolute pragmatism; a notion of getting beyond what was immediately present and allowing any thought of what might come next to be suspended until it was directly faced. It wasn't overly fatalistic any more than it was practical for men grown used to the lack of any certainty beyond one moment to the next. Glad, perhaps, to be on our way home, but not overjoyed at the prospect when thought was placed on what it had cost to secure return passage, and on such a lengthy voyage there was little else to do than think. No longer having to conserve mental resources to the functions of the present, there wasn't a shortage of things to think about. For the first time in anything like recent memory, it would become permissible to put thought towards the future. That is, in a sense of possibility, beyond the next few moments, a great unknown lay within time yet to come. And though it wasn't fixed and awesomely uncertain, it was far better to imagine what might be rather than dwell on what had been.

With all of that behind through time's passage, this ship, which I only supposed might have been likewise converted for war, had reverted to the glory of its purpose. Fittings returned and replaced; deeply varnished wood accented richly painted walls on which in lounges and cabins, paintings of oily art, hung glass and brass fixtures, lit plushly upholstered chairs and heavy oak tables dressed with crisp linen. It made a brilliant contrast to the Spartan appearance, safety and expediency had deemed required. I was also not under the same sort of restrictions as had been in place the last time I had traveled. Aside from a few areas sensitive to the ship's operation, I was free to go where I pleased and was under no obligation to what times I was required to be one place or another. Which was entirely a good thing as about halfway over, I was bored out of my teeth. Bill was on for nothing, save attempting to discolor our cabin walls one cigarette at a time and I couldn't abide being in such funk to keep him company. There's very little to look at mid-Atlantic and only so much reading I can do at any one time. I found myself wandering about this ship for no other purpose than to run the clock on the afternoon of the fifth day I was on the aft deck at the rail, watching the surging, turning wake of the ship, a path of foamy water stretching back over the length of ocean we just covered. I suppose that somewhere below, far, far below where no light could pass was the resting place of the brother-in-law I never met. Merchant Seaman Gordon Fitzgerald lost, as with all hands, when his ship was brought under by a torpedo in the winter of 1917. As I was standing there figuring that point of interest, it occurred to me that this ship I was traveling on would also pass the area where on my journey home from the war, standing much as I was on the stern of a converted liner I cast into the water the single souvenir I could not bring home. With one great pitch, the pistol tumbled away in an uneven arc; its splash insignificant and almost hidden by the rolling wake.

When I had finally told Adelaide the truth of her father's death, I was not entirely sure how she felt about the fact I had kept the weapon for my own use. It was rather good forethought on my part to have tossed it overboard. I was on my way home on my way to meet her for the first time, this lady of my affection whom I only knew through her letters. Even if I never told her, keeping the pistol which had killed her dad would never have sat easy with me.

I thought I heard my name being called, just able to pick it out over the roar of the engines turning.

"Felix! Felix Strachan! Catscratch!" Well, that was for me, alright. I turned from the rail and set eyes upon a friend I hadn't seen since Final Muster.

"Bert!" My goodness, it was Bert Ellins, one of the very few men of the King's Own Canadian Scots who, like me, had gone all the way from start to finish. We shook hands, which wasn't enough for everything we had been through together, so we embraced and laughed, spilling over with joy at the unexpected reunion.

I hadn't liked him all that well at first. We really didn't interact that much early on as it was more common to be friendly perhaps even cliquish with one's section mates than others in the same platoon assigned to the other sections. He and I had been sent on a course together just before the Ridge, to qualify for our corporal's stripes. The both of us had been tagged to lead sections for the attack. We were the only two of Six Platoon in attendance and by that measure of familiarity stuck together. Being honest, I found him a bit tiresome at times. Bert was very well read and offered no hesitation to add this acquired wisdom to conversation. Sometimes, I felt a whiff of superiority, particularly above someone such as I who had not as much time in books. As it went on, I began to realise that his display of intellect wasn't anything showy, it was just how he expressed himself; and he didn't have any notion he could come across as a blowhard. I know because we had words about it. I forget why, exactly. It would have been a moment in which—as he did so frequently—he was able to relate to the present situation some like scenario from the depths of history or philosophy. I don't know any of all that; if only for not having had time or inclination to have absorbed such a wealth of information. I told him what he could do with all his smart words by inviting him to engage with them an anatomical impossibility. The look he had given me in return was as if I had torn him open with my bayonet. Bert had professed that he had not considered his expression as belittling, and was crushingly apologetic that I had seen it that way. Truly, he saw me as his intellectual equal, and sometimes misremembered that I lacked much in education. From thinking he had been about putting me in my place, I wound up having him do so in a way I was the one needing to extract foot from mouth. By then, there were so few of us left from the early days, we became friends by the default of there being no one else who had lived through the same trials. We of that minority were able to understand each other purely from the familiarity of events which defied understanding by those who had not been present. Surviving continual challenging situations bred an intimacy among those remaining not at all unlike castaways adrift from a shipwreck.

"I couldn't believe it was you," he said. "I almost thought I was mistaking you for someone else. How are you?"

"Fantastic. Just a quiet wee life. You?"

"Yeah, grand. I qualified in twenty-one, been in general practice since then."

"A doctor? Well, we all knew you were a bright one. How about family?"

"Oh, yes. Married, three daughters and a son."

"I've two sons, and a daughter."

"So, was it her you married? O'Leary's girl?" I was smiling in a positively ludicrous way. I nodded. "I hope," he said, "it didn't turn out like I had teased you." God Almighty, how was it he remembered that? I mean, it was no secret I was in correspondence with Kelley's daughter and I'm sure Bert had only been making a joke when he'd asked me:

"Has she sent a picture?" This was just after getting our mail, where I had been handed another letter from Adelaide to add to a growing collection.

"No," I answered. "Never thought to have her do so." Such a thing had never occurred to me. Bert shook a cigarette out of a crumpled packet, offered me one, I refused.

"Still off them, eh? She's got you that far."

"Ah, no, Ma's been after me on the smoking far longer," an excuse he didn't buy.

"They're conspiring against you, Catscratch. First the smokes, then, well, you haven't that many vices to get at you for. You're in trouble, mate. Especially," he added, "if you've no idea what she looks like."

"What difference does that make?"

"That's very noble of you to say so, Felix, but has it ever crossed your mind that she might well be her father's daughter?" There was a thought. Kelley was no looker, sure. He fit his nickname "Bulldog" with letter perfection. Everything about Kelley was thick; his stature, his accent, his hair. He had a heavy forehead populated by wiry dark eyebrows, a nose of withering cant from more than one break which ended in a widely

244

splashed tip of cavernous nostrils. His looks were unflattering enough on himself but would be devastating to any femininity if passed along to his daughter. At the point Bert put the idea in my head, Adelaide and I had been sending letters back and forth for well over a year. It had not come to mind that there was a possibility of a strong paternal resemblance, and Bert's comment had forced me to consider how shallow my attraction could be.

"Well," I had answered carefully, "I certainly can't ask for a photo now. What would I say? 'Dear Adelaide, please make proof you're not as ugly as your Old Man'?"

"Never took you for much of a gambler."

"Sometimes, you pays your money and you takes your chances."

It was coincidental, but not unreasonably expected that besides having booked passage on the same ship as I, Bert had also hired a room at the same hotel. These voyages had all been arranged by agents to be inclusive packages and the appeal for the one I had opted for was that lodging in the days running up to the dedication was within the town my battalion had been billeted before our attack on the Ridge, a pleasant piece of France near the Souchez River called Petit Séjour sur Bois. Returning to these fields so many years on, I gained no notion of 'hail the conquering hero'. It was not that sort of war and we were not that sort of people. An argument could be made to whether or not any of us were heroes. There was no doubt we didn't conquer a damned thing. All I recall feeling at the end was relief, and despite having won the war, a tremendous sense of loss. We who had lived to see the end had done little more than merely surviving would merit. In that way, it would not be right, nor indeed tasteful to swagger about, as if we could be imagined our efforts here were owed something. I can't make opinion for anyone other than myself, so it might be my view alone that I had been here, I did what had been asked of me and I deserved no recognition beyond my status as a participant in past events. I gathered that many of my compatriots held the same view because the air about us had an intangible urge to silence, even in the gladness of seeing old sites or meeting old friends, such as a feeling one gets upon marking a familiar face among mourners at a wake. No tourist was really of a holiday attitude, nor was the tone completely and collectively somber. It was a very tense and not entirely authentic mixture of the two. Any exuberance I saw an of that, there was little in peak of laughter or tuneless wailing of old, dirty songs seemed false, nearly forced; no truth of appearance to a genuine mood of celebration, but rather a comedy mask worn and held onto desperately to prevent the nature of why we all made our way here from knocking us loose. We weren't here for ourselves, for any idea of pride and whatever greatness we may or may not have had a part in. We were here for what had been left behind.

My second morning at Petit Séjour I scheduled to myself alone. I walked along the main town road, which was still stone surfaced and much worn, in the direction of the old front line. The town had been fortunate that its locale had not been in direct path of the war, nor of any great significance to make it a target for destruction. Inasmuch as the war happened to it, the events of the conflict more often passed through Petit Séjour than tarried. There had been occasions when it was shelled, but these were incidents so infrequent and of no great intensity such as to consider them mistakes of aim. Our artillery did have a battery of super heavy howitzers at the railyard, so any German bomb descending on the town had probably been meant to silence our guns rather than to terrorize the population. I knew Sweet Fanny Adams about artillery anyway, but what I do know is that after we took the Ridge, our possession of the high ground gave the Germans something more important to shoot at. This had spared Petit Séjour from the fate of so many other towns in France and Belgium; those which had been reduced to nothing but dust and ruin from four years of destructive intent. In turn, this fortune of circumstance made it entirely familiar. As very little of it had to be refashioned, Petit Séjour had not been required to act the Phoenix, although it must be said I had spent very little time within the town. The King's Own had been stationed here for less than six months, but the regiment as a body was encamped beyond the town itself. We visited local establishments when given leave of duty to do so, and I had been required to report to Battalion HQ at the Hotel du Ville on a handful of occasional errands; but other than that, it remained largely off limits. So, in facing another irony caused by years apart, what I recognized most for remaining unchanged was an area I had been least familiar with. If the recovered countryside appeared in its rebirth, somehow dreamlike, walking the stone streets of the village, which remained much as my memory painted it was as in the same fashion alike to having woken and realizing the years gone by as the dream.

After some time, I began to believe myself lost, even though I had been certain I was on the right road and had not deviated from it. The one thing I was consistently forgetting was the passage of time, and it was a very powerful urge to expect to see things as I remembered them, not as they might be now. Sheepy Baa Woods was completely gone. The town had swollen and swallowed the forested allotment, which had marked an old boundary and had provided shelter for our battalion whenever we had been out of the line during the months spent preparing to assault the Ridge. I never did figure out why it had such a name. Places took on designations, usually wrestled into English from the French or Flemish pronunciations. Having first come to the woods years after it had been so named, there'd been no one to ask who would know why. Now the woods themselves were gone, and thus only existed in the memories of men like me. When we had all gone ourselves, it might well be as if such places never existed at all. Smart new houses and shops stood where great trees once loomed almost mockingly made tribute by a tiny greensward. Had I actually applied any thought towards the provenance of the name and my destination for my walk this morning, I might have resolved that inconsequential mystery, for laying along a groomed path off the newly extended main road at the very edge of where the woods had once begun and the town now did end was an iron railed gate marking the entrance to Cimetière du Septième Bois. A stone alcove of the gate sheltered the steel box within which was the registrations book. I consulted it to find the correct plots before letting myself in. The creak of the gate was a small noise, though its grating scrape of thickly painted metal, moving over equally treated stationary parts, cut through a reverential silence in what seemed an improper wail. It turned the heads of the small collection of men milling through the rows of silent stones just enough to see what had disturbed them before returning to commune with the dead.

This place and only this place, was the reason I had come this great distance. That huge edifice, standing tall and alone atop the heights, might be the inspiration for the journey, its nature and promise of recognition of our missing was central in appealing to Bill to come with me. The monument didn't capture my desire so much as a smaller, tremendously more modest testimony to the war's cost. An immense effort had been made to create these spaces with the immeasurable respect deemed appropriate to such a level of sacrifice. As destructive as a war it was, both Andy Ferguson and Kelley O'Leary were fortunate to have a known place of rest. Off to the far side of the main yard, along the short stone wall, which enclosed the cemetery were a small number of markers different from the plain stones of the other graves. These were onyx crosses, most marked with several names, group plots of Germans, including Ulrich, who had been given a decent burial.

It was strange to be here. I've had years to imagine what this reunion, if it could be called such might allow me to feel. Those years had been steeped in the guilt of my failure and while at times I might have supposed putting myself before the spirits of those who my mistakes had punished would absolve my own, I'm not certain I have as deep a belief in such matters as to be able to imagine forgiveness by standing in the same place in which lay what was left of the material vessels the beings they were had once inhabited. There was nothing here aside from memories I had with me which gave any indication of these men's humanity. Nothing in the inscriptions displayed personality. Smooth granite described in the most basic terms the men who lay below in death and forever after these stone markers would declare that Once Upon a Time a person had answered to a number, rank and name, and had been part of a particular unit. It told nothing of who they were, what kind of person they might have been. It was sufficient for purpose, but woefully not enough. Unless I let it be known, there would remain a peculiar anonymity to these graves, and if I kept within that I was alive because of what they had done while still living, my friends would sink into history as only what their headstones stated them to be, with others in precisely set rows, named and nameless under carefully tended grounds returning to the earth from which all life had come. I've been taught to believe that the body is fallible, the soul indestructible. While I can't claim to know that as truth, as an article of faith such an idea could mean that these men buried here collected in yards like this one or still undiscovered afield had outlived the war, by existing in the most pure and immutable form, while someone such as myself, transporting the memories of experience with me, so that even years beyond those events I was keeping the past from gaining any real distance from the present. With that past never being far from mind, and indeed sometimes so powerfully present that I could feel it more real than anything current, I could argue that the only way I could have outlived the war would have been if it had outlived me.

I didn't stay long. Not being the sort to blether at a headstone as if it could listen to me in place of ears beyond hearing. Although I did indulge Adelaide's request to leave a rosary-- Mother O'Leary's-- at Kelley's grave. It might only be a token, a physical object endowed with a power I'm none too familiar with, but if it would help Aidie in any way to know I had united wooden beads with a slab of stone, I would do so. My beliefs and understanding of faith would never allow me to exclude or diminish the rectitude of hers. Making that visit resolved nothing for me and I remained in a state of paradox. Because of what they had done in protecting my life, I was in the only condition, that is, alive for which I could feel such a thing as guilt. For them, things were infinitely simpler. Nothing mattered to them, no questions of gain or loss of right or wrong had any bearing on these men anymore, and they never would again for the remaining term of eternity. And with that realization that while there is a lot to be argued for the value of being alive, death seemed to be a much less complicated and more stable state of Existence. I departed, leaving my friends to lie quietly in the ground for which they had died.

It was quiet, and strange that I had not noticed. If the sites I remembered had vanished, so the sounds. Noise of the war varied from loud to deafening to mind shattering depending on what was going on at the time, but there was never a moment without the blows and blasts, both near and distant, right up to that epochal hour before noon on one November day. As time went on, as war progressed, every action was preceded by and supported with an ever-increasing number of large guns firing an exponentially greater number of shells, and those were made incrementally more potent. It's any wonder I can hear anything at all. It made me realize that some things are remarkable for their absence as much as they might be for their presence. This silence, save for the ambience of nature and a permanent barely audible high note which floats just inside my ear canals, was in contrast to all my memories, adding to a deepening feeling of new strangeness in the oddly familiar, making it impossible to believe there had been any cacophonous violence visited here.

France, August 1918

I was being told not to worry. That in itself was often a fair sign there was plenty to worry about. We were going to be moving up to our jumping off points in a few hours and things would become really busy after that. In the longest two years of my life, I had come to never expect anything to the letter of a plan. This was reinforced by where we happened to be, as if things had gone to plan a year ago or the year before that, our divisions would not have to need to muster up for a fight along the same bloody stretch of ground bordered by the same bloody stretch of river. Although, the cautious adage of things never going to plan was usually saved to apply to a plan in progress, not one yet to begin.

"Don't worry about it, Sergeant," he told me again as if repeating it would help somehow. "Not much changes. Six Platoon remains in Company reserve. Attack goes well, shouldn't even have need of you."

I held my tongue, which is not an easy thing for me to do, especially when smart remarks to punctuate my disdain or frustration could burst forth with the suddenness of seeming to have lost control of the noises my mouth makes. As usual, a smart remark wouldn't have helped anything except to annoy the Lieutenant, and if I could get beyond myself for a moment, it was he really who had more cause to worry than I. Thorncliffe had just told me that Captain McCormack was no longer in command of 'B' Company and he was stepping up to replace him. This adjustment left me as de facto head of 6 Platoon. Granted, Lieutenant Thorncliffe was now charged with the direction of four platoons instead of a single one, as he was used to, at least he knew how such things worked. Less than half a day before going into what might be a very big fight and I was being let known that my level of responsibility had increased well beyond my preparedness. I did not want to do this. I tempered that thought when I said it out loud as,

"I don't think I can do this."

"Of course you can. How would you cope if I was lost to you under the gun? Like as not, I'll only need you to keep Six Platoon in place and if I do need to push you up front, you'd be going in to support our advanced platoons and would fall under the command of whichever one that might be. There is no one else but you who can do this Catscratch. It's a Hell of a hiccup at the last moment, and we're going to go ahead by not upsetting the cart too much. Organize your platoon Sergeant, and even if you are worried, which you shouldn't be, don't let your men catch whiff of it." That was a lot of ifs he presented, each one a hinge on a host of things that could unfold against expectation. "If," in that regard, may as well stand for "I'm Fucked." Strangely, the thing which worried me most was the Lieutenant hadn't told me how much fun we were going to have.

I went away from where the Lieutenant had brought me aside for the chat we'd just had over to where Six Platoon was assembled, methodically going through the solemn rituals of departure. Men were securing the kit they would need going forward and weeding out items of no tactical use, personal stuff like, to be put in their large packs and be given to Battalion Transport. These would be returned when next we came off the line or forwarded to next of kin should we not.

"Gather 'round, Six," I told them, trying to put into practice what the Lieutenant had told me in parting. Thankfully, the racket of the big guns working through a preparatory bombardment, disguised any nervous tone in my voice. "Lieutenant Thorncliffe is taking over 'B' Company. Which means, at least for the time being, I'm handling the platoon. The overall plan doesn't change. We remain last in order of march in the company on route to the jump off and will move out in rear of Company HQ on the advance. The battalion is still doing an alphabet advance. A on our left, C on our right, and D in Battalion Reserve behind and at the right flank. Everything will go as we've been told, so your jobs won't change, except that Corporal Tremaine will take my place as Platoon 2 I/C. Which leaves Lance Corporal Brentwood as head of One Section. You good for that, Lonnie?"

"Yes, Sergeant," he said without hesitation. As I wasn't giving him the choice it helped that he was positive.

"Any questions?"

"What happened to Captain McCormack?"

"No one told me. Doesn't matter much, save for curiosity. Nothing else?" I checked my watch. "Still about an hour and a half to the off. Let's make use of the time to be sure we don't forget anything." Then, perhaps because I had heard it so often as had my men, that perhaps it was expected, even anticipated, the final words of my update to Six Platoon spilled out of a wide grin. "Don't worry about it, it's going to be fun." I hoped, most likely against reason, that while it might not be fun - it never was- our next little bit wouldn't unfold into chaos.

I was the right sort of chap that made a good NCO. I knew the intricacies of the work required of ordinary soldiers, having spent time in that role myself, which lent authenticity to my council and instruction to both subordinate and superior. Granted, I could be by experience well-disposed to my function and be a howling menace while performing it. The complete equation of suitability was made up of how I carried myself and related to those I worked with and for. Like so much of everything, the proper attitude of leading NCOs was a balance, in this case of authority and compassion. Success depended on knowing when and having the ability to lean more towards one end or the other. My particular mandate, that is, of a Platoon Sergeant, was the administration and discipline of the body of men who made up the platoon, and my interposition between them and the platoon commander also made me their advocate. It was upon me to possess practical insight into what men might reasonably be expected to accomplish, and what limitations would make accomplishment difficult. It would be my job to temper my officer's requirement to prioritize mission before men by insistence that without men, no mission can succeed. The army, by necessity, is an autocratic body but it is not without a reasonable number of checks to ensure it is an autocracy bound to successful outcome with minimal misuse of resources. Simplified, an NCO was in a position to apply a measured cynicism versus an officer's unbridled optimism to the benefit of mission completion. Where I had been placed that morning was to duplicitly drop the one attitude in favor of the other. Having already prepared for the day as the leading NCO of the Platoon, I had my mind fixed on conducting myself as such. Now that I was leading a platoon outright, any shift in my outward comportment then placed me in the contradictory position of lying to myself while being fully aware of my dishonesty. It had me envy the lunatic. They act in whatever way their madness dictates without sense to what might be correct and when their senses are contradicting reality, they unfailingly believe what these senses tell him is true. Unfortunately, I have those senses which they lack, which only serves to complicate matters.

The Lieutenant had made a good point. In my role as the Platoon Sergeant, one thing I had to be prepared for was to take command should Thorncliffe be absent for any reason. Aside from filling in when he'd gone on leave, the prospect had not surfaced. Those few days had been quite some time ago, before spring, and mercifully coincided with the battalion being out of the line. It did not really amount to very much except me getting the daily briefing at Company HQ in place of Thorncliffe. This was all kinds of different. We were going into action. Not even the quasi-routine of a front-line tour, but an honest to goodness advance against enemy positions. It was a big deal, this, involving in one respect or another, most of our Corps, which itself was part of a larger mixture of corps within an army working in cooperation with other armies, and that was saying nothing of the French who were committing a few divisions themselves, and assorted bric-a-brac of other national forces. That all amounted to a staggering sum total of men involved; well into the hundreds of thousands, putting the thirty I had with me into a sharp perspective, except it had never been my responsibility to lead them, that until I had been so informed that they were not in terms my men, and that shift had taken away a critical factor. Not only had Six Platoon not ever gone forward without an officer in command of it, the platoon had never gone forward without the only officer to have commanded it. Consistency in such things as structure of command meant a great deal. The war was a source of continual inconsistency, a confusing mass of contradictions and changes of situation as fickle as which way the wind blew. As a problem, it was one of compound interest which accrued more the further down the ladder of organization it went. Those of us at the lower rungs not only had to put up with what we encountered day to day, we were subject to the whims of the larger units to which we belonged, who directed us to act according to their understanding of events. This complexity was also influenced by elements no amount of will, desire or application could make any difference upon, chief among those being the combined will desire and application of the enemy. With all of that in play, it's a marvel we ever get anything done at all. What helps, what keeps us from flying apart into distracted individuals is an iron grasp on those small number of things within our control of a monumental effort against innumerable and unknown agents of change. Six Platoon had always an immovable rock to which we could chain ourselves when the tide of circumstance flowed in. For me, just being brought to light about such a sudden change in the teeth of a coming battle, it was doubly worrisome. The platoon was now without the steady centre around whose immense gravity we all orbited- bad enough in itself- it was now me alone who was to be counted upon to keep the circulating planets of the platoon from colliding or whipping off into oblivion.

Not being certain I possessed the right amount of gumption to rise to this occasion, I had some stern questions to put to whoever was responsible for placing me in such a tight spot. If granted such an audience, it would surely be pointed out that it was I who had volunteered for service in the first place. Anything which it happened to me since, for good or ill, was tethered to that initial decision, so I had better shut up and get on with it.

At large nothing could overcome the desperate nature of an inconsistent environment. Thorncliffe had a knack for dispelling that for us as he'd maintained the personality of certainty in action, clarity in purpose, evenness of temperament, regardless of what bastard situation had fallen into our laps. Despite having seen how he worked; that I had studied and deeply admired his coolness of conduct, the ease with which he had not only led his men, but also exuded some intangible spirit which inspired others to follow that lead, I had a nauseous bubbling doubt that any attempt I could make in emulation would be anything more than a pale and hollow imitation. The quick change of command and no explanation given to its cause was just another thing among the events of the past week in which most everything laid before us was clothed in an element of mystery. Normally we would not know specific time and date of an attack right till last possible moment. Still, we usually had days or weeks beforehand to rehearse and reconnoiter the objectives. It seemed to me, though, that we were on a diminishing return of such preparatory time. For the Ridge we had the better part of three months getting ready. That time was spent with the emphasis on a specific target, which was perfectly fine if every attack was to be identical and our position relative to the enemy remained stable. While most big operations were still worked up to much the same way; all of our training had to be flexible enough to permit making decisions as the situation unfolded and we had to develop the ability to be as flexible as operating in such a way as required. Rote rarely has a place on the battlefield. It was hard to see precisely at what ratio old stood against new in the subjects we were taught. Progress could be as rapid as a day's difference between doing something one way to another. All the same, we were barely a generation removed from scarlet tunics and forming up for an advance dressed off regimental flags. We'd stop wearing Glengarry caps for field use only because the sheep hasn't been built whose wool will stop a steel ball. Anything else we could reasonably cling to as symbolic or traditional without interfering upon present conditions and method were retained. The process was a matter of going with what might work in order to find out what would and unapologetically getting rid of what didn't. Really, in a gradual fashion, we lost our tails and started walking upright.

Luckily for us, we weren't the first ones out of the gate for this attack. The Corps was advancing on a narrow front here with two divisions up and two back. The leading divisions in successive waves would take and hold objectives on one reporting line "Green" and the other "Red." We would pass through them and move to take a third line "Blue." The lines were notional, our own invention, and only vaguely described the enemy's defensive network. Fritz had found that far from being a wall of men at arms upon which an attack would break, a densely packed firing line resulted in a loss of manpower for no result should it be overrun. The problem on their end was that a well-coordinated and adequately supported assault had the potential to smash through even the most determinably held trenches. As the Hun still stood upon much of Belgium and a good bit of France, they were able to cite their defences on terrain of their choosing. The real hitch was that they had designed them to best suit every advantage a defender could ask for. At the very front, there were two things: Wiring and concrete. The latter was thickly poured, reinforced with an iron frame and stood up to a good walloping. Each of these block houses placed within sight of at least two others would be armed with machine guns. Of the wire, it was between the bunkers except where lanes had been left open under the nose of automatic weapons. It was no use trying to get through fifty yards or so of mixed entanglements. If possible, the attack was to be deflected here. At the very least, the blockhouse crews would force the attacker into smaller groups, easy enough to push back using dedicated counterattack units. The delay at this Outpost Zone was all which would be needed to move their stormtroopers forward. Should it appear that this line wasn't going to hold, the bunkers would be evacuated to a second layer of defences; a properly built trench system which would have little difficulty in swatting away disconnected bands of attacking troops who would now need to cross a subsequent frontage of wire under direct fire all the way. This was the "Main Line of Resistance", a fortress from which a counterattack could be directly committed. These two lines, Outpost and Resistance, were the day's Green and Red report lines. We had no intention of playing to Fritz' game, though. Our boys attacking the Green Line weren't going to go any further than that and would be succeeded by fresh units who would take the Red Line. Staging our advance to meet each line as a separate phase of operation negated their mutually supportive nature. It really came down to who was both more clever and more determined. To that end, German doctrine was that if the Resistance Line could not hold against an attack, they would withdraw from it, leading their enemy into a third area again of isolated strongpoints like their Outpost Zone, with the same delaying purpose. This was called the Battle Zone, and within this particular arrangement was our units' objective. So, while we weren't to be the first or second in line of advance, we did have a difficult task. Each successive zone of defence in this type of layout was designed to be tougher to crack than the one previous. Meaning, for those of us tasked to take the Blue Line, the worst might yet be ours to face.

The speed at which we had gone from "nothing going on" to "going on to battle" was remarkable, there not being any time to do any physical run throughs of our assigned tasks. It was apparent that speed rather than deliberation was the day's imperative. The series of creeping barrages-- the moving wall of artillery fire we infantry would advance behind was set to move twice as fast as at the Ridge. Again, this was something we had not practiced. Fine thing would be if it all went as it should and Five, Seven and Eight Platoons secured our little bit of the Blue Line without a hitch. Or, fingers crossed, without a hitch requiring commitment of Six Platoon. I should know better by now to be having such dreamy expectations. First of all, everything had to proceed apace and a slight twitch in one of any number of parts moving either too quickly or too slow was going to cause a ripple effect, much like a stone dropped in a pond, such things were most powerful at the point it occurred and dissipated as it moved outward. However, that tiny outward wave could be enough to start stones dropping elsewhere. It bore no thinking about how much could go wrong when even the tiniest thing had the power to precipitate absolute disaster. My problem was, in order to be effective, I had to be able to consider the maddening number of the tiniest things both to the general situation and specific to my sudden elevation in authority, and be prepared to meet any or several of them with a workable response.

This was a big show made such not entirely by the weight of numbers involved so much as it was the concentration of mass along a narrow frontage. For us, intending to take the days final objectives, there was a lot of waiting and moving in stages queued behind the leading divisions. In the march out from our assembly area to jump off, we had most of the way use of a road which marked the boundary between us and the French units South of us. It was intensely strange to be marching forward in such a plain fashion, not but a few hours after sunrise on exposed surface of highway, which had been under enemy control until perhaps an hour or so before we passed along it. While taking an established route made the march quicker, easier to manage and control, all elements much better than moving over untracked ground, I wasn't confident that those rewards were worth the risk. There was a heavy mist that morning, a dewdrop blanket obscuring everything at distance. While it did help to keep us shrouded as we trod forward, I realized the weather's cooperation was entirely coincidental. We would have moved out on the same route regardless. Thickness of fog was of a washed blurry quality. Everything we approached or which approached us from the opposite direction came into resolution from outline to shadow to form like God's first day on the job. The scrap was still a long ways off, a distant but vocal threat. From our remove the din of the fighting was only a rumour of war, always just far enough away to seem a low rumbling over the horizon. It was part of the living battle moving forward, as we came loping after not at all in a hurry to catch up. With five hundred yards, perhaps slightly more, between where we were and the fighting up ahead, there was little to tell from rippling crackles and resonant booms how well things were progressing. Other clues to gauge what sort of fight we could expect once we got to it had to be looked for. The first thing was how urgently we were moving, which wasn't such at all. Our pace remained consistent, set by the arranged timetable. This was not like Bell Hill the year prior, where the frantic nature of a quickly developing situation had set everything carefully plotted out of whack. Along the ground to our left, much of what was closed in from view by the fog, there were palls of thick and very darkly black smoke standing out in the wispy white mist like exclamation points. These blooms were rude, oily streams reaching nearly straight to the sky, undisturbed as if too dense for wind to shift them. What breeze there was pushed the flavor of the reek in or direction, a grisly smell of petrol, hot steel and burnt flesh. Counting them as we passed, it became apparent that these pyres, as such they really were, indicated a huge loss of the tanks which had been committed to the opening phases of battle. However, traffic in the opposite lane passing us as we went along was far more encouraging. Few motor ambulances were driving by, although the wounded may have been directed to another route, rearward. It does little good for those moving into battle to meet those being brought out. What proved most heartening, where the long columns of disheveled pale and dirty men in gray shuffling past under escort. At first, their approach through the heavy mist was a shock, slightly confusing as they moved towards us through a mire so thick anything beyond a furlong was invisible. If were not for the escorts shouting, "Prisoners! Prisoners!" as a foghorn, there might not have been as many collected in cages arear. I was surprised at how pleased some of them looked. Many of them appeared far too young, underfed and wearing clothes which seemed to properly belong to larger men.

Before coming to the Green Line, we were required to make a river crossing. A large bridge was available to vehicle traffic, so we went over one of the two narrow footbridges. They were solidly built, robust and stable, and yet another miracle performed by the Engineers. Neither one of those bridges had been in place for more than an hour before we came to them. As neat as they were, we were still went over cautiously in file two abreast, one company at a time. The whole division needing to get over meant a fair deal of waiting our turn. Fritz must have had some notion of where we were moving as he sent the occasional salvo of artillery fire around the bridgehead. This was not his best effort. Many shells were well off target and not a few plunged into the river itself. None of these interludes of fire gave rise to any panic, and we moved ahead in line as steady and sedate as a crowd moving from platform to train. There were a few casualties, but most that happened was a soaking from a geyser of river water sent up from a poorly placed shell. Patience was required as thousands of men in small parcels made their way across, and once we were formed up on the other side, our walk forward continued. On reaching each reporting line, we were held in position for a pause. These were contingencies for keeping any knock-on effect to a minimum, allowing each attempt at a line to be a battle of its own. It didn't help me all that much that the Green Line had collapsed under the ferocity of an unexpected attack, or that the Red Line had been mostly manned by inexperienced troops, or that our tanks, despite losses, had thrashed all kinds of fresh Hell out of the Hun. No mistake, it was entirely a good thing that the attack had gone exceedingly well, but I couldn't disregard that the enemy occupying our objective within the forbiddingly named Battle Zone had to be aware of the fighting by now, and could reasonably conclude it would be coming their way. Beyond the Blue Line, there were no further tiers of organized defence. There would be strong points, fortified woodlands or villages though these would be protecting lines of communication and logistics. Cracking this successive type of defences would then put Fritz's administrative apparatus at risk of being overrun, crippling their ability to continue resistance. Therefore, as the Blue Line was the last thing between us and their tail end, it was reasonable to surmise the enemy would hold it with a determination. Whether to do so would have the intent of repulsing our attack or to fix us in place to be swept aside with a deliberate counterattack didn't make much of a difference to those of us about to assault the Blue Line. One way or another, they were going to be inclined to not give easily. It might even be that the Germans awaiting us were under implicit orders to hold at all costs. If that were so, things stood to get very ugly.

Four hours after setting out from our assembly areas, we reached our jump off points a short distance from the Red Line. In a fashion of order and organization which made my mind reel to think about, we had come to be exactly where we were supposed to be exactly when we were supposed to be. Then we did what we spent most of our time doing. We waited. Our battalion was being held on open ground in the lee of a little rise that peaked with a wide road running roughly perpendicular to the boundary road we had come down to get here. To my left and right and for distance behind our formation were, as much as I could see through obscuring damp nothing but men, a stadium's worth of khaki figures, a loosely arranged crowd of uniforms. The mass of numbers was nothing short of awesome, interrupted in place with heaping outlines of the tanks coming forward to support our advance. In the case of old meeting new units of mounted cavalry and light horse were in place as well, drumming of heavy engines roaring over huffing whinnies and the jangle of tack. There was an almost electric sense to the power of all this. The men, beasts and machines just building in the waiting moments with more and greater potential, ready to burst forward in a blinding flash once the flow of current was opened. For a very short moment as I witnessed this, I was not afraid. What I seemed to feel right down to my marrow gave me a tantalising taste of what it is to be ten foot tall and bulletproof. It was heady, yet fleeting and had run its course when Sergeant Major Gordon found me to fetch me to company HQ for final orders.

Now all I felt was out of place. Aside from the company HQ section of Clerks and Signallers, who were only present and not actually part of the orders group, I was the only non-com among the company command structure. Both Lieutenant Douglas of Five Platoon and Lieutenant King of Seven, had been sergeants before taking field commissions. It was I who replaced Douglas as Platoon Sergeant of Six last October. It didn't matter who they used to be, who they were now put me as an outsider, a very junior and segregated member of this fraternity. Such as my alienation of status, when Thorncliffe said "Gentleman, orders," by default of correct extension of terminology, I was not included.

"Now," he said, producing a map, "look here." He began naming features and pointed them out to us, "Le Quinsel," a substantial town, "Divisional boundary and final objective of 11 Brigade." He traced a line, which went from the town in a meandering fashion East NE North. "Le Quinsel-Caix Road. In order to protect the flank of 11 Brigade, assault on the town and gain control of access routes, 16 Brigade will be moving against fortified positions along this road. Our battalion's objective is here," he tapped a square on the map just beyond the dashed line marking the boundary between 11 and 16 brigades, a delineation about halfway between the villages that road serviced. Widely spaced contour lines showed the terrain as a low hill slowly rising upward with the road running through the widely flat high point.

"Elevation Thirty-Three. Placed along its crest in advance of line Le Quinsel-Caix are three interconnected redoubts." These were drawn in red, a series of intersecting jagged lines meant to illustrate communication trenches running into each other and punctuated by red squares at the leading ends, enemy bunkers. "This system is known as Roadblock, and has been divided into three sections, each a target for a company attack: Abbey, Buttress and Cloister. Each of these positions is mutually supporting and is anchored either end with MG emplacements. Buckshee Company will assault and destroy the redoubt known as Roadblock Buttress. As you can see, Buttress has excellent fields of fire on our axis of advance, which makes it imperative that we gain control of it to allow A and C companies a clear approach to their objectives of this system. Five and Seven Platoons will reduce the bunkers along Buttress Five left, Seven right. Eight Platoon will provide base of fire, Six Platoon in Company Reserve. Our zero hour's now fixed for 12:10. Keep your platoons clear of the road. No. 5 Squadron from the Duke of Markham's Horse will be moving through at zero minus ten. Right, that's it."

We weren't looking at anything new. We had seen such things before, a defensive arrangement which was the hallmark for effective efficiency. A small group of mutually supporting machine gun pillboxes with generous fields of fire could cover a frontage several times wider than what they presented as targets. That kind of wide coverage demanded a requisite amount, at least of strength, to stand a chance of carrying the whole works. In that way, for the expenditure of half a company's worth of men, the entirety of Roadblock Redoubts was evenly paired with an attacking battalion of three companies forward and one in rear. The three redoubts spaced fifty yards apart, straddled the road, running along Elevation Thirty-Three. Buttress was dug into the road's natural embankment on the side nearest us. The other two positions imposed upon the road itself, along either side of Buttress and at 45-degree declines from it. They were all built to the same plan. Each consisted of two sheltered machine gun positions, which could have been poured concrete just as much as they be some other material. Knowing what they were made of was information which would have been handy to have and only a proper reconnaissance could have confirmed. Again, in the interest of speed and surprise, the possibility of a recce was made moot. They weren't made of candy floss, that much was certain. A firing trench cut in a zigzag connected each pair of bunkers and the entire system was linked by means of communications trenches reaching a central gallery, which had its own protective structure and underground shelter for the position's garrison on the reverse slope. Roadblock did indeed interdict the road, controlling its length from Le Quinsel at its southern end by Cloister to a point about a third of the way to Caix where Abbey's arcs of fire were intersected by those of the next bunker system to the north. These largely independent fortified sites reduced the rate of loss from our preparatory bombardments by providing good cover, being an optimal distance from one another and having low manpower requirement. Additionally, they were so well armed and protected it was usually not wise to bypass any of them. Even if our Gunners managed to knock a few of these strong points out, we'd still have the remainder to be rid of. Things like this were the nuts given to us to crack.

I moved back to Six Platoon, let them know about our start time and had little to do but continue to wait, which was nothing but time for me to worry about all that could go wrong. At noon we were marshalled aside to clear a path for the cavalry which cantered past in echelon of sleek, trim bay mounts, men upright in saddle; sabers drawn, and flankers out, with guidons flapping. Pure and beautifully majestic. Up the lee they cantered, the rhythm of hooves roughing the turf and clopping over the stony path, leaping beyond the opposite bank, the ground pulsing and trembling through the soles of my boots. The echo of their movement faded, overtaken by the next phase of the artillery barrage. Moments ticked away and we wrangled the platoons back in order. Precisely to the second, whistles blew and our pipers began. The great mass surged forward. We still had a small length of ground to cover before reaching the Red Line where we'd pass through Third Division. Once that was done, we would at last become the forward edge of battle. Midday heat had won its own battle against morning damp in just enough time for our advance to begin with the clearing away of the soupy mist and the restoration of visibility over distance. I might have known we couldn't have had such luck. Fritz would know we were coming, and now he'd be able to see us.

Mister Thorncliffe always liked to give the impression that any advance we made was little more than a walk in the countryside. His attitude was never brashly false overconfidence so much as it was a sly wink at the gut stabbing reality of it. Once we were past the Red Line, everything ahead of us would be ground still under German control. Except for isolated spots which the horsemen had galloped towards ahead of us to screen our move forward, this bit of France was to be thought of as under lease to the Hun. After we stepped beyond the Third Division, who were making the usual effort of turning defences to face the right way, we would no longer be just advancing, we were advancing to contact. What that really meant, if broken down to the most basic of definitions, was that we were going to keep walking forward until someone started shooting at us. Basil Douglas, who now newly commissioned commanded Five Platoon, had become Six Platoon's Sergeant, the job I nominally held were it not for whatever happened to Captain McCormack, after our first advance to contact just almost two years ago with Spoon Farm. Bas liked to give such a move the appropriate level of significance.

"This is your bread and butter," he would say, although his drawl softened t's to d's. "This is what the infantry is all about; This is what we're for." Which if considered with any care, raised some interesting questions about the intelligence or sanity of any man who had ever gone into the line of work which was the infantry, including –no, especially- myself. What a blessedly stupid thing to be doing. It countered all instinct, all notions of preservation held by the self-aware. It was plain that was precisely why Lieutenant Thorncliffe hung such sunshine of lovely country outings above moves like this. Somehow it was less crazy to think of a crazy thing as something it clearly was not. If nothing else, it serves to confuse me on which parts of the whole were the crazy bits. As far as this day went, the Lieutenant's notion of a cross-country jaunt was at least believable by half. It was the other half which would prove problematic. The immense concentration of strength, seemingly invulnerable host of men and machines at our jumping off point had solved quite a bit as units moved into waves of depth in line of advance. Tanks lurched into gear and rumbled off to their destinations, the towns bordering our axis, which had been converted into bulwarks. Better, I imagined, tanks than us. The infantry following up those beastly things would only need to count the dead and prod prisoners to the rear.

Beyond the Red Line, we moved into more spacious formations. This was to cover the widest frontage while not being too close for the danger of one strike of shell or burst of shot causing multitudes of casualties at once, nor too far apart to risk losing visual or vocal control of all pieces in play. This compromise put hundreds of yards between battalions scores of yards between companies and dozens of yards between platoons. From the stadium crowds of the assembly areas and jumping off points, there was now more space between men as much as there had been men between space. The numbers were the same, but we'd become so dilute as to reduce my earlier feeling of invincibility to an exposed isolation. In company reserve I was directly behind Thorncliffe's HQ by measure of fifty yards at the head of Six Platoon with five yards between each man. My nearest neighbours to left and right, the reserve platoons of 'A' and 'C' companies were a football pitch distant. If the fog of the morning had remained, I would not have been able to see them at all. The barrage obscured vision up ahead as completely as had the mist; a thick mash of shells, mostly shrapnel set by the gunners to burst while still airborne. Usually this was at the height of 20 feet when the charge would blow through the casing and vomit a funnelled cascade of bearings downwards. We here behind this show of pops and puffs were entirely reliant on good practices of men well beyond our sight back along the gun line. A fuse trimmed to fine, or a barrel elevation out by a fraction would do us more damage than Fritz. The first few minutes went swimmingly. Quickness of everything began to tell not long after. At twice the speed we were used to the lifts and drops of the barrage were moving faster than we could keep up and our lack of practice with this type of fire plan put a good deal of uncertainty into our pace. Like our spacing between units, our forward movement had to be a balance between too fast or too, slow maintaining a distance by which we benefit from the protection the shrapnel provided without it moving beyond us and the enemy while also not risking being caught by our own fire. Even optimally placed, errors still occur. At best it was as benign as the occasional steel ball having struck a really solid surface, sailing back to us invisible with speed, singing out an overhead, a whistly 'whee' as it went. At worst, it shredded our own men into liquid and rags, saving the Hun the bother of having to do it themselves. Lay of the land beyond the Red Line was open wide and plain, dotted hither and yon with small copses of trees and thin boxed forest. Our advance went over undulating ground, first rising up a lazy incline to a road now under control of dismounted horsemen, one man in four minding the animals on the leeward side. Over this road, the land banked sharply down with another rise ahead putting us in a shallow valley before moving up over a higher slope than last. This went along even for a distance towards another road crossing. Before we had got this far, our flanking cavalry had turned right at the road and made a charge towards an outlying wood one hundred yards South of where we met the road, which was still being contested and a fair bit of the ground between us and the wood was marked with a felled horse. We pressed on over crossroads and down a gently sinking grade, still a mile or so from our objective, which we could see plainly as we moved downward. In brief flashes between the drop of shells, parts of Roadblock Buttress stood menacing facing towards us, lining a third road which passed along the highest ridge yet, Elevation Thirty-Three.

Briefly we were in the shelter of bottomland and protected by the continuing barrage. On the next time it shifted, it would give us leave to proceed, our leading platoons required to rush up the high bank and hit the road out before the Hun could mount a challenge. In behind I couldn't see much up front until Thorncliffe blew the series of whistle blasts to signal the assault and the men of Five, Seven and Eight Platoons leapt upward along the slope in bounds, firing and throwing bombs as they went into their attack, climbing the hill and going beyond my sight over top. The ringing whirl and thumping crush of our shells continued into the distance and were replaced by the mechanical metronomic of machine guns and the slamming thud of hand grenades. Where I was, those fifty yards behind company HQ, I could only rely upon sound to assess the progress of the assault. Noise of small arms fire increased to become a singular rolling, rippling tumult. A few minutes passed without it abating.

"Six platoon!" Came a call, Lieutenant Thorncliffe's voice, "Six Platoon up!"

Oh, bother. I gulped, a parched swallow with my gullet trapped by the bite of my helmet strap and my tunic's tight collar. The entire interior of my mouth had gone dry as dust, the rest of me lashed with sweat. It was not but a few hours ago that Thorncliffe had insisted that I was the only man capable of taking over the platoon. I found myself in an odd duality of mind. I couldn't countenance doing anything which would prove the Lieutenant wrong while I was equally certain that in this case, and nothing else, he was. My hands were shaking.

"Right lads," I told the men in what I hoped was a cool tone, that nothing of my unwinding nerves was transmitted, "that's us." They spread out under the guidance of the section commanders and followed me without hesitation as I closed the distance to Company HQ.

"We're hung up on the right," the Lieutenant told me. "Leave a Lewis gun and one of your runners here. Take all else forward, reinforce Seven Platoon and push on to the objective."

"You're not coming, sir?"

"What? No, Sergeant, it's your platoon, now; this is my company. Go!" Well, so much for that. I turned to my men.

"Lynch, Carney, Dewey, stay put here. The rest of you, fix bayonets. On me, One Section left, Two, right. Four Section directly behind, Three Section rear, prepare to move." It was alright, I told myself; no big deal. I was only moving forward a wee bit and would hand my men over to Lieutenant King. the men rallied into the formation I had called for. I couldn't tell if the firing up front had changed in any way.

"At the double-quick, follow me!" I ran up the slope, moving slightly right oblique to pass around Eight Platoon. Taking their positions as far ahead of Company HQ as I had been behind, Eight were fully at their business of providing base of fire, essentially a volume of bullets and bombs to pin the occupants of the redoubt in place, making it as dangerous as possible for any chance of accurate return fire. Their effort gave me ample cover to shift around to make my approach towards Seven Platoon in the way they had gone in to flank the MG position on the right edge of Buttress. Five Platoon had already done the same thing in mirrored fashion on the left. They were in, they'd managed to hit that bunker and were holding firm, pouring aimed fire on Redoubt Abbey. Seven Platoon had mis-stepped somehow; both ends of Buttress should have been jumped at the same time, which put Five in a tight spot. They only had the slightest although tenacious hold on a slim portion of the whole position. Eight's base of fire was helping, if nothing more than ensuring a delicate situation didn't change for the worse. It was a stall which couldn't be permitted to last for long. Both ends of Buttress had to fall or nothing further could be accomplished. Failure of one platoon to meet its objective would hold up the other attacking companies, starting that stone in the pond upsetting the ability of the other battalions in our brigade to meet their objectives, leaving a hole in the middle of our division, and on like so ever upward. That didn't matter so much to me as did the possibility that failing to gain the whole of Buttress would leave Five Platoon isolated and exposed to a counter attack they would not be able to repulse. I was under pressure of time to get my men tagged up with Seven Platoon before the bottom fell out. I skirted around the rise, trying to keep my platoon lower than the crest. Rushing all the way uphill would have done nothing so much as shouting "I'm here!" to a Hun machine gunner and I would lose my platoon in the first handful of minutes after I had led them into battle for the first time. It was a move which worked to put me behind as well as below Seven Platoon. While it kept my men out of direct line of fire, it kept me out of line-of-sight of our friends to the front. The air was getting thick with dangerous things the closer we got.

"Go to ground!" I yelled, and my platoon melted into the hillside. All I wanted to do was to sink deep into the earth; sink so far that nothing could touch me and stay there until the war ended or the world collapsed. Either suited me just fine. Unfortunately, either were options open to me. I had to see what was ahead, and that meant moving closer. It meant doing something all of sensibility screamed at me not to do, crawling uphill in the direction of an unhealthy level of lead travelling the wrong way.

Seven Platoon was in trouble. I clocked a few khaki bundles between slope's edge and the wire traps fronting the bunker. Our barrage, mainly shrapnel, wasn't meant to be anti-materiel. It made for a good barrier to move behind, as so it was named, but of little use in destroying enemy hardpoints and impediments. The bombardment, on the other hand, a targeted shelling of emplacements and gun positions which had preceded our attack was specifically designed to blow aside any obstacles the infantry would be slowed up by. The cracking force of the blasts of high-explosive shells snapped and sundered the steel pickets between which barbed strands had been suspended. The way wasn't completely clear. It wouldn't stop us, but it would slow us down. Had to get there, first; which is something

Seven Platoon hadn't managed. What they had done was balked, and made for cover in the fresh shell holes our bombardment had left. Now they were pinned, in groups out of touch with each other, unable or undirected to move, even in the little bit required to return fire.

All of that I took in within all the time it took to blink, though it felt much longer. I pushed myself downslope with a singular thought. Unless I could make direct touch with Lieutenant King or Sergeant Dundas; who, even if they were about seemed to not be affecting any development, I had to treat this as if my platoon were alone responsible for committing to the attack. Just wait until I see Thorncliffe again with his "Don't worry, Catscratch, we won't even need you." If, sir, if, if, if. It takes a while to set these thoughts and sights out in a way to be understood. At the time, in the moment, however, it is a rush of colliding things, smashing through the mind in instant flashes. A proper bloody miracle that a human brain can filter and assess such a collection of mental noise. Delay, though, no matter how tempting, to take time to gather all available data and construct a response, was death. I had to act, right in that moment, without any luxury of deep analysis.

Step one was to win the firefight. Simple ideas are best at times as such as these, and the army excels at simple ideas. What I had to do, using only what I had to hand was to put enough fire on that bunker so that it couldn't interfere with what would follow, the assault. One thing before the other, though. My best bet to complete that first step was to get my Lewis gun into a good position for supressing fire. I had One Section on my left, Two to my right. Four, my Lewis gun section had stuck tight with me, and Three Section, my rifle bombers, was in behind us, a little further down the rise.

"Corporal Taylor!" I shouted in the direction of Three Section.

"Yeah?"

"Can you put a volley on that bunker from where you are?"

"Sure can!"

"Good," a concentrated hit with rifle bombs might not knock out the target; it would give Fritz something to think about. "Load up, fire on my signal." I turned to Corporal Tapscott, "I'm taking Atherton, Robbins and the gun with me. Once those bombs hit, I'll dash forward. Follow up with your section the moment we get the Lewis in position."

"Right, Sarge."

"Ace, shell hole, five yards from the crest, directly in front. You ready to move?" Atherton gathered his Lewis, gave me a thumbs up. "Taylor, now!" Four little barks, the noise of blank cartridges, came from behind, followed a hanging moment later by the explosions of the bombs they had launched. I moved without pause for second thought, Ace and Robbins stuck to me like flypaper to a deep shell hole crowded with men from Seven Platoon, most of whom were not doing much but hugging earth. While Atherton put his gun up on its bipod, after clearing a path through the inactive men, I looked back to see that Corporal Tapscott had the remainder of Four Section up. Taylor's bombs had bought only enough time for myself and the Lewis team to pass unbothered. The German gun at this end of Roadblock Buttress recovered and fired a long burst right into Tapscott, Grant and Coxwell, all three went down. I looked about at the men I found myself with, no officer nor an NCO with them.

"Ace, get some fire on that bunker!" In seconds, he was pouring measured rips on target, Robbins standing by to reload. I hoped that Taylor, below us, had hearing equal to my dry voice.

"Necktie!"

"Yeah?" Thank fuck.

"Gie us another volley and take a bound forward to me," another four coughs, another four blasts, another pause in machine gun fire.

"You, there," I addressed an idle lump, "where's Mister King?"

"I think he's dead."

"What about Sergeant Dundas?"

"Don't know." A wealth of information, that one.

"Anybody?" I canvassed the remainder of the—quick count—seven men with me here, besides Ace and Rob. No one had an answer. "Where are your Lewis guns?" Again, no one seemed to know. As best I could tell, Atherton was the only automatic weapon we had. He was putting up a good show, but I couldn't expect him to carry the whole game. "All of you," I extolled the Seven Platoon men, "be of some fucking use and give me fire on that objective." They weren't cowards, they had only needed someone to tell them what to do, to show them that action countered fear. Three Section hadn't come forward.

"Catscratch!" I heard from Taylor.

"Yeah?"

"Got three down over here." Damn. Those men were Atherton's lifeline. Riflemen, yes, but primarily they were porters, carrying a stack of magazines to keep the Lewis fed full of bullets.

"Ace, how're you doing?" He didn't answer, his attention in focus to working his gun. He made a slight movement of his head, which passed my question on to Robbins, in better position to give an answer.

"I've four left, Sarge." That wouldn't do, I'd need to get them a few more, at least.

"I'm coming back, cover me!" A third volley of rifle bombs went, and I flew back down the way I had come. The only man left able in Four Section was Endicott. Coxwell, Grant and Tapscott had taken hits. None were too bad, but that was them out of this fight. We couldn't do much for them; not until the SB's could move up, and that couldn't happen until we had that bunker out of business. I needed to bring the rest of the platoon forward, and increase the level of fire so as to make the final assault with as little enemy interference as possible.

"One Section!" I yelled, my request echoing in a jungle telegraph. "Move up to the crest. Two Section!" The same shout worked in the opposite direction. "Prepare to move, shell hole, front and right." I drew a breath, looked left to see Brentwood had moved One Section into position. Time to go. "One Section, fire!

Two Section, move!" Rapid rifle fire snapped out on one side, Corporal Ellins and his lot jumped forward a length on the other.

"Two Section, fire! One Section, move!" Same process, opposite ends. Half my platoon was now five or ten feet closer to the objective. Just another five or ten yards to go.

"How are you for bombs, Necktie?"

"Not bad, but I can't be at this all day. I can give you another three volleys."

"Alright. McCulloch!" I called for my runner.

"Yes, Sergeant?"

"Move beyond the ridgeline right. Take a bound and make contact with Corporal Ellins. I want him to put everything he's got; bombs, rapid fire, pocket change, the lot, directly on that bunker when I give the signal."

"What's the signal?"

"He'll know it. Now, go, and be careful." McCulloch sped off, and with Ace still hammering away and my two forward sections adding their bit, my runner was well covered.

"You have a plan?" Taylor asked.

"Almost. Let's get the Lewis pans from Tapscott and his men. Nelson! Stuff these about yourself and be ready to follow me. Nick, fire one to cover me and Nelly while we jump forward. Wait thirty seconds, then fire your last two rapid."

"You got it."

"Good stuff. Tremor, stay here with Three Section. If I go down, take the assault in." I grabbed a sling bucket of Lewis magazines to take with me. "Ready, Nelson?"

"Aye."

"Now, Taylor." His men fired again, and Nelson was on my heels as we came back up the rise. I had half a minute to explain my notions to men I'd never worked with. I went through it, quickly, while setting out the ammunition Nelson and I had brought for Ace.

"Two more rifle bomb volleys will hit, and we'll go forward at the charge. Cover fire will come in from our right. You, you and you," I singled out some Seven Platoon men, "bombers. Sling arms, and when you see me hit ground, throw into the trench. You, and you, with me on bayonet. those bombs go, we follow. Stick anything soft. The rest of you stay put and move with the Lewis." How much time? Not lots. "Ace, once we've got that gun, come forward. Nelson, tune up 'All the Blue Bonnets'."

"Aye, Sergeant." From a protective canvas bag, he produced his set and gave it wind. Taylor's boys shot their rods, buffeting the MG bunker with their final offerings.

"Now, Nelson!" In one move, my piper was on his feet and playing out, Bert's section took the cue and poured fire right on target.

"CHARGE!" I couldn't believe it was my own voice, or that it was my own body I had willed to move. We traipsed over the tangles of wire and right at the trench's edge, I went prone. Two Mills bombs were cast overhead and landed deep into the trench. The third took a heavy bounce and came to rest not a foot away from my nose. Had I needed time to think about it, I wouldn't have had enough time. Even though it was my hand that reached out and urged the short-thrown bomb that final yard to drop into the redoubt, I'm not convinced it was my brain which told it to do so. I'm not a big man, but I could stand to be a lot flatter at times such as. The blast was close, and while the trench walls absorbed it, a great shock seemed almost to lift me off the ground. Made it easier to get to my feet, I suppose. Fucking Seven Platoon. No wonder we beat them at baseball all the time.

I jumped over the parapet and fell into the fire bay, there was no place to make a landing. The pasting this trench had received with the preparatory bombardment, and our creeping barrage had torn the wood revetments loose, shattered the floorboards and incited landslides. The effect was heaps of muddy spoil impaled by various slats and branches, broken and tossed; flattened and burst tins and steel cans; a liberal spread of dull brass from spent and live rifle bullets, their sparkling tint under afternoon sun not quite matching the shine from a gold band upon the finger of a hand half-stripped of flesh standing out among other debris. It was as if a giant had scooped the whole extent with both hands, raised it up to a great height and let it drop. I quickly corralled my troops, sending one of the bayonet men and two bombers to work left towards the centre of the redoubt where Five Platoon would make contact. The other two I had follow me as I picked my way across the mess towards the machine gun bunker which was our ultimate goal. It was never an encasement of much substance; a work of packed earth and scrounged wood. A good deal of it had been caved in and much of it added to the larger bits of scattered flotsam which required me to vault over it all along the trench rather than making a headlong dash to the collapsed bunker. I saw a pair of hands from within push aside a heavy beam, clearing an exit from which three battered men tumbled out, puling themselves through the wreckage, and once clear, got to their feet, unbalanced and stumbling. They all looked in my direction, locking eyes on me, and came to reckon, through minds stupefied by close explosions, just what was taking place.

It was one thing to give in; to have no want for a fight, throw down arms and put hands up as we came upon them. It was another thing entirely to expect clemency in surrender after tearing through us with their machine gun; only giving up the ghost when at last it was smashed. If they showed no fear in killing, they should not be afraid to die. As those three filthy and ragged men struggled out of the toppled bunker, before they could decide on making an attempt at surrender, I pulled out my .45 and shot each one where they stood.

France, July, 1936

I lay awake in the unfamiliar bed, a mattress of such solidity and little give I might well have kipped on the floor for better comfort. The realisation that I was half a world away from my home took a moment to gain purchase in my mind, alongside correct measure of time; to understand that the past was where it should be. Damned thing only seemed to be receding in measure if not intensity. I missed Adelaide very much, as having her near was reassurance enough I hadn't at last tumbled into a madness in which I could endlessly repeat the crucible of my youth. There's no lie in saying I was seriously concerned with such a possibility.

With morning yet to show itself, I quietly dressed and went out from the hotel and into the street. This time of morning, twenty years ago, we would have been up and active, already engaged in the business of the day. The war was a twenty-four-hour enterprise, anyway; there was not ever any complete break from the event. To find myself alone on a street devoid of any traffic just reinforced to me the idea that in a warped fashion I had never actually been here before. There might be some truth to that. When I was here, this place, though not entirely physically different to the present, was wholly dedicated to the purpose of the events in which it was an active part. I had never seen it as a village, which it had been before the war began and which it became after the war ended.

Petit Séjour had not been a very populous town at that time, and that had been much reduced by systemic levees of its young men. Our presence easily outnumbered the remaining population to near invisibility. As many of the buildings had been requisitioned for military use, they may have looked as houses and shops, chocolate box images of quiet charm on the outside; while within they had been made to serve as billets, offices, mess facilities and store houses. Traffic, in and out and within the town was almost entirely for our purpose and strictly controlled. Although it was their village, the locals had been under our direction; needing passes to travel and subject to a lengthy curfew. With everything we had brought into the town as well as what came through the rail station or occupied outlying areas, Petit Séjour as I knew it had been nothing less than an armed camp. Now, having reverted, rebuilt and regrown, it no longer was the place I had been familiar with, and seeing it as it was meant to be was like not recognising a person of some vague acquaintance in good health after having only known them to be sickly.

It might well be I was coming at the feeling of unfamiliarity from the wrong end. My alienation from this environment may not have so much to do with how it had all changed since I was first here, but rather how little I had changed in the same lapse of time. In many ways, without a real ability to comprehend why, I was not by temperament at the same remove from my past as I was by physical age. My war was, as far as time went, a fraction of my living years which was now sandwiched between lengthy periods. On the one side were the experiences of youth, all the phases of growth and learning to come to a relative understanding of the world I inhabited. The other was the passing through into adulthood, that of responsibility, family and being not just a part but an influence upon that world. Both lengths were drastically overshadowed by those few years in the middle. That miniscule measure was so outrageously steeped in extremes its content, not duration, was the imperative as to how it remained so current with me yet. Bert Ellins had made an interesting case of this when I had accepted his invitation to meet for drinks the evening before.

He'd selected a place we had both known back in our old times here. It was one of the few establishments which had remained under civil direction and of those, the only one Other Ranks had been permitted to frequent when actually allowed into the town. We had treated it rather poorly, it must be said. Young, with the very real prospect we might not get any older, we were far away from home and any decent supervision, our pockets lined with money most of us had no practical use for, and full of violent energy absorbed and kept in potential from constant duress which tended to react explosively kinetic when infused with drink many of us were not accustomed to. Not a few times had the provost been called upon to save us from completely wrecking the place. L'Oie du Nord in that fashion had been the most thoroughly and consistently damaged building in Petit Séjour, a remarkable if not ignoble distinction as no German bomb ever struck it, despite looking as if it had. It's a bit tongue-in-cheek to suggest our exuberance had done the place a favour, but in order to keep running, it did have to replace quite a lot in the way of fixtures and fittings, which at present had been done in the 'oh, so modern' fashion Adelaide was fond of. I liked it, too. The combination of toned woods and polished metals was clean; the flourish of delicate etched lines in frosted glass was decorative, yet undemonstrative. Also, it no longer smelled of spilled beer and vomit, which did wonders for the atmosphere.

Bert and I had talked, in small ways, about our shared history, a little on life since then. This sort of conversation can be bittersweet, as names not thought of for years are brought to mind; men with whom I had lived through times which were so poignantly to remain.

"I was really sorry to hear about Tim," he'd said. Tremaine, Bert and I had made quite the trio in Six Platoon, all of us becoming leading NCOs within its structure. Bert provided his bookish intellect, Tim his patient wisdom of age and paternalism, and I'm certain there were qualities I added to the mix.

"I remember you sent a wreath; that was kind of you."

"Thanks. It was far too difficult to get away to come east for the funeral."

"It is a long way to come from-"

"Medicine Hat," he reminded me. "How's his family?"

"Well. The boys run a good business, and look after Sarah as would do their dad proud. I go out to see them, now and again."

He raised his glass. "To Tremor," he proposed.

"Aye, to him, and all our absent friends." We clinked and had a solemn drink. After having gone to see the graves of friends earlier in the day, it helped to be in the company of someone still living who had been to the same places my memory continues to vividly visit. What we had collectively experienced could not be really understood by anyone who hadn't been there with us, which created a comfortable solidarity. Everything I failed to relate in a directly comprehensive way to Hamish's curiosity of my war and what Adelaide struggled to accept about my acquiescence to the possibility of being called to war again, Bert had intimate and immediate sympathy. I can't fault my son or wife for such an inability, that they tried was what mattered; trying to better understand a complex person because of the importance I had to them. Going along a conversational route of our departed companions seemed to be putting on a mood of melancholy, and wishing to steer us both away from a greeting match, I tried to bring up something to lighten our evening.

"Do your kids listen to 'Antoine and Belfry'?" He pulled a face which betrayed a modicum of distaste.

"Those idiots? My kids never miss it. I usually try to be in the other room when that show is on. Why do you ask?"

"Don't you know that 'Antoine' is Llew Dewey?" Bert laughed.

"Oh, you're joking. Really, Dewey? I had no idea. Can you imagine getting paid to act the fool day-in day-out? What a racket that must be for him. Doesn't make me want to like the programme any more than I do."

"Nor I." Our chatting remained for a spell quite benign, something to fill the air between taking on liquids, nothing of any real depth until he put a deceptively simple question to me.

"Can I ask you, frankly, how you've been? I mean that towards your personal well-being; your satisfaction of life."

"Alright, I suppose." I wasn't sure how much I wanted to talk about such things, very private things, even to a comrade, regardless of him also being a doctor. I left my response as blank as that, and turned the question back onto Bert. "Why?"

"I'm genuinely interested. When I got back home, my only goal was to get on with things the war interrupted. All the aspirations I had for life; these were the very things that I not only had thought my efforts would direct me toward, they were the reasons I wanted most to live through the war to be able to do."

"I think we all had much the same thoughts." All I had wanted to do was to be able to get back to Inchmarlo. Whatever I had to suffer or sacrifice just to survive was always put up to that being the light at the end of the tunnel. Except, when indeed I had squeezed through the gates of moral and physical ruin to live my life in peace...

"It wasn't enough," Bert completed my thought. "Becoming a doctor had meant everything to me, since I was very young. Yet, there was this strange sort of hollow feeling, a lack of enthusiasm for anything I wanted to accomplish or enjoy with my life." He was describing something very familiar to me.

I had put any sense of dissatisfaction to my work at the family vineyard in that it was an obligation I didn't really want, caused by a failure of having any other option which kept me in a place I had staked my existence upon reaching and perversely hadn't any wish to be. In retrospect, that feeling of being chained to an unwanted obligation causing me to believe I was both trapped and unfulfilled was false on two fronts. The first being that neither Uncle Isaac nor Bill had ever made my employment explicit. I hadn't known how either might have viewed any expression I might make to carve my own path, simply because I never brought the notion forward. It was precisely as Paddy had told me when he'd dangled a commission in front of me. Not doing anything for fear of my own inadequacies was just cover for never having to try, and it was he who put the matter unavoidably in my path. He'd telephoned a few days after I had gone to that town meeting in the Spring.

"I heard you made quite a stir the other night," he'd said.

"From who?"

"Who do you think? The Padre. Got some sort of building scheme in the works. He told me all about it."

"Ach, I was only putting forward what Bill had sent me there for. Most of it I made up as I went along."

"Galbraith said you spoke with passion and conviction. I'd put it to you that you care more about this than just getting some asphalt laid because your cousin told you to." Damn him, he was right. I had no strong feelings to giving Bill and his like what they wanted nothing objectively for or against. I did have an abiding notion that we were in a position to offer those going without work the opportunity to make a wage doing something for the betterment for all of Falls Parish. It was, if passion was the right word, that of a lesson the army had taught me. Waste nothing, as even the least has value and always promote the welfare of the men, as nothing can be gained without their efforts; essentially the whole philosophy of concentration of resources to directed purpose.

"I knew you'd been paying attention," was Paddy's response when I explained to him what had motivated me to speak up at the meeting.

"Bunch of old men looking out for their own pockets. I'd only been trying to give them my mind on their self-interest. Now I've got to see the Mayor about it."

"Don't mind that, he's a friend of mine," no surprise. "Spoke to him too, when I heard from the Padre."

"What did he say?"

"He wanted to know more about you, and I obliged him. Try to act surprised when he offers it; he's of a mind to appoint you Director of Public Works."

"Come off, Paddy."

"No fooling. His idea, but I saw no reason to not agree, as long as he'd be okay with you scheduling office hours around your military obligations and any university courses you might be attending." I could almost hear him winking through the phone. I wanted to ask, but couldn't find the courage to why he cared so much. Really, though, I knew the answer. It was why I cared about getting those civil projects going. Our experiences together had shown the both of us the merit of looking out for the well-being of others. If he or I had failed to provide for our men, we'd have no cause to expect them to fulfill their tasks. If he didn't push for me to improve myself, he could not use me to my best potential to the benefit of the Regiment; just as we couldn't expect Falls Parish to thrive without using potential resources to improvement. All I had done was to apply a lesson learned in war as a practical solution to a current problem. What I believed at the time that this would require, should I take on such a commitment, would be to bow out of working at the Estate; which meant I would be in for a difficult conversation with Bill.

"Ah," he's said after my telling him, "good for you. Adelaide will be pleased."

"Haven't told her yet. I wanted to tell you first."

"Why?"

"To let you know I won't be taking on the Estate."

"Okay."

"Eh?" Such a response was not the one I had been bracing for. I'd expected a berating of my ingratitude, a betrayal of the family name, geese and golden eggs, biting feeding hands, any number of proverbial rants. "You're not upset?"

He looked at me quizzically. "Should I be? Felix, when I'm gone, I don't care if you swallow the keys and burn the place to the ground. What will it matter to me, if I'm dead? It's a business, not a legacy. Besides, I never much thought it was for you. Chas and Hen have been doing most of the running of things the past few years anyhow. If this is what you want, laddie, go on to do it. I'm not one to tell you your life."

Before I had this new opportunity, any of this lack of satisfaction Bert and I were talking about at L'Oie du Nord I could ascribe to feeling as if my life had been set for me. Clearly that wasn't true, and lacking courage to move beyond the safety of predestination made any resentment of circumstance self-inflicted. That, though, was only half of it, the obverse side of the coin. The reverse was that in all other things, this 'hollow feeling,' as Bert had put it, remained. After a long pause to reflect, I told him

"I see what you mean. That no matter what, life was empty in a way. I would have thought that after such a thing as we had gone through, we might be deserving of a little inward peace. Of all I've done since, there's been very little of that."

"Would you say, Felix, that you're happy with life since the war?" Being asked that was rather direct, so I took a moment to think about my response. I finished my drink and ordered another.

Was I happy? It was a question which carried a lot of weight. If I were to have answered 'yes' without hesitation I might not be entirely sincere, just as much to say 'no' wouldn't be exactly true. I might well have to decide what the idea of the thing itself meant for me before I could offer any assessment of how I fit within any definition of the condition. I had no cause to complain, while at the same time I had long been part of a professional culture which had a very narrow view of complaints. Maybe there were things I could take issue with but I was still uncertain I had the freedom from scrutiny to raise. Satisfied, certainly. My family and I wanted for nothing, which was much to be said. Loved, definitely; as much as I loved those who loved me. Not particularly joyous, but I've never been the demonstrative heel-kicking, chirpy whistling type. Didn't mean I was miserable, either.

"Don't worry about not having an answer, Felix," Bert said, putting an end to my considerations. "That you really have to think about it tells me you're not so sure; which is fine. Not knowing was the point I was wanting to make."

"I didn't want you to misunderstand any answer I might give. I'm glad of all the things I have in my life; I have such deep gratitude for my family most of all, but deep down, about myself, I don't think I can say I'm altogether that happy."

"I understand," he said, which made me feel better, in a small way. "I've come to find that what you and I are talking about is rather more common than one might expect. We went through some pretty serious shit and it's damned hard to come away from it clean." Bert's tone changes to one freckled with the gravity of his profession. "What do you know about Shell Shock, Felix?"

"Not a lot," I admitted. "Got some fellahs pretty nervous, like. Explosions, wasn't it? Knocking the sense out of folk, right?"

"Yes and no. Initially, it was thought the cause was physiological, uhm, that the force of blast was damaging the brain. More doctors, myself included, are beginning to believe that the condition is emotional in nature, from prolonged exposure to stressful circumstances."

"Really?"

"Indeed. See, a lot of men diagnosed and given psychological therapies made good, if not complete recoveries. We really have to thank the Germans in this, I'm afraid. The clinical information their medical establishment collected on these sorts of trauma cases when added to our own really paint the picture of us being misinformed. To the extent—and I've seen our own wartime clinical reports to verify—that acute cases could be able to resume effective duty after a period of rest away from the battle area. If the cause was strictly physical, the damage wouldn't reverse itself. Plus, it wouldn't explain the presence of symptoms in those who hadn't been directly exposed to shellfire predicate to diagnosis."

"That so?"

"Absolutely. With that being the case, that it's a question of emotional exposure rather than a physical injury, it's hard to assess any damage unless it's of the most extreme disturbance, because it relies upon the individual recognising signs that aren't outwardly visible. I'm seeing a lot of this in my practice, enough to be very concerning. Many of my patients who are veterans describe much the same flatness of being; a lassitude with life, even with taking on the same things they enjoyed before the war. Quite a few admit to a troubling emotional instability; intense and vivid memories coming unbidden, difficulty sleeping, nightmares." It was as if he had climbed into my brain and had a good look around.

"I'd say that's fairly accurate to me, Bert."

"I'm not immune, either," he confided, which leant me another measure of strength in solidarity. "Trouble is, Felix, this is all very new. Both cause and cure are a matter of some debate among my colleagues." It was his opinion, he explained, that regardless of the origin of the problem or an agreed method of recovery, there was a paucity of activity to a solution. This was on the part of the afflicted, in some ways, for not recognising or being able to express what were quite personally intimate difficulties. All of us had come through that system of antipathy to any sort of complaint or grumble and Bert had pointed out that system was itself inadequate to address this as a concerning and legitimate problem. A problem, he felt, which was equal to the challenge of returning to an active and productive life faced by a man who had lost a limb. Which if true—and I had little doubt of Bert's veracity—did very little to help.

"If it doesn't result in you presenting me with an invoice, what would you recommend, Doctor?"

"I sometimes forget you're Scottish," he jested at my supposed inherited parsimony, "so I'll give this to you for free. Find someone to confide in."

"I'm guessing my cat doesn't count."

"No, and you didn't let me finish. Another vet who can understand the nature of what you've been through and how you're still struggling with it. My experience—personal experience, not clinical—has shown me how beneficial this type of mutual support can be. The other advice is to push yourself towards something, a job or hobby, whatever, that you can get a kind of altruistic reward from. I like to think of it as helping yourself by helping others." I told him then of my work with the town council and the frequent chats I had with Paddy.

"That's a damn good start. I should have charged you."

"For what, following advice you'd hadn't yet given me?"

"Is this your first time getting advice from a doctor?" Damn. With Bert it was often I found myself in a battle of wits for which I'd arrived without adequate logistical support. He sank the rest of his drink and stood back from the bar. "Anyway, it's late, I'm off. I'll see you tomorrow for the bus to the monument."

I don't presume that everything in my life would be worry free if I merely had a good chinwag with Paddy every now and again and threw myself into a life of civil service. On the other hand, it wouldn't hurt anything if I did. Should any of that effort result in a few less sleepless nights I'd be daft not to give it a go. Knowing I wasn't alone with these troubles helped, and while it was worrisome to be told they were prevalent there was a backhanded comfort that we were not few. It had a twisted way of making something which seemed abnormal less so and thus not something to hide from.

Morning was beginning to really show itself, my wandering the streets while wandering my mind having consumed the early dawn. I struck back towards the hotel to get ready for the day ahead, for the grand ceremony we had come all this way to see. If I realised anything from talking to Bert the night before, I finally had an answer to a question so often put to me when I was here twenty years ago that I was satisfied with. The question, that is, of what I would do after the war.

France, September, 1918

The question which was raised every so often seemed harmless enough. If, though, it was to be examined with any realistic scrutiny, the answer given was entirely contingent on two factors beyond reasonable control. Those being, that the war would end and do so before one's own mortality did. "What will you do after the war?"

"Helps to get to know your men better," Captain Thorncliffe had explained, taking opportunity to advise me on certain nuances of command; inside tips I might find useful considering what he had opened with: "I'm keeping you in charge of Six Platoon. Only one subaltern has shown up, and Seven is more in need of leadership." Lieutenant King had been killed that day at Buttress, and Sergeant Dundas seriously wounded. Unfortunate as that was, it had put the Captain in the tight spot of having to manage the entire company while at the same time handle one of its platoons which had not nearly enough NCOs to run efficiently. As a stop-gap, Sergeant Major Gordon had filled in, although leading platoons wasn't something company sergeant majors were supposed to do.

"You're getting two," Thorncliffe said, on the subject of new men, shuffling through a heap of papers, "let's see. McAdam and Laredo." I scribbled the names in my notebook.

"Yes, sir." A small batch of replacements had arrived earlier that morning to supplement the losses we'd taken over the past month. I would have required three times the two I'd been allotted just to make good on empty files from our actions in August, and twice that to bring Six Platoon to full strength. My company commander would well know that, which meant if he was only giving me two, it was because he only had two to give me. I knew better than to attempt to broker for manpower that didn't exist. Thorncliffe was in a position of having to share out these arrivals across all four platoons of 'B' Company, and mine was by no means the worst off for numbers.

"We are pretty low in order for a front-line rotation and it might just be we'll get more reinforcement before we next go up. All the same, the situation overall is incredibly fluid; meaning we might be required to change our plans with little notice and go ahead with what we've got." Well, that was just business as usual. Maybe I should count blessings and be happy with only getting the two replacements rather than a full establishment. A sudden influx of manpower would be a sure sign we'd be headed for action. The army being the most economical of concerns it would not part with resources it might have to hand if the elements of its organisation could function adequately without them.

"With all new men, meet with them one-on-one as soon as practical. Be informal, ask questions of familiarity." This was where the post-war interrogatory had been brought up as example. Not only would doing so allow me to gain a little insight to the arrivals, "it gives them a chance to understand that you, their leader, is in a position of care as well as command. It's very important that you also inquire about any administrative deficiencies; shortages of kit especially, and waste no time in correcting them. Knowing that you're looking out for even the smallest issue goes a long way to endear your men to you. Having their absolute confidence is the only way to be certain they won't let you down at a bad time." That Thorncliffe devotedly practiced what he preached gave no room to doubt the correctness of his advice. I had thought enough already to attempt to emulate his style, if only from the point that I admired it so much, which only made further proof to his instruction. All he had done in making it explicit was to connect the line between cause and effect.

"That's all, Sergeant. Regular Orders Group here at five this evening. Have Corporal Tremaine submit an administrative report based on your findings to CQMS before then." I saluted, turned about and left, picking up my rifle where I had left it leaning on the outside wall of his office, an army bell tent set up in the lee of the tumbled brick walls which once had been a house. 'B' Company HQ was under canvas as there were no other available structure of suitable integrity in the whole of our surroundings. Where we found ourselves at present, I supposed must have been a nice country villa at some point. The war had lingered in these parts for much of the duration and that consistent presence had eroded almost everything which had stood upright. Most of the destruction was the result of shelling that had pounded to dust and blasted to splinters every single construction. Whether it had been by our guns or the enemy's was something I didn't know, and I don't imagine responsibility would matter much to those whose houses and livelihoods these remnants had been.

Anything of use or value had long vanished, most presumably any items portable enough to flee with the inhabitants had taken with them. Furnishings left behind and not smashed in a bombardment would have been coveted for making trench dugouts homier, and all else left behind were subject to the long understanding of soldiers having light fingers for abandoned items. What price thievery when far wore actions were sanctioned? Beyond household fittings and forsaken possessions, any decently intact building material was also absent, most certainly to have been re-used as parts of defensive constructions. The only thing close to a normal state were the roads, swept clear of debris which had been roughly piled along the verge into lumpy embankments; a lengthy slag of mixed and broken rubbish stacked to a height of several feet. Nothing could be left which would impede traffic. This was a continual project, taken on by gangs of Chinese workers from the Labour Corps. The Front was miles beyond us, pressing ahead in a wildly mobile fashion none of us who had been here a while was used to. As the fighting continued forward, it was essential that all lines of communication, growing ever longer, were not interrupted in any way.

Such unusual momentum was precisely what Thorncliffe had meant when he'd called the situation fluid. It had led to, of late, rumours about the state of German affairs; specifically, that our recent gains were being made by pushing against a spent force. I wanted so much to believe that even if I had nothing aside from conjecture to give substance to such claims. For the most part, the Hun were still giving a good account, performing just as stubbornly as usual in defending their positions, such as we had seen last month. Either they would hold to the last or manage to de-camp in good order to other prepared works further arear. While we might have been making huge forward strides, they'd done little to make it easy. On the other hand, large bodies of prisoners were being taken, which some might say showed an eagerness to surrender borne of weariness. From these I had seen for myself, it would appear that many of them were recent call-ups from expanded age categories, both younger and older than previous levees who might not be well suited or acclimated to life at the front and had little keenness or fortitude to withstand the demands upon moral strength required by war. I thought it unlikely the idea that any German of lengthy experience would ground arms unless no other option existed. That belief I was projecting on them from how I felt about such things. After all, they were men such as we, with the same depths of strength and weakness. There were far too many factors at play to make any kind of certain idea of how things might unfold, and all too easy to be overly hopeful or despondent depending on which way the wind blew. Best case would be for nothing to happen to upset any sense of regularity or pace beyond what had already occurred. If our efforts pushed the front lines further or faster than intended; or indeed if the fighting became stuck in place, our battalion's rest period among this rubble could be cut short. It might not mean throwing us into the thick of things in one leap of naught to full steam, however, if reserves local to the fighting were committed, everything else behind would take one pace forward. The longer we were held arear, the better, and not only because it kept my mother's son away from present danger.

Six Platoon as a whole remained in a delicate state. From a strictly numbers perspective, this was obvious as we were drawing rations for just about two thirds of what our full strength should be. Even so, lacking a more complete establishment wasn't an isolated problem. Effectiveness relied upon experience and leadership, qualities no number of replacements could make up for. We could have all the men we ever wished for, but they would be of no good use without those to tell them what to do, or having been sent out to us lacking all the skills requisite to function in a front-line unit. My particular difficulty wasn't one thing or the other, it was both, and I had to include myself in that. I was beginning to believe that I indeed had the capacity of directing a platoon in the absence of an officer, and whether or not this was true, Thorncliffe's reassignment and casualties of late created the need to appoint two men to command of sections. I didn't have a lack of faith in either Brentwood or Atherton as both had been with the platoon a good long while and had performed well enough. The only thing they might be lacking was a test of the qualities beyond ordinary soldiery a position of authority required. This really meant that I had more than one person having to learn new responsibilities while at the same time coping with the astounding lack of preparation endemic among my platoon's newest arrivals. Not much longer than two years ago, all that had been required of an infantry private was mastery of the Rifle, Short, Magazine, Lee Enfield; practice in the techniques of fire and movement which enabled closing with the enemy, and skill with the bayonet. Modern war had made demands of a change in means; though method remained more or less the same. A rifle platoon now carried a more diverse set of tools to counteract the difficulty of attacking well prepared defensive positions defended by automatic weapons. Tremendous advantage was bestowed upon well-protected men employing mechanical firepower. I would not likely have been able to successfully reduce Roadblock Buttress without a Lewis light machine gun, rifle bombs and hand grenades; certainly not without taking far more casualties than I did. Just as well, then, I did have those weapons, and in the hands of men well trained in their use. So intrinsic were these things to the operation of a platoon that each man was required to know, completely, how to use them. It would do me no good, as an example, to lose Atherton should he have been the only man who could work a Lewis. The two such guns I had made up to near fifty percent of my platoon's firing power. To ensure that rate of fire never diminished, every last one of us had to be able to load, fire and clear stoppages on the Lewis, as that weapon would still need to be in operation even if it came down to only having the last of us about. Same went for bombs, both hand-thrown and launched via a device adapting a rifle for the purpose, with the added concern that these objects could be far more dangerous to a novice user than the enemy if mishandled. None were complicated pieces of kit to learn; but all these things required practice to build skill into talent. That would take time, and time was a commodity of which I was unsure of how much I had.

This was growing into a critical problem concerning taking new men on strength as more and more arrived to us lacking proficiency to even the most basic of standard acceptable for assignment to the Front, and that standard barely being met was that of time past; before we had adjusted doctrine and introduced new weapons. The rate at which losses occurred taken against the need to keep units in the field at an effective level of manpower meant that time spent in training was condensed, substantially undercutting a man's preparedness. Hell, we'd been getting new men who'd not fired live on a range any more shots than were the minimum to qualify as 'passed.' That would be the same number of bullets a fellow could blow through in an instant out this way, and said nothing towards any proficiency—and in some cases even familiarity—with other weapons and equipment. Under-trained troops might look and march like soldiers, but those superficialities were hardly sufficient to a quick integration with a fighting unit and were rather something of a liability. Everything encountered between Spoon Farm and Roadblock Buttress had been lessons learned through drawn blood. The journey, albeit not one of any distance, had been of trial and error paid for in the heavy excise of men's lives. As the cost was so high and so absolute, it infuriated me when we were given a practical examination of the lessons we had gained without those arrived to take the place of the dead having at least theoretical knowledge of what we had paid so much to learn. I had no bones about the war causing casualties, I'd be in the wrong business otherwise. I do take issue with needless casualties which is what happened when insufficient time was given to teaching men what they might need to know. Such things were akin to repeating a mistake, which might have at first been caused by ignorance; meaning to revisit the same errors was loathsome negligence. More aggravating than that was there supposedly being a system in place to rectify those shortfalls which was itself falling short. All men arrived in France for assignment to the field were being transited through depots ostensibly set up to acclimatise and deliver remedial instruction. It was generally accepted that these 'Bull Rings,' as they were known, were designed with the intent of being so insufferable to the degree that no man would wish to linger; the prospect of going towards the guns seeming a better option. Rushing men through wasn't as much of a problem as was the program of instruction during a soldier's tenure at such a depot. Those in the position of instructors were not liable to front-line service and many of them understanding which side their bread had butter deigned to prove continued usefulness in their roles and thus away from the more dangerous parts of France. Blacklegs, the lot of them, they contrived to create a mandate of a martinet's approach to the minutia of soldiering more pleasing to the review of those in the rear, such as sharpness of foot drill and smartness of dress rather than to focus on fieldcraft and battlecraft, the very things their charges should have to grips by the time they were sent to us. This was of no practical use for operational units. I didn't need men who could put a good shine on a brass button, I needed men who knew how to duck. There was no pretending that any level of proficiency was sufficient to prevent a man from becoming a casualty, all it would do is narrow the odds.

Strictly speaking, as a leader—whether of a section, platoon or otherwise—it was not my job to keep my men alive, or even free from harm. My paramount function was to make use of the resources at my disposal to carry out the tasks I had been ordered to regardless of what the human cost might be. Just because I could shelter under that proviso did not make the idea any easier in practice, and I struggled with being certain I could always place duty ahead of desire. In some ways, it was moot, as how long I would be able to keep my men alive or that I might be called upon in the course of circumstance to be an agent of their demise was out of my hands. Really, the only thing which might relieve me of such a grave imperative would be the war's conclusion. Despite loose talk, proselytizing and innuendo, there was nothing to signal such a thing was foreseeable any time soon. I had been in the belly of this beast for just over two years and I saw nothing to evidence any side about to give way; although I'm not knowledgeable enough to guess at what was required to cause a definite end. Should this conflict prove attritional rather than territorial, there can be much fuss made over numbers and measures, but without including the obstinacy of human will, especially when such a force as that is blindly dedicated to purpose, prediction made upon figures alone had little meaning. Men are not numbers and often fail to act in such an absolute fashion as does arithmetic.

Recently, affairs did appear promising. Just in those first few days of August, we had made advances which were equal to or greater than gains made previously over periods of months, certainly, years, perhaps. This intoned little as we had only been reclaiming the huge gains Fritz had made against us earlier in the year. I brought out the latest map I had. I think we had walked off the edge of it before we got here. If I was uncertain to where I was in France, I could only guess how far into the hinterland we had gone. Soon enough we would be moved forward and see for ourselves this fabled line of theirs with deliberate attention to the style of defense we had experience with; but on a much wider frontage. Concrete bunkers watched over ground set with wire traps so dense they barred passage. Being that it was so well done, both bunkers and wire would have been placed to use the terrain to conceal outposts and hardpoints while creating channels to force attacks to disperse into pre-sited killing zones. What I knew was that intimidating set-up was the prize needed to be carried in order to push things right open, and it could be tomorrow, or next week, but we would be going that way eventually. It put us at a tipping point, where either we could succeed or wind up resuming an everlasting battle over the same places again, and again, and again. If it had to be we go all the way to the Kaiser's front door and oust him, this might turn out to be a very long process. All I can do is be able to have a part of one solution or the other. At my little mouse's view of the war, that reduced to continuing to move forward until an end was met; even if it came to me tending a garden from the wrong side of the soil.

The knowledge that we would go until told to stop required a strength beyond physical measure; a quality somewhere within which none could be certain wasn't finite in supply. In its most basic form this fortitude was just a matter of putting one foot in front of the other, while fully aware that the best was being done to make each of those footsteps the last.

What will you do after the war?

Had to get there, first; then I might have reason to put thought to that question, as having an answer only made sense if I were present at the end. If I didn't make it, that put any post-war plans or dreams beyond concern. There is nothing of me which desires or covets death, but I shall admit it seems a much simpler state of affairs. Death alleviates all uncertainties, resolves everything for better or worse. Regardless of how the war was fought or won, the dead would always remain as they were, unchanged by circumstances, whereas each new moment I encountered made its impact upon me and I would carry all those moments with me for the extent of my life. Inescapably, the longer I had to move through these collected moments was that much more of

315

a burden on my soul. The dead, in spite of the detractors inherit of their condition are at least absolved of the suffering weariness it is to be living.

Belgium, July, 1936

I took up a handful of earth from the pile, allowing it to sit in my open palm a minute. Crumbling, dry and granular, specked with tiny stones, it wasn't a substance of any particular quality for what it was physically. What made it different was what it represented. This dirt was only an ounce or so of the ground over which the greatest event of human history had been fought. It also had a more profound and more personal significance to me, this handful, as I cast it downward. Turning to Bert, after he had done the same, I told him,

"Thanks for coming with me." He certainly didn't have to. After all, he had spent a great deal of money to come from home for one purpose. I suppose we all had, even if that purpose wasn't the same for all of us. To that, it was entirely decent of Bert to have abruptly changed his plans for my benefit. The huge and lavish ceremony, presided over by the new King had gone by without our attendance, specifically because the Monument's dedication had not ever been anything but secondary to Bill's true intention for taking this journey. His actual design was to pull us away from one part of the old Front to another. It was a rail hub town just over the Belgian border with a name no two people seemed to agree upon a consistent pronunciation. Unlike Petit Séjour, this place spent the entire war under fire, its concentrated transportation lines coveted by both sides and what stood now was completely re-built from ruin. I couldn't say as to what difference new was from old for appearances sake as I had only seen the place once, at a distance at night and in the rain, its shadow of skeleton buildings only visible because of several intense fires. It hadn't been part of my war, nor did it have any direct connection to Bill, but our individual experiences were not the point. Bill himself had finally made that clear, at last letting his true reason for his pilgrimage be known. In his own fashion, it was a reason he kept close to his chest until there was no longer any way to keep it hidden.

"Looking forward to it?" I had asked Bill when we'd had dinner the night before the dedication.

"Guess so," which was as enthusiastic a statement he'd made on the subject as ever he'd made. I attempted, then, a sentimental appeal which finally got a reaction; though not of the sort expected.

"Get to see Alec's name up there, eh? That'll be something."

"Doesn't matter," he said, remaining implacable, seeming to dismiss the idea altogether.

"Pardon?"

"Doesn't matter," he repeated, more firmly than at first.

"I don't understand," this was the entire reason I had sought to bring him here. "Don't you want opportunity to say good-bye?"

"Has it occurred to you that I never wanted to have to in the first place?"

"I hadn't thought of it, no."

"Besides, he's not there, now, is he? He's out yon; nowhere near this place. His name on some sandstone doesn't matter a whit."

"Alright, so he isn't," I said, trying for a placatory tone. I might have guessed that bringing up Alec's uncertain whereabouts would upset him but for the reason we had never, in fact, spoken of it. Bill's temper was easily provoked and while I hoped to not deliberately make him cross, it was sometimes difficult to know what might do it. Once past his threshold for anger, Bill would become troublesome to deal with, and thus a lot of effort was put into not upsetting him or trying to wind him down if he was becoming too agitated. It seemed to me just then I had been doing this sort of thing rather a lot throughout this whole trip. Bill's irritability wasn't anything unusual for him and maybe I'm the fool for expecting him to adopt a different attitude when going abroad. The man never took a holiday; he hadn't even left Inchmarlo for more than a few hours at a time in the last ten years or so, which meant that I had wrested him from the comfort he'd insulated himself with. Certainly, there was nothing about this journey in the way of pleasure, but it didn't have to feel as though Bill was being inconvenienced by everything. All that served was to make an already delicate time even more so and his brusque attitude was wearing thin upon my annoyance of how much I had to work at keeping him from being annoyed. There were my own things I had to deal with, the elements of this event which I had thought might help me heal. I hadn't come all this way to devote my attention to him.

Everything being fair, I was starting to think it might have been better had Bill remained at home, particularly as he had just dismissed the importance of the central point of this whole affair.

"Damn it, Bill, if you're not pleased to be here, if you don't care, why for Christ's sake did you come?"

"Mind your language, and watch your tone with me, laddie."

"Well?"

"Well what?"

"If the Monument doesn't matter, why did you bother to come at all?"

"I will tell you later."

I was incredulous. The same answer he'd been giving me for months now, word for word.

"We're bloody well here now! Why do you keep saying that?"

He only looked at me straight on and thumping the table just enough to jostle the cutlery to point out each word, he said it again.

"I will tell you later." He stood, threw his napkin down and absented himself from the table. I settled the fare and then went to my drinks meeting with Bert.

Fact was, he did tell me, albeit indirectly. The morning of the ceremony, I struck back towards the hotel to get ready for the day ahead. I drew back the curtains and was faced with the sun washing through the windows in dazzling early morning brightness. Our window overlooked a laneway which wound its way down to the main road, which was just starting to greet the day. A small crew of men in grubby overcoats were sweeping up with huge straw brooms. Shopkeepers and café staff pulled their awnings open, scrubbed their doorsteps or brought tables and chairs to set on the pavement for customers soon to arrive. Pushing the sash outwards, I caught a breeze scented by baking bread, the clatter of opening up work scored with conversation between business neighbours. Aside from my inability to understand the chatter going back and forth, it was so entirely normal and because it was so, there was something altogether odd about it, compared to how it was from my memory of this place. I stood there a bit at the window, admiring the scene below. A cyclist pedalled by, waving and receiving cheerful "Bonjours" as he passed. All of it was rather charming, quaintly twee in the way foreign vistas can be, from my point of view; whereas this was no different from any other morning for them and was probably nothing other than mundane. Looking at these folk going about their regular day made me realise something. It may not have amounted to very much on its own; the whole thing having taken the effort and sacrifice of many millions, but whatever part I had in what happened here so long ago was, in its infinitesimal way, responsible for this day being the most usual. What I had done was to contribute to the ability of ordinary people to live ordinary lives.

I don't suppose I had taken much time to think about the war in that way. My concentration was always upon my immediate experience, an understandably narrow perspective being that it was consumed by the concerns of survival. At the time, I didn't consider much on the course or conduct of the war, and less on what the results would be. Having done that, I came away without any real sense of the purpose of what we had accomplished. It had taken twenty years, but there, in the street beneath my window, it was to be found in the workaday routine of strangers. I had helped create that, and seeing it for only what it was satisfied me more than all the time I have tried to put any sense to having been through such a terrible war.

With only an hour or so before needing to meet the bus, I cajoled Bill to rise. He made no response; the room remained quiet. I didn't take a cue from that straight away, but in a moment of standing by the window, across from where Bill lay in his bed, I slowly put it together that the room was too quiet; entirely devoid of his heavy, congested rumbling breaths. I crossed over to him, placed my hand on his cheek. It was shockingly cold. Picking up the telephone, I called the front desk and had them connect me with Bert's room.

"I think you should come see me, Bert. My cousin is dead."

He was along very quickly, and made some examinations.

"I'm very sorry, Felix," he said, pulling the bed clothes to cover Bill completely. "I can't be certain, of course, without a proper look, but it appears he expired some time in the night to heart failure. Do you know if he was taking any medications?" I shrugged.

"No idea."

"Do you mind if I look?" He indicated the bedside table. I shook my head no, and he fished into the drawer, from which he produced a brown glass bottle which rattled with pills. Bert drew out a pair of spectacles to read the label.

"Oh, dear," he said.

"What is it?"

"Bill should have been taking these several times a day. This prescription was drawn from Falls Parish Pharmacy more than two weeks ago and it's nearly full. If he stopped this medication, it's given to wonder how he managed to keep from having a cardiac arrest before now."

"That doesn't seem right," I replied. Bill might be obstinate and all but immovable on certain things, particularly in taking advice, but he did have a good respect for doctors and typically abided by their directions. This was looking a lot like Bill had deliberately invited death, which was, despite him being the calculating sort, not something I could think him capable of.

"No medicine is perfect, Felix, but these pills would have been a safe bet against having a heart attack. This is all dependent on what shape he was in when his doctor prescribed this medication, of course. Academic at any rate now, I'm afraid."

"I can't see the sense of this. Honestly, Bert, he had been pretty certain he was dying. He told me so, but I thought nothing of it beyond the sort of complaints grumpy men like him make." I had put his claims to nothing more than hysterics, forgetting the fact that Bill was not given to hysterics. "It's a bit late to believe him now, but that being the case, if he was in such poor health, why did he come all this way and then not do the least to keep him right?"

"I can't posit why he might stop medication, but maybe he took this trip despite his condition because it was important for him to do so."

"That's the thing. He didn't care one way or the next about the Monument. It took a long time to convince him to come along. I'd been after him for months before he finally agreed."

"If he didn't want to come, what changed his mind?"

"Don't know. He never told me. Each time I asked, he said 'I will tell you later.' His last words to me, as a matter of fact."

"Really?" He picked up something else from the drawer.

"What's that then?"

"An envelope marked 'Later'," which Bert handed me to open. It seemed Bill had meant it to be found, mentioning within he'd deliberately kept it by his medicine for that purpose. In his note, Bill described how he had not expected to live very long and he had quit his pills because he believed them to be only prolonging the inevitable. All he had hoped to do was get himself this far, to at least outlive the journey outward, without any expectation of returning home. Once he'd known how serious his condition was, Bill had faced the choice to stay put and wait for the end or take this opportunity to do something he believed would have a greater meaning. He'd wanted this, his note made that entirely clear, closing the letter with a final request:

"Tell the family that you left me in the same ground as Alec. My grave is to be for the both of us. Tell them that he is there with me."

Planned to the absolute end, which was most certainly his style. I allowed myself a small smile that despite Bill being tough to warm to at times, he was never anything but true to who he was.

"I have to get him to Belgium," I said to Bert without knowing how I was going to do that. My old friend nodded.

"I'll need to make some calls to get in touch with a coroner to have the death certificate made out. They'll likely know a mortician who we can employ to see to the details on putting him where he wants to go. Why don't you go down to the desk and have them take down a telegram back to your family. Bill's alright where he is, I won't leave this room until everything's finished here."

"Thanks, Bert. I really appreciate you sticking by, especially as it means you missing the unveiling and all."

"The Monument won't be going anywhere. My profession does oblige me to certain standards of care, but even if it didn't, I wouldn't think of leaving you. You wouldn't, t'other way around."

I was privileged to have a friend like Bert. Heaven knows how I would have been able to get everything done without him. That he was a doctor was entirely fortunate; that he spoke French was indispensable. He got all the right sort of people involved, the mortician in particular taking great pains to prepare Bill for his final journey. These arrangements involved a train cross country and securing a plot in a small Flemish church yard near to where Alec was last known to have been. I don't know who it was that managed to have a guard from a Belgian artillery regiment meet us alighting from the train. Impeccably turned out in their finest uniforms, with admirable dignity they bore my cousin's casket upon a limber and escorted us to the prepared grave. We laid Bill there, the plot marked by a stone which I'd had inscribed with both his name and Alec's. That's where I left them, at a place where the both of them could wait together, unchanged in death, until the end of all time.

Author's Note

The preceding story, although hopefully enjoyable, is entirely a fiction. Fall's Parish, Petit Séjour and all the Western Front landmarks of Felix's war are my own inventions; as are the military units of 16 Canadian Infantry Brigade-- the King's Own Canadian Scots, West Prairie Rifles, Fort La Salle Regiment and the Duke of Markham's Horse.

These fictions have allowed me the latitude to tell this story without borrowing too directly from actual events or real personal experiences of the war.

I attached 16 CIB to the extant 4th Canadian Division, which requires the reader to imagine France about a mile or so wider, roughly North to South, than it is in reality. The situations and actions of Felix's experience are entirely reflective of the actual events being faced by the Canadian Army between September 1916 and September 1918. The weather, as well as tactics and equipment of both sides have been reproduced faithful to reality; thus, the reader can be satisfied that this story is accurate in those details.

I wrote Felix to be a person contemporary to the time he inhabits. He is considerably progressive in his views on individual religion and both racial and sexual equity. However, from time to time, his own ignorance is exposed in his use of racial terminology we in the present would find outdated and insensitive. The irony is that I wouldn't use the terms myself, but felt that it would be inauthentic for Felix to have a modern-day awareness on such matters, placing me in the position of apologising on behalf of a fictional person for any real offense his language might cause.

Manufactured by Amazon.ca
Bolton, ON